SILVER

SILVER Bells

Sometimes love needs
a Christmas miracle.

DEBORAH RANEY

summerside
PRESS™

New York

Songs of the Season™

Songs of the Season™ is a line of inspirational romance fiction that overflows with nostalgia, warmth, and Christmas cheer. Each novel will have you humming a lovable holiday song and longing for an old-fashioned Christmas.

A Merry Little Christmas
ANITA HIGMAN

A cozy holiday read about two people from different worlds. Franny Martin is an Oklahoma farm girl, Charlie Landau the wealthy city boy who shows up one day and offers to buy her farm. As Sinatra croons from the radio and snow blankets the ground, Franny teaches Charlie the curious and sometimes comical ways of country life. In the process, they unearth some discoveries of the heart—that sometimes love comes when you're least ready for it.

Silver Bells
DEBORAH RANEY

Elvis croons from the radio as Christmas descends on a small Kansas town in 1971. Michelle Penn has started a job at a tiny weekly newspaper, where the boss's son, Rob, helps her forget all about her former sweetheart in Vietnam. Rob is forbidden by office policy to date Michelle, but if he were to quit his job, he'd have nothing to offer her. It seems that the gifts Rob and Michelle most desire—each other—are out of reach. But then, they didn't count on a small Christmas miracle.

Silver Bells

ISBN-10: 0-8249-3437-7
ISBN-13: 978-0-8249-3437-8

Published by Summerside Press, an imprint of Guideposts
16 East 34th Street
New York, New York 10016
SummersidePress.com
Guideposts.org

*Summerside Press™ is an inspirational publisher offering fresh, irresistible
books to uplift the heart and engage the mind.*

Distributed by Ideals Publications, a Guideposts company
2630 Elm Hill Pike, Suite 100
Nashville, TN 37214

Guideposts, *Ideals*, and *Summerside Press* are registered trademarks of
Guideposts.

This a work of fiction. References to actual people or events are either
coincidental or are used with permission.

Cover and interior design by Müllerhaus Publishing Group, Mullerhaus.net

Printed and bound in the United States of America
10 9 8 7 6 5 4 3 2 1

DEDICATION

For Tavia and Collin.
May the Lord bless you
with many, many happy years together.

CHAPTER ONE

"Good morning, Kansas!" The radio scratched out static over deejay Kris Kristiansen's lilting baritone. "Keepin' cool on another hot, hot August day. Thanks for waking up to KGRV... music to get you in the groove and out the door."

Out the door? Michelle Penn squinted at the clock on her nightstand. Six thirty. She flopped onto her belly and covered her head with the plump feather pillow. *Too early.* And she'd thought Mom's "Yoo-hoos" were bad, floating up the farmhouse stairs at the crack of dawn every morning. Now, while she *was* glad to have her own place in town, no deejay could serve up the aromas of bacon and French toast that had always come with Mom's wake-up calls.

Outside the window of her third-story apartment, the leaves of the locust tree brushed the window screens and some sort of yellow-breasted bird sang his heart out. Already it was so hot that she was tempted to turn on the air cooler propped in the window of her kitchenette. But by the time the cool air made it back to her bedroom, she'd be out the door. Besides, her landlord had warned her to watch her electric bill if she ran the cooler. And her budget didn't leave much room for error. At least not until her first payday.

But it was all worth having her own place, and she did love her cozy apartment over the Jacksons' nineteenth-century Victorian. The pitched ceilings and unique nooks and crannies in every room—all three of them—had a charm the new apartment complex on the edge of town could never offer. Not that she could have afforded one of those places.

She rolled over onto her back and said the short ritual prayer that began every morning. "Please, God, keep Kevin safe, wherever he is today." She snoozed through Mungo Jerry's "In the Summertime," but when Tony Orlando and Dawn "knocked three times," she took the hint and eased her legs over the side of the bed.

Instantly, the butterflies in her stomach fluttered to life. First day of her new job, and she couldn't have felt less prepared. Especially when she thought about Kathy and Carol. Her best friends were no doubt sacked out in the dorm, slumbering with the sweet knowledge that they could skip class if they didn't feel like getting up till noon.

Two years of that life had spoiled her, but there wasn't enough money for her and Allen both to go to college. Dad could use her brother's help on the farm, but being in college just might keep him out of Vietnam. So, today, Allen would take her place at K-State. She didn't mind that much. Dad was right that college was a waste of money for her. She'd been there for two years, and she still didn't know what she wanted to do with her life.

Well, that wasn't true, either. She knew. She'd known what she wanted to do with her life from the time she was twelve years old, and she'd been on a fast track in that direction ever since. But Kevin Ferris derailed her dream when he signed on the dotted line at the recruiters' office two years ago. It still hurt like it had happened yesterday.

But now, armed with only a few undergrad credits and the dubious experience gained during a work-study job shelving books in the campus library, she would begin her first *real* job at Bristol's weekly newspaper.

"I'm the city reporter for the *Bristol Beacon*." She rehearsed the words aloud, hardly able to make them seem true. Why they'd had her start on a Thursday she didn't know, but at least she only had two days before the weekend. Not that she had anything exciting planned. With all her friends away at college and her love life down the drain, she may as well work every weekend.

She staggered to the shower, and twenty minutes later, peered into the mirror in the tiny bathroom. If that snooty lady who'd hired her could see her now—cardboard orange juice cans pinned to her head at various angles and an army of freckles brazenly at play on her nose—she'd surely have second thoughts about hiring Michelle Penn.

Singing along with B.J. Thomas on the radio, she unwound her hair from around seven orange juice cans. "Raindrops keep fallin' on my head," she crooned. "And just like the guy—" She stopped mid-verse and stared at a frizzy lock of hair. Those stupid raindrops may as well have been falling on *her* head. *Seventeen* magazine had promised the juice-can method would smooth her unruly curls into sleek perfection. Fat chance.

She ripped the remaining cans from her head and tossed them into the trash. Tugging a hairbrush through the dishwater-blond mess, she tried to coax it into submission. She finally gave up and pulled it all into a frizzy ponytail on top of her head.

Taking one look at the clock, she gasped. She pulled on a miniskirt and peasant blouse, stuffed her feet into the new wedge sandals she'd bought for the occasion, and flew out the door.

* * * * *

Despite large box fans in each corner of the *Beacon* office, the air barely stirred. The space felt like a sauna and smelled a little like a library-turned-locker-room. Michelle blew out a breath that ruffled her bangs. She could feel her hair frizzing and her makeup melting, exposing every last freckle.

Robert Merrick Sr. eyed her as if he was afraid she might faint.

And well she might.

"Sorry about the air-conditioning," he said. "They were supposed to have it fixed last night. Didn't happen."

"It's okay. I'm used to the heat." True, but air-conditioning was also the number-one reason she'd opted for an indoor job. She'd spent one summer detasseling corn in triple-digit temperatures. That was enough.

The *Beacon*'s owner ran a hand through gray-streaked black hair and motioned for her to follow him through a labyrinth of file cabinets, type-setting equipment, and slanted stand-up desks to the rear of the building. The place seemed strangely deserted for eight o'clock on a weekday.

"Your desk is right back here," Mr. Merrick said, unsmiling. She remembered Dad talking about the man who'd moved here from St. Louis to take over the *Beacon* around the time she started junior high. Apparently eight years hadn't been long enough for her boss to absorb even a smidgeon of small-town friendliness.

Mr. Merrick showed her to a makeshift cubicle in a row of three that held a dusty desk piled high with folded newspapers and stacks of catalogs and manila envelopes. He made a halfhearted effort at clearing a one-by-one-foot space on the desktop then merely walked away.

She looked after him, her mouth agape. "Excuse me . . . What am I supposed to do with all this . . . stuff?"

He looked over his shoulder and shrugged. "I guess that's your first assignment."

"But—"

"Figure it out. Your résumé said you were a self-starter."

She'd heard he was square, but she hadn't expected him to be such a jerk. She watched him disappear into his office. Maybe this was a test.

The man in the cubicle next to hers had his nose to a Selectric type-writer and seemed not to notice. Once Mr. Merrick was out of sight, she peeked over the low divider and cleared her throat. The man looked up briefly but ignored her and went back to typing, hunt-and-peck style.

Well, if the boss wouldn't introduce her, she'd do it herself. She stuck a hand over the partition. "Hi, I'm Michelle Penn. The new . . . city reporter." The title sounded more pretentious than it had in the privacy of her apartment this morning. She didn't have a journalism degree. Or any degree for that matter. Still, that *was* the position she'd filled.

"So I heard." *Tappity-tap-tap-tap.*

"So you heard?" And so much for small-town friendliness. What was wrong with these people? This was Bristol, Kansas, "a little town with a big heart"—according to the sign marking the city limits. She drew her hand back to her own side of the cubicle.

The collection of sports memorabilia decorating Mr. Hunt-and-Peck's pegboard walls confirmed her suspicion that he was the sports reporter. Well, that explained a few things.

He finally stopped typing and looked up. "So where're you from?"

"Right here. Well, I mean, I live here in Bristol now, but my dad farms, so I grew up west of town. Northwest, actually. But I've been away. At college. K-State—"

"Slow down. Slow down . . . " He held up a palm like a school-crossing guard.

She blushed. She was rambling like the roses on Mom's trellis. "Sorry. More than you needed to know."

"No problem." How could he sit there looking so cool and col-lected? In neatly pressed khakis and a crisp white dress shirt, his only concession to the heat was rolled-up shirtsleeves that revealed tanned forearms.

She tucked in a curl that had escaped her ponytail. "Do you know where I'm supposed to put all this stuff from my desk?"

He bobbed up to peer over the five-foot-high partition before plopping into his chair again. "I guess you could stack it over by the Xerox. Just don't let Merrick catch you."

"Junior or Senior?"

He studied her. "Um . . . Senior. There is no 'Junior.'"

"But I thought—"

"It's Senior and Robert Merrick the third." He etched a Roman numeral "three" in the air.

"Oh." She made a face. "Whoop-dee-doo."

That made him laugh.

She glanced over her shoulder at her desk. "Well, they surely don't expect me to work with all these piles on my desk."

Looking amused, he motioned to his own desk, where a similar jumble of papers and unopened mail cluttered the desktop.

Rolling her eyes, she scooped a pile of dusty newspapers into her arms. She headed for the corner where a behemoth copier loomed but stopped long enough to poke her head into Sports Guy's cubicle and risk another question. "Where do I get a typewriter?"

"You don't."

"I don't? Then how am I supposed to—"

"Just kidding." He shot her what could have been a grin. "You requisition one from Myrtle in Reception. Just be prepared to sign your life away."

She eyed him. "Kidding again, right?"

"I wish I was." He went back to hunting and pecking.

She took the hint and left him to his life-changing sports stories. Besides the receptionist and Mr. Merrick, they seemed to be the only ones in the office today, but the third cubicle looked as if it belonged to someone.

For the next half hour, she moved stacks off her desk to the corner by the Xerox machine, taking furtive glances over her shoulder for fear of running into Robert Merrick Sr.—or Robert "the third," whom she'd yet to meet. She didn't relish the thought of getting fired her first day on the job.

When the desk was clear, she polished it with a rag and a can of lemon Pledge she'd found in the restroom. Satisfied with the results, she went to sign her life away to the receptionist—who apparently also served as personnel director, since Myrtle Dressler was the one who'd hired Michelle.

"I see you've made yourself at home." Myrtle looked her up and down, peering over cat-eye glasses that hung from a chain around her neck. "Now, I don't like to mention this, but we do have a dress code here, Miss Penn. Or are you one of those who prefer *Ms.*?" The way she said it, with her nose wrinkled like a prune, left no doubt as to how she felt about the "feminine mystique."

"Oh, please . . . just call me Michelle."

"Well, Michelle, as I said, we do have standards, and that skirt is *this* close"—she pinched two well-manicured fingers together—"to breaking our dress code."

Feeling self-conscious, Michelle tugged at her skirt and prayed this conversation would not get back to her father.

What was wrong with her? She was almost twenty-one. Why did she still care so much what her father thought? Besides, the skirt wasn't even that short. And it was in style. Myrtle just needed to get with the program. "I assure you, I won't be breaking any dress codes. Now, I have my desk cleared off, and I'm ready for my typewriter. The sports guy said you were the one to talk to. . . ."

"The sports guy?" Myrtle's brow furrowed deeper, if that were possible.

"Hey, Myrtle." Sports Guy appeared beside her as if by magic.

Michelle felt his hand on her shoulder, its pressure just light enough not to be inappropriate.

"Let's get this young lady set up on a Selectric, shall we?" he said.

"Of course." Myrtle practically saluted. "Right away, sir."

Sir? Talk about discrimination. Well, at least she'd get her typewriter.

Myrtle curled a finger over her shoulder, beckoning. Michelle followed, mouthing a "Thank you" to Sports Guy as she passed.

He gave her a friendly wink, and she decided he would be a very nice next-cubicle neighbor.

Half an hour later, she was tapping away on a Selectric identical to the one she'd used in college. One fear down, two hundred and ninety-nine to go. Myrtle had given her a news release to "practice" on. She was an accomplished typist and could have tapped out the whole thing six times by now, but she paced herself and did her best to look busy.

Sports Guy was on the phone in a serious conversation—if one could consider football a serious topic. From what she could make out over the noise of her Selectric and the awful classical music wafting from the reception area, it sounded like he was doing an interview with someone about the upcoming Bristol Bears football season.

He hung up and left his cubicle, but when he returned a few minutes later, the unmistakable aroma of coffee floated over the partition that separated them.

She hit the carriage return, pushed her chair back, and peeked over the divider. "Hey . . . Mind telling me where I can get a cup of that?"

"Myrtle didn't show you where the break room is?"

She shook her head.

He looked at his watch. "Coffee break isn't for another twenty minutes, but I can show you where it is then."

She eyed his cup. "We take staggered breaks?"

"No. Break is at ten."

She looked pointedly at the porcelain mug in his hand. "And you get coffee now because . . . ?"

He looked down, as if he hadn't realized till this moment that he was drinking coffee. He stuttered and shrugged.

She put her hand over the divider. "By the way, I didn't get your name."

He shook her hand and a grin bloomed on his face. "I'm Rob."

"Rob—" An odd sensation niggled at her.

He tightened his grip on her hand and looked her in the eyes. "Robert Merrick III . . . I know, I know . . . " He let her hand drop and twirled his index finger in the air, mimicking her. "Whoop-dee-doo."

CHAPTER TWO

Michelle could feel her palms sweating even as Robert Merrick III pumped her hand and grinned like Howdy Doody. If she'd thought it was hot in here earlier, now it was a veritable oven.

"I—I didn't realize . . . " She would have paid a thousand dollars right now to disappear into the federal witness protection program.

She should have recognized him. Rob Merrick. *Of course.* Heaven knew she'd watched him aplenty when, as a high-school freshman, she and her friends sat moon-eyed in the bleachers while the hunky senior won every tennis match on his way to State. He was a Bobby Sherman look-alike back then, and it seemed as if his photo had been in the *Beacon* every other week. Now she knew why.

Looking at him with this new information, his chiseled jaw and muscled forearms were suddenly all-too-familiar. But his hair was dark and straight now, and it touched his collar. A little surprising given that he worked for the straitlaced Robert Merrick Sr.—and Myrtle Dressler.

And he was no regular "sports guy." He was the boss's son. No, worse. As far as she was concerned, he *was* the boss. The *Beacon*'s masthead clearly listed him as *Managing Editor*, directly under Robert Merrick Sr.'s *Publisher* designation.

First day on the job and she was toast. Burned-to-a-crisp toast.

* * * * *

It was all Rob could do to hold in the laughter that came every time he thought of the look on the new reporter's face when he'd told her his name. He wasn't sure he'd ever seen anyone blush such a deep shade of scarlet. Poor girl.

It probably wasn't very nice of him to let her suffer that way. He would make it up to her before the day was over, but right now, he could almost hear her discomfort on the other side of the divider, and he was enjoying it too much. *Whoop-dee-doo.* Laughter threatened again, and he distracted himself by going through his notes for the football feature one more time.

Satisfied he'd accurately quoted everyone he'd interviewed, he checked his watch. Ten fifteen. An idea struck and he popped his head over the partition. "Hey, it's past time for that coffee break now. Come on. I'll show you where the break room is."

She didn't look up from the stack of news releases she was shuffling through. "Thanks, but I don't care for anything right now."

He rolled his desk chair out of the way and leaned over the divider. "You're not still sore at me, are you?"

She looked up at him, those hazel eyes of hers narrowing. "Of course not. Why would I be 'sore' at you just because you humiliated, embarrassed, and patronized me? Not to mention, deceived me."

Uh-oh. "Okay . . . I'm going to take that as sarcasm and assume that you are, indeed, still sore at me."

"Indeed? Wow. Nice vocabulary."

He wanted to laugh, but he wasn't sure that would go over so hot right now.

"And another thing," she said, obviously going for broke. "Would you please explain the whole Robert Merrick III thing to me, because that's just guaranteed to trip people up."

"Oh, so we're back to *whoop-dee-doo* again? Listen, I'm sorry. But I thought you knew who I was."

She ignored that. "Why is your dad 'Senior,' but you're the third?"

He propped his forearms on the top of the partition and regarded her. "Have you been talking to Myrtle?"

"No . . . Why?"

"Because she gives us a hard time about that too."

"Well, I looked it up, and it doesn't make sense."

"Looked it up?"

"Emily Post." She tapped a blue book on her research shelf.

He laughed. "Ah, the *Pocket Book of Etiquette*. You *have* been talking to Myrtle. Or my dad."

"No, I haven't. I swear. It's in the book."

"So I hear." He sighed. "Apparently Mrs. Post ascribes to the convention of the names and numerals—"

"Post-nominals."

"*Whatever* you call them. Talk about vocabulary," he muttered. He cleared his throat. "Anyway, Emily Post—and Dad and Myrtle— say that when the original 'Senior' dies, everybody moves up a notch; therefore, when my granddad died, my dad became Robert Merrick Senior."

"That's right. Making you 'Junior.' And if your son is Robert Merrick, *he's* the third. Until you die, and then he's 'Junior.'"

He curbed a smile. This girl was adorable—but he wasn't about to let her know he thought so. Not yet anyway. "I don't have a son, and I'm not planning on dying anytime soon."

"I'm being hypothetical."

"Fine. But I don't *want* to be a junior. I've been Robert Merrick III my whole life, and I'm not going to change my Social Security card and driver's license and bank account every time a Robert Merrick drops dead."

"That's terrible!"

"I'm being hypothetical," he deadpanned. "And there are plenty of sources that say I can keep my Roman numerals if I choose."

"Name one."

"Listen, I feel bad about that coffee." He looked pointedly at the mug on her desk. "Let me treat you to a fresh cup, okay?"

"Don't change the subject."

"I might even be able to rustle up a couple of cookies. Myrtle usually bakes for Thursdays."

She fell for it. "What's so special about Thursdays?"

Nice parry, Merrick. Well done. "Boy, do you ever have a lot to learn about the newspaper business. Thursdays are celebration days because the newspaper has been put to bed, mailed, and delivered."

"It was awfully nice of you to let me start work on a celebration day."

He grinned, suddenly not so annoyed at Myrtle for filling the cubicle next to his. Michelle seemed to have forgotten she was mad at him. He wouldn't tell her that not only did he have nothing to do with her starting work today, but he hadn't wanted to hire her in the first place.

"Let's go find a cookie, then." He flipped off the lamp on his desk and came around to her cubicle.

He led her through the office, giving an abbreviated version of the guided tour that someone should have given her before sticking her all alone in a cubicle.

"Mrs. Dressler said I'd be covering school-board and city-council meetings?"

"Are you asking me or telling me?"

Her face flushed pink again. Pink was a very good color on her.

"Sorry. I'm feeling a little . . . " She shrugged. "It's just that I don't know who I answer to, and I'm not sure what I'm supposed to do. I–I've never been a reporter before, and that's what I told Myrtle when I interviewed for the job. But I feel like I've been tossed into the ocean and told to do the backstroke when I barely know how to dog-paddle."

Nice metaphor. The woman was obviously a writer. "And things will really pick up tomorrow."

She made a face. "That's supposed to make me feel better?"

"Or would you rather spend another day typing the same news release over and over?"

More pink cheeks.

"Don't worry," he said. "Your secret is safe with me." He opened a door and motioned for her to go through. "This is the break room."

She lifted the empty carafe. "But no coffee?"

"Oh. I guess I sort of . . . drank the last cup."

"That wasn't very nice." But she smiled when she said it.

"Here . . . I'll show you how to make more."

"I think I know how to make coffee."

"Be my guest. I'll be over here eating cookies."

He took two cookies from Myrtle's gilt-edged plate, put them on a napkin, and placed them into the microwave oven. He turned the dial to twenty seconds. The oven rumbled to life.

Michelle whirled to face him, sloshing water from the coffee carafe. "What in the world is that racket?"

"It's a microwave oven." He grinned. "You've never seen one?"

"Is that like that radar range I saw at the state fair?" She took a step backward. "Those things are dangerous, aren't they? I read somewhere that you can get radiation poisoning from them."

"It's perfectly safe. Watch and learn." The noise stopped and he pulled the cookies from the microwave's glass tray, warm and fragrant.

"Wow! Amazing." But she kept her distance, watching him from across the room.

He offered her a cookie. She accepted one and took a bite. "Mmm. Delicious. Like it just came out of the oven."

"It *did* just come out of the oven. Our Selectrics and adding machines may be as old as dirt, but when it comes to the break room, the *Bristol Beacon* is state-of-the-art all the way."

"Speaking of which, I shouldn't have spoken so soon about making coffee." She pointed back to the stove. "I've never seen a percolator like that. Where do you put the grounds?"

"I wondered if you'd figure it out," he said. "It's a prototype for a new coffeemaker that'll be on the market soon. My dad knows a guy who knows a guy. It's pretty slick, actually. Here, let me show you."

He filled the carafe with water and poured it into the reservoir.

"But—that's cold water. Don't you have to heat it up first?"

"That's the beauty of it. The coffee brews right into the pot, ready to drink."

"That, I've got to see."

"Well, it takes a while to heat up. Why don't you warm up a couple more cookies while we're waiting?" he said, spooning ground coffee into the basket.

"I don't know how to run that thing." She eyed the microwave as if it might start shooting flames at any moment.

"It's easy. Just put the cookies on a napkin, pop them in, and turn the dial."

Michelle mumbled something unintelligible as she ratcheted the dial, but he heard the microwave come to life again.

The coffeemaker started sputtering, and he motioned her over. "You want to see this work? Come here."

She bent her knees until she was eye-level with the counter and watched as the first thin stream of coffee dripped into the pot. "How does it do that with cold water?"

He took advantage of the awe in her voice. "It's complicated. You see, there's an electric element inside that heats the cold water right in the machine. That heat creates pressure and siphons the heated water up through a tube, where the hot water sprays over the coffee grinds, then drips through into the pot."

"It smells like coffee." Closing her eyes, she breathed in the steam. He did the same, but when he inhaled through his nose it wasn't coffee he smelled. Something was burning.

He turned to see smoke seeping out from the door of the micro-wave. He crossed the room in two strides, depressed the oven's latch, and yanked open the door. "How far did you turn that knob?"

"Obviously too far."

Two charred lumps of coal sat on the tray. The napkin had turned to ash. "Obviously."

Pungent gray smoke filled the room and hung in the air. Michelle covered her mouth with one hand and fanned with the other, her eyes huge and watery. "What do we do?"

"Open the window!" He went to the room's one small window and tried in vain to raise the sash.

She got on the other side and braced her feet. "One, two, push!"

He squinted at her through the fog. "What happened to three?"

"Okay, on three. One, two, *three.*" She heaved on three.

He was waiting for *push.*

Finally they got the window open a crack. Michelle went to the door and swung it back and forth, using it as a giant fan.

"Robert!" Through the haze of smoke his father appeared, glaring. "What on earth happened in here?"

Michelle stepped in front of him. "It's my fault, sir. I . . . must have turned the knob too far on that machine."

"What machine?" Mr. Merrick cast about the room.

"The microwave oven, Dad."

"Well, get it cleaned up before somebody sends the fire department over." He threw Michelle a disgusted look then turned it on Rob. "Robert . . . I'll see you in my office."

Rob didn't dare look at Michelle. And now it was his turn to blush.

CHAPTER THREE

Michelle wrung out the dishrag again and swabbed down the micro-wave oven. *Cookie-scorcher* was more like it. Or *firebomb*. She could have burned down the whole building! She might have found the whole escapade funny if she wasn't so afraid she'd lose her job over it. All she could think about now was how she would explain to her father why she couldn't pay her rent.

She took her time cleaning up, not wanting to interrupt whatever discussion Mr. Merrick Senior and Merrick "the third" were having.

She was only paying seventy-five dollars a month to rent the third story of the Victorian home behind the United Methodist Church. The house had served as the parsonage until a few years ago. When she'd discovered the apartment was available, even her parents had agreed that it made more sense to rent in town than waste gas driving into town and back every day. But if she couldn't manage to pay her own rent, she knew Mom would love an excuse to get her back home.

And Dad would love nothing more than to say "I told you so." She could almost hear him now. "I have plenty of work for you on the farm. Why you ever came up with the harebrained idea of working in town, I'll never know."

She actually felt kind of sorry for Rob. His father was an intimi-dating figure. But Rob had to be at least twenty-three or twenty-four. She doubted anyone had twisted his arm to come back to the old hometown and go to work for dear old dad. Maybe Merrick III needed to get a backbone.

He was probably still living under his father's roof. At least she'd had the good sense not to move back home when she dropped out of college.

She remembered hearing back in high school that Mrs. Merrick had died when Rob was just little. At the time, she'd thought it the worst fate possible, losing your mom like that. Rob was an only child too, with no brothers or sisters to help him through. From what she remembered of him, he'd grown up more than a bit spoiled, but she had to admit that college had only improved his good looks. Kathy and Carol would go ape when she told them who her new office mate was. Well, office mate for one day, anyway.

She rinsed the dishrag and draped it over the sink to dry. Taking a deep breath, she steeled herself to face the music and went to find the publisher's office. If she could have walked any slower without standing still, she would have. But finally there was no stalling. She needed to find out whether she still had a job after nearly incinerating the news-paper office.

She walked out into the office and was mortified to realize that the horrid burnt smell wasn't confined to the break room—it had seeped into the newsroom too.

Myrtle was on the phone at the reception desk, and behind her Michelle could see Mr. Merrick in his office. The venetian blinds cover-ing the window between his office and the reception desk were tilted just enough that she could see his dour expression.

He must have seen her too, because he rose and came to the doorway, beckoning her with a curl of his index finger. Still on the phone, Myrtle gave her a look that said, "Good luck, sister. You'll need it."

Before she was even through the door she started apologizing. "Mr. Merrick, I am so sorry. It was an accident, but I had no business operating that thing. I should have let Rob—Mr. Merrick . . . the *other* Mr. Merrick, I mean—run it. But, well, he asked me and I—"

"Miss Penn, are you always this talkative?"

She thought for a minute. It was a trick question. But she heard her father's voice in her head. *Honesty is the best policy.* "Yes, sir. I'm afraid that's one of my faults. But I'm working on it, and I think I'm getting a little better at—"

"If you're finished, Miss Penn."

"Sorry." She clamped her mouth shut and winced.

"Have a seat, please." He indicated the chair in front of his desk.

She took it and waited while he straightened a sheaf of papers.

He looked at the ceiling as if trying to decide what to do with her. Finally, he leaned forward and leveled his gaze at her. "I accept some of the blame for your little incident in the break room this morning. I should have seen to it that someone showed you how to operate the equipment. Robert said—" He cleared his throat. "Well, never mind what Robert said. Suffice it to say that I'm going to pretend this never happened. We'll start fresh from here."

"Thank you, sir. I—" She caught herself. "Thank you."

"I understand you were not properly introduced around?"

"I—I guess not, sir."

"I think you've met everyone who's here today. Thursdays are down days after we get the paper to bed. But I promise tomorrow you'll be given a proper introduction to your coworkers."

"Thank you, sir."

"You may dispense with that 'sir' business. Just address me as Mr. Merrick."

"Yes, sir—Mr. Merrick."

She thought she detected a ghost of a smile in his eyes, but she couldn't be sure.

"Now get back to work. Myrtle can give you some news releases that need typing and show you how to clean off the layout banks for the next issue. I'll have Robert figure out your reporting assignments for next week too."

"Okay. Thank you." She bit back the "sir" that was on the tip of her tongue.

He pivoted in his chair and began typing. Was he finished with her? Or was he typing something for her?

After an awkward moment, he looked up. "That will be all. Please close the door when you leave."

"Oh." She pushed her chair back. "Sorry."

She went to the door, but before she could open it, his voice came behind her. "One last thing, Miss Penn."

She turned expectantly, grasping the heavy doorknob.

Mr. Merrick cleared his throat loudly. "If you value this job, you'll keep your relationship with my son strictly professional."

CHAPTER FOUR

Rob parked his Pinto behind the newspaper office and checked his hair in the rearview mirror before getting out of the car. He recognized Michelle Penn's '65 Delta 88 two spaces over and smiled. For the first time since he'd started working for his father nine months ago, he actually looked forward to coming in to work.

He went through the back door and headed straight for the break room. The smell of burned chocolate chip cookies lingered ever so faintly in the air, but Myrtle had the coffee going and that aroma quickly won out. He poured himself a cup and carried it through the newsroom to his cubicle.

Michelle was already at her desk. Her ponytail from yesterday was gone, and in its place, a cascade of blond waves tumbled past her shoulders. Her hair was longer than he'd imagined. And even prettier.

"Good morning." He was determined to start the day on the right foot.

She looked up from her Selectric. "Good morning." That was all he got.

"Has anyone introduced you around?"

This time, she didn't even look up. "Yes. Myrtle took me around. I'm set." She went right back to typing.

He shrugged, fed a new sheet of paper into the Selectric, and tried to salvage his story about the Tigers' upcoming season. Bristol High had a new football coach, and the man had not been very forthcoming with material or quotes. Rob was scrambling to come up with even two inches of decent material. At this rate, the page he was supposed to fill was going to be mostly photos. And he still had a column to write before Monday night.

He heard rustling in the cubicle next to him and looked up. Michelle's head bobbed on the other side of the partition. He turned in his chair to watch her walk by. She was wearing hip-huggers today. The hems almost dragged on the floor, but judging by the way she tottered, he suspected the bell-bottoms hid a pair of those stupid platform sandals that made girls look like you could knock them over with a feather duster. Still, he had to admit she wore them well.

She threw him a closemouthed smile as she passed by, and when she came back five minutes later, balancing a steaming mug, she ignored him and walked right past his cube. But a few seconds later she was back, standing in his doorway, arms folded, still holding her mug.

"Okay." She breathed out a sigh. "Since I survived the burned-cookie incident and it looks like I may be employed here for the foreseeable future, I need to put in a request."

"What's that?"

"I need to take my coffee break before you take yours. I don't care when it is. I can adjust, but just let me know before you take your break. Please."

"Why?"

She held her mug under his nose. There was barely an inch of sludgy coffee in the bottom.

"You already downed a whole cup?"

She glared at him. "I've barely had a sip. I went back there right after you, and the dropolator is almost empty."

He cracked up.

"What's so funny?"

He cocked his head. "For a supposed journalist, you sure do bungle your words."

"What did I bungle?"

"First, it's *drip*olator."

"That's what I said."

"No, you said *dropolator*. And second, it's not a dripolator anyway. It's called a coffeemaker."

"You're just trying to change the subject because you know I'm right about you guzzling all the coffee."

"I'm sorry about that. I should have made another pot—"

"And what exactly do you mean by *supposed* journalist?"

"Well, you did quit college and settle for this small-town rag." He was teasing, enjoying their repartee, but he was also curious about her choice to drop out of K-State.

But the hurt expression that shadowed her pretty face made him cringe.

"If you really want to know, I settled for this 'rag' because I couldn't afford to stay in college. I–I'm trying to save up, but for now, it's my brother's turn. My dad couldn't afford to send us both."

He closed his eyes, feeling like a jerk for touching a sore spot. "I'm sorry. I didn't mean to . . . That was thoughtless of me. I'm sorry."

She shrugged. "It's no big deal. I'll get my degree as soon as I can."

"I'm sorry about the coffee too," he said, hoping to get back to a more pleasant subject. "It won't happen again. In fact . . . " He jumped up and took the cup from her hand. "You go back to work. I'll bring you a fresh cup."

She started to protest, but he put a hand at the small of her back and steered her to her cubicle, wishing it wouldn't be misinterpreted if he gave her a hug.

But he refrained and instead pulled out her chair, motioning for her to sit. "You relax. I'll be right back with coffee."

* * * * *

Rob hadn't been gone three minutes when Michelle heard a high-pitched beep coming from the other side of the office, followed by static and voices. She stopped typing to listen. It reminded her of the squawking on the CB radio Dad used to stay in contact with his harvest crew. She couldn't understand what the voices were saying, but it sounded like someone was pretty worked up. Sirens wailed, and it took her a minute to realize they weren't on the radio but right outside the office on Main Street.

Rob reappeared—without her coffee—and poked his head into her cubicle. "Come on, Penn. Hear those sirens? Here's your first big break."

"What?" She jumped up and went to her doorway.

Rob darted into his own cubicle and emerged lugging a camera with a huge lens. He slipped the wide strap around his neck and jogged toward the back door. "Come on."

She grabbed her purse and a notepad and hurried to catch up.

"Let's take your car," Rob yelled when they got out to the parking lot. "That way I can shoot pictures."

"Pictures of what? What's going on?"

"Didn't you hear the scanner?"

"I heard the sirens, but I couldn't hear what they were saying on the radio."

"The police scanner, you mean." He opened the passenger-side door and folded himself into her car. "There's something going on at 358 Donner. Do you know where that is?"

"I think so. Just a few blocks east, right?"

"Yes. Drive!"

She started the car, backed down the alley, and drove around to Main Street. Donner Avenue was already clogged with traffic by the time they got there. All three of Bristol's patrol cars were there, along with two fire-department vehicles and an ambulance.

Rob rolled the window down, scrunched low in the seat, and balanced the camera on the ledge of the door panel. She heard the *click-click*, *click-click* of the motor drive attached to his camera as it captured shot after shot.

Adrenaline put her senses on high-alert, and even as she composed an opening to the news story in her mind, she also composed letters to Kathy and Carol, bandying Rob's name about in a way she knew would have them green with envy.

"Pull up into the alley. You can park right over there." He pointed behind the ramshackle house that seemed to be the center of attention.

"I don't see any fire."

"No. The scanner said 'domestic altercation.'"

"But—the fire trucks . . . ?"

"The fire department responds to all emergency calls."

"Domestic altercation. You mean like some guy beating up on his wife?"

"Or some kid beating up on his mother. Come on . . . Let's find out." He flung open the car door and ran across the overgrown lawn.

She followed, wishing she'd worn more sensible shoes. As they rounded the side of the house, police were bringing out a man in handcuffs. Rob ran up the porch steps, snapping pictures as he went. But when Michelle caught up with him, she saw why they were hauling the guy in. Behind the man, in the doorway, stood a young woman. Tears and mascara streaked her cheeks, and a giant goose egg protruded over one eyebrow. A tiny wisp of a girl with jet-black hair clung to her mama's knee, screaming. It took every ounce of restraint Michelle had not to run up on the porch and take the little girl in her arms.

Rob moved in closer. He knelt and adjusted the camera. Michelle heard the *whirr* of the lens as he zoomed in on the child. What was he doing?

A police officer who looked as if he couldn't be a day over seventeen tried to get the woman to go back inside, but she fought him off, shouting something Michelle couldn't understand—though she was pretty sure it was profane.

"Are you getting this?" Rob shouted, his eye still to the camera. "We need some quotes."

Surely he didn't expect her to stop one of the authorities and ask questions now. Every person in uniform was doing something important—far more important than answering some reporter's questions. She could call the police station for information when they got back to the office, after the situation here was under control.

She pulled the notepad from her purse and jotted down a few key words—more for Rob Merrick's sake than her own. She would remember the important details. This kind of *altercation*, as the scanner had called it, wasn't an everyday occurrence in Bristol. Usually the most exciting thing in this small Kansas town was when the ice cream truck came through once or twice a week.

She stood at the corner of the porch and watched as the police dragged the man to the squad car.

The young officer left the woman and approached Rob. "I'm going to have to ask you to leave the property, sir. If you want pictures, you'll have to get them from across the street."

Rob ignored him long enough to shoot another series with the camera's motor drive.

Michelle felt paralyzed. Everything in her wanted to carry the little girl back into the house so she wouldn't have to witness what was happening. But the mother's battered face told Michelle that the child had probably already seen the worst thing she would ever witness.

The little girl appeared to be about two, maybe three. Michelle tried to recall any memories from when she was that small, but the only things that came to mind were supremely happy times—Christmas at Grandma Penn's in Missouri, with bubble lights on a real cedar tree and hot cocoa sipped by a crackling fireplace. And the first time she'd ever ridden a horse. She'd been terrified of the tall bay mare at first, but then Mom lifted her up into Daddy's arms and she rode in front of him in the saddle, feeling safer than she'd ever felt. What must it be like to grow up watching your father beat up on your mommy, then watching him being dragged off to jail? She shuddered.

The policeman warned Rob again, and this time he pulled the camera away from his eye and backed away. But Michelle thought she heard the shutter clicking again even as he stepped off the porch.

She looked past Rob, and her gaze locked with the swollen, haunted eyes of the young mother on the porch. Without uttering a word, the woman seemed to be pleading with her to help. But there was nothing Michelle could do except turn away and walk across the street.

She felt like a traitor.

CHAPTER FIVE

Rob stood beside Michelle, watching from the street for a while before he directed her back to her Oldsmobile. They sat in the car in silence until the last emergency vehicle pulled away. From what he could tell from their vantage point in the alley, the battered woman had refused medical treatment, and she and the kid remained inside the house. Her brute of a husband had gone for a ride in the back of a patrol car, but the man would no doubt be back home in forty-eight hours. And who knew what he might do then.

In the driver's seat beside him, Michelle clutched the steering wheel, her face pale.

"You okay?"

She merely nodded and turned the key in the ignition.

"Wait . . . " He motioned in the direction of the house. "Do you want to try to talk to her?"

"The victim?" She looked incredulous.

"Who else would I mean?"

"I don't know"—her eyes flashed—"but the last thing that poor woman needs is some reporter making her relive the whole thing."

"Who *did* you talk to?" He didn't know what she'd written down in that notebook, but he was pretty sure she hadn't gotten one quote.

"I–I'll make some calls later."

He shrugged. "Suit yourself." He could only guess what his father would say when he found out they'd come back with nothing but a roll of film. But that wasn't his problem. She could learn the way he had—the school of hard knocks.

She rolled through the alley and turned onto Donner Avenue. Only then did he notice that her hands were trembling.

"Why don't you just drop me off at work and take the rest of the day off."

"I don't need the rest of the day off. I'm fine." She gripped the wheel tighter.

"Whatever you say."

They rode the rest of the way in silence, but before they got out of the car, he thought of a way to give her an out. "Do you know how to develop film?"

She shook her head, still looking a little shell-shocked.

He opened the car door and got out. She did the same. He held the office door open for her. "Go put your stuff away and meet me in the darkroom. Let's see what we got."

* * * * *

The single red lightbulb over the door illuminated Rob's face as he inspected the strips of film clipped to a length of clothesline strung above the developer pans. The chemical fumes burned Michelle's nostrils, and she rubbed her nose in protest. But the images on the negatives provided a distraction from the unpleasant odor.

Even in miniature and with the odd black-and-white reverse of the negative images, she was shocked at the violence the photographs depicted. Rob must have used the telephoto lens, because most of the photos were zoomed in on faces.

Rob's voice beside her broke through her thoughts. "First we need to decide which photos we want to print, so we'll print a contact sheet."

He showed her how to make the print of all the photos in miniature, explaining how the developer, stop bath, and fixer worked. She found it fascinating—and a little exciting—to think about developing her own photos.

But half an hour later, when Rob slid the still-damp contact sheet down the clothesline for her to view, her breath caught. The camera had captured the woman's swollen forehead and haunted eyes. And the little girl's hands clutching her mother's knee. They were powerful photographs . . . but heartbreaking.

And invasive.

Surely he didn't intend to publish these in the *Beacon*.

"What about this one?" He pinched the edge of the strip near a frame that showed the little girl crying, her face half-buried in her mother's skirt.

"You mean for the paper?"

"What else would it be for?"

"It just seems like that would be—a little cruel."

"Cruel?"

"How would you feel if you were that little girl's mother?"

His expression was inscrutable in the crimson light, but his silence gave her hope that he'd taken her point.

They stood side by side in the darkroom while he studied the film he'd shot. Rob was an artist with the camera, and she didn't mind having him peer over her shoulder, close enough she could smell his spearmint chewing gum, as they viewed the images of the event they'd experienced together.

"Why don't you choose the one you think works best," he said after a few minutes. "We'll print out the contact sheet and a few photos and decide later."

She nodded, feeling oddly guilty.

They emerged from the darkroom almost an hour later with four photos hung to dry. There was no doubt which photo would grip readers, reveal the heart of the story, and, most importantly, sell newspapers. Still, it made her sick to her stomach to think about that photo running with a story that bore her byline. When she put herself in the shoes of the young woman—or even the little girl—she could almost feel their anguish.

Following Rob back to their cubicles, she felt the eyes of the three other newsroom employees on them. The two middle-aged typesetters merely looked curious, but Michelle was pretty sure she wasn't imagining the less-than-friendly gaze Joy Swanson turned on them. Joy handled advertising sales and layout and occupied the cubicle on the other side of Rob, though most days she was out of the office selling ads.

Michelle's time in the darkroom with Rob had been completely innocent. And yet it had felt intimate at the same time. She'd only known him a couple of days, but she had to admit, it had been quite pleasant standing beside him, their shoulders touching, while he taught her the magic of making an image appear on blank paper in poignant, evocative shades of gray.

The thought warmed her face, and she ducked into her desk chair hoping no one had noticed. She was pretty sure the images in her head right now were not what Mr. Merrick had meant when he'd told her to keep things with Rob "strictly professional."

"So . . . are you going to be upset if I use that photo?"

She whirled at his voice. Rob must have followed her into her cubicle. She knew exactly which photo he meant. "Upset?"

"Upset: to be angry or agitated." One corner of his mouth turned up in a grin.

She returned it, even as she scrambled for an honest way to answer his question. "It's a beautiful photo, Rob. It makes me want to cry. You captured the emotions of the moment amazingly. But I—I don't think it would be right to publish it. It would feel like we were exploiting that poor woman's pain. And the little girl . . . "

He looked at the floor briefly before meeting her eyes. "But don't you think that photo could help people understand the woman's plight? What if the photo made people think?"

"Think what?"

"I don't know. About that kind of . . . violence, about how hard it is to be a single parent. Stuff like that."

She thought for a moment about the point he made, not wanting to overstep her bounds. "I could understand if the picture was just an image of some random person that no one knew. But this is a small town, Rob. And that little girl will likely grow up here—with her mother. For all we know, the grandparents live here—or close enough that they'll see the paper."

"What if I didn't use their names?"

She shook her head. "Even if we don't use their names at all—in the photo caption or the story—you know that everyone will know who it is. The mother's probably not much older than I am, and I can tell you how I'd feel if a photo of my little girl appeared in the paper with that story about me. I'd be mortified. I'd want to move away. But the sad thing is, they may not be able to move away."

"What do you mean?"

That got her hackles up. "Because, Rob, not everybody can just up and move whenever they feel like it. They may be tied here by law because of that sorry excuse for a father. And they may not have the money to make a move. Not everybody is made out of hundred-dollar bills."

He clutched his heart. "Ouch."

"I—That wasn't very nice. I'm sorry. You can't help it if you're filthy rich."

She could tell he was trying to be civil, but her attempt at a joke failed miserably.

He held up his hands in surrender. "It's your story. If you don't want me to run the pic, I won't. We can run the one with all the emergency vehicles instead." His dejected tone left no doubt how he felt about that option.

"I don't see why we have to run the story at all. It's a private matter. But if we have to, I'd feel a lot better about the other photo. Thanks for understanding." When she considered her words, it seemed absurd. She'd been employed here barely two days and she was trying to call the shots? But he was right. It was her story, and her byline on it should give her some rights as to how that story was illustrated. "Speaking of my story, I'd probably better go write it."

"Good point." He raised his eyebrows, conspiring. "And I've got an important front-page football story to write." His smile and his joke—at least she hoped it was a joke—seemed to suggest a truce.

Rob went back to his cubicle, and she heard his typewriter clicking away. But she sat in front of her Selectric keyboard for twenty minutes before an anemic opening paragraph for her story formed. What had ever made her think she could be a reporter?

CHAPTER SIX

"You look so thin, Michelle. You're not anorexic, are you?" Beth Penn smoothed the gingham tablecloth in the kitchen of the farmhouse where Michelle had grown up. "I just read an article about that in *Redbook*," her mother said. "It's becoming almost an epidemic."

"You can't be serious, Mom. I've *gained* at least four pounds since I moved into town."

"Don't be silly. You can't gain four pounds in a week."

"I've been there two weeks. Can you believe it?"

"No, I can't. But you be careful. This *anorexia nervosa* stuff isn't anything to mess around with."

Michelle rolled her eyes and laughed. "Mom, I assure you, I am in no danger whatsoever. In fact, what's for supper? Can I stay?"

"What kind of question is that? Of course you can stay. I was hoping you'd spend the night and go to church with us in the morning."

"Thanks, but I've got too much work to catch up on. I'll stay for supper, though. When will Dad and Allen be in?"

Her mother blew a damp wisp of hair off her forehead and looked at the clock. "Dad's cultivating on the east eighty, but he promised he'd be in before dark. Allen didn't come home this weekend. Help me set the table, would you?"

"Sure."

It felt weird being back home. It had been one thing to come home for a weekend every now and then while she was in college, but now that she had her own place in town, she felt like a guest in her parents' house. She'd stay long enough to see her dad, but she was anxious to get back to her apartment. And she did have a long to-do list to accomplish before she went to work Monday morning.

Getting down the plates and glasses from the hutch, she noticed the weekly edition of the *Beacon* lying on the window ledge in the breakfast nook where Dad read the *Wichita Eagle* every morning and the *Bristol Beacon* every Thursday evening. Her mother hadn't mentioned her byline yet, but Mom would tell her that her story was terrific even if it stank. Dad was the one who'd tell her what he really thought. It was his opinion she valued most.

"So why didn't Allen come home? I thought he was going to work for Dad on the weekends."

"Have you talked to your brother since he started classes?" Mom's attempt to sound casual failed.

"No. Why? Is school going okay?"

"I think so. I just wondered if he'd said anything to you about a certain girl."

Her jaw dropped. "Allen has a girlfriend?"

Her mom looked worried. "A pretty serious one, it seems."

"Are you kidding?" Her brother had been on exactly one date during his four years of high school. Just like she'd had exactly one date during her two years of college . . . and that had been a disaster. Now that she was finally ready to consider dating again, she was stuck back in her hometown, where the possibilities were zilch.

The irony was not lost on her. She opened the silverware drawer and counted out three of each utensil. "So my baby brother has a girlfriend. Anybody we know?"

"No. And it's nobody I *want* to know."

"What do you mean?" This was getting interesting.

"Her name is Piper Something-or-other and she's older than you. Already graduated."

"He's dating a twenty-something woman?" She almost laughed. "How did he meet her?"

"At the college. She's taking some nursing classes there."

"Have you met her?"

"No. And Allen hasn't said one word to us about it, so don't tell him I told you."

"Then how do you know about it?"

"Sylvia Branson has a sister who works in admissions at the college."

"Mom, don't blow things out of proportion. If Sylvia's sister is anything like Sylvia, she probably saw them wave at each other and jumped to conclusions."

"No. She saw them—" Was her mother blushing? "Let's just say she saw them do a lot more than wave. I tried to tell—"

"Hey! Look who's here." Her father's booming voice made them both start, and Mom's expression said the subject was closed.

"Don't tell me the prodigal daughter has returned," Dad said.

"Just for a while. I'm headed back right after supper." She went to the door with arms outstretched.

But he took a step backward and took off his cap, revealing a line of dirt streaking his forehead. "Save that hug for me. I'm too dirty from the field right now."

He disappeared into the basement where the farmhands' shower was, and by the time she and Mom had dinner on the table he was back upstairs, smelling of Lifebuoy soap and Aqua Velva.

Dad claimed his hug and they sat down to eat. After blessing the food, he stabbed a forkful of scalloped potatoes and turned to Michelle. "So how's city life, Mish?"

She couldn't hold back any longer. "Did you read my story?"

He chewed thoughtfully. Finally he put his fork down. "I did."

"Well?" She tilted her head, waiting. "What did you think of it?"

"The question is, what did *you* think of it?"

Uh-oh. She swallowed hard. "You didn't like it."

"The writing was good, Mish."

"But . . . ?"

"But I'm not sure that was a story that needed to be told."

"What do you mean?"

As if on cue, her mother slipped from her chair and went to the sink.

"I just don't think people pay twelve dollars a year to read about some guy beating up on— About situations like that," he finished lamely.

She swallowed back sudden tears, embarrassed—and surprised—that his words cut so deeply. "Are you saying I shouldn't have written the story at all?"

"Not necessarily," he said. "I don't think it needed to be a front-page story, though. And the photo was completely unnecessary."

They'd ended up going with a photo of the emergency vehicles gathered in front of the Preston home. She hated to think what Dad would have said if they'd used the picture Rob wanted to use.

"I know you probably don't have any control over those decisions, but—"

"No, I don't. And I didn't take the picture. Rob Merrick did. It's not like we used names or anything."

"Bristol is a small town, Mish. Anybody with a brain could figure out who that was."

Just what she'd told Rob. "Do you and Mom know them?" She'd seen the police report, but she didn't know the family.

"That's not the point." Dad reached for the paper and unfolded it, spreading the front page between them. "How long do you think it would take somebody to put two and two together after seeing this?" He thumped a finger on the photo.

For the first time, she realized the house number was clearly visible in the photo, along with a distinctive half-barrel planter on the porch next door. She knew Bristol well enough to know there were people who'd make entertainment out of driving around town until they found the house and the definitive planter in the photo, just so they could brag that they knew who the story was about.

"Like I said, Daddy, I didn't take the picture." She hated the defensiveness in her voice. She turned to her mother, who still stood at the sink with her back to them. "Mom, do you agree?"

"Agree about what, honey?" Mom came back to the table with a dish towel balled up in one fist, but she didn't sit down.

Michelle sighed, frustration rising within her. "Do you think I shouldn't have written the news story?"

Dad gave her a stern look. "Now, don't put words in my mouth, Mish."

"That's what you said, Daddy. You said it was a story that didn't need to be told."

"I said I'm not *sure* it was a story that needed to be told. There's a difference."

"Mom?" But even as Michelle tried to rally her mother's support, she knew Mom would side with Dad. Like she always did.

Her mother sighed and pulled out her chair. "It's just that there's already so much bad news in this world—the war, the drug problem . . . It seems like the local paper would want to focus on what's *right* with the world."

"But ignoring the problem won't make it go away. Maybe my story will get people to thinking about how they could help. Or maybe it will help people understand that woman's plight." She realized she was parroting the arguments Rob had given her. Arguments she'd shot down one by one. And hearing herself repeat them, they still sounded feeble.

"The only thing that story will do is get people gossiping." Dad put down his fork and looked across the table at her. "We're not saying the problem should be ignored, Mish. We're just saying it doesn't need to be aired on the front page of the *Bristol Beacon*. People subscribe to the paper so they can find out about church events and keep up with school activities."

"And the football games," Michelle said, not even trying to hide her sarcasm. "Don't forget the football games."

"Michelle . . . " He put down his fork and shot her a warning glance that made her feel as if she were fifteen again. "We just don't think this is what people are expecting when they subscribe to the *Beacon*."

From the way he said "we," she knew he and Mom had talked about this before she arrived.

"Well, it wasn't my decision to report this story. I just wrote what they assigned to me. It's not like I've been there long enough to decide what gets published and what doesn't."

"Now, you don't need to get defensive, Mish."

"I'm not." But that wasn't true. She felt like they'd ganged up on her. And it hurt.

Her mother folded the dish towel into careful fourths, not looking at her. "So you're saying Mr. Merrick told you to write all those details? Told you to describe the battered woman and that poor little girl in such detail? I just wonder if you couldn't have taken a different angle with the story."

Michelle scowled. "If you're going to patronize me, Mom, I'd just rather not talk about it."

Dad drained his iced tea glass, set it on the table, and looked at her—hard. "Your mother is not patronizing you. It's a fair question. I just hope you're praying about this job and making sure that it doesn't cause you to compromise what you believe. I wonder . . . " He stopped, as if he'd thought better of what he was going to say. But then his eyes softened and he went on. "Just pray about it, Mish. But if you *were* under orders to write those details, maybe the *Beacon* isn't the right place for you."

She racked her brain to recall what details she'd put in the story that her parents found so offensive. And remembering, she felt as if her own words had struck her in the face. For, with words, she'd drawn a picture that was every bit as graphic as Rob Merrick's photograph. The one she'd convinced him not to publish.

Chapter Seven

Myrtle Dressler scowled at Michelle over her cat-eye glasses. "This is at least the second time I've reminded you, Miss Penn."

"I'm sorry. I keep forgetting."

"Well, I can't complete the paperwork without the official, original Social Security card. If you want a paycheck, you'll have to get that to me."

"I'll see if my mom can track it down."

Myrtle looked down her pointy nose. "You mean to tell me your *mother* still takes care of those details for you? How old did you say you were, Miss Penn?" It was said with a smile, but Michelle knew a lecture-disguised-as-a-joke when she saw one.

"I'll try to find it. But . . . it might be Monday before I can get it to you." She felt exactly as small as she was sure Myrtle intended her to.

"Well," the woman huffed, "I guess if I have to issue a separate check, I can, but just keep in mind, you won't be getting a paycheck tomorrow when they're handed out to the other employees."

Great. She was already two days late on her September rent. Michelle slinked back to her cubicle to get her purse. She'd officially been employed at the *Beacon* for two full weeks now, but some days it still felt like her first day on the job. And Myrtle seemed determined to keep it that way.

She started out the back door then remembered she wanted to pick up a few things at the corner drugstore before she went home. She traipsed back through the building, ignoring Myrtle as she passed the reception desk. She pushed through the inside doors and stepped into the air-lock entry just as Rob hustled through the outside doors.

"You leaving?" he asked.

She nodded. "Have a good weekend."

"Um . . . last I checked, your car was in the back lot."

"Thanks for keeping track of it for me. It's nice to know I won't lose it."

"Sure. Anytime."

That crooked grin of his was going to get her in big trouble. He held the door for her, and she swept past him and headed for the drugstore. But before the door closed completely, she heard Rob holler her name.

She stopped on the sidewalk and turned to see him jogging toward her. In spite of the calendar's declaration of September, the sultry air still felt like August, and by the time he caught up with her, sweat beaded his brow.

"You want to go get a Coke or something?"

Or something? "Um . . . is this business or pleasure?"

"Totally pleasure. Cross my heart." He drew an *X* over his broad chest.

"I'm not sure that would be a good idea."

"How could it possibly not be a good idea? Come on. . . . It's Friday night." He narrowed his baby blues at her. "Unless you already have a date."

"So now it's a date?"

He studied her, as if trying to decipher what she wanted him to say. "Sure."

He apparently didn't know about the warning his father had given her . . . or maybe he was attempting to spite his old man at her expense? His expression gave away nothing.

"I'll tell you what. I need to pick up a few things at the drugstore. I'll have a quick Coke with you—dutch treat—because there are a few things I'd like to talk to you about. Strictly business."

"Yes, ma'am. Business meeting it is." He wore that enigmatic half smile again—the one that said he was just playing along with her but knew he had an ace in the hole. And an ace on the table, for that matter.

He led the way down the street to Bristol Drugs, then up the main aisle of the drugstore. Michelle hadn't been inside the store since the week before she left for college, but when she looked up and saw the soda fountain, she felt as if she'd instantly been transported back to high school. She could almost hear the mellow strains of Tommy James and the Shondells and Neil Diamond playing on the jukebox. She felt certain if she simply spoke Kevin's name, he would whirl around on one of the patched vinyl bar stools and give her that trademark Ferris grin. She closed her eyes, surprised at the power—and the pain— of the memories.

"You okay?"

Her eyes fluttered open to see Rob Merrick's face inches from hers, his brow knit in a worried expression.

"I–I'm fine. I just . . . haven't been here for a while. It hasn't changed one bit in two years."

Two adolescent girls bent over the jukebox in the corner, giggling and feeding coins into the machine. When they sat down, the smooth vibrato of "Crystal Blue Persuasion" filled the air. Michelle wanted to cover her ears. If "Crimson and Clover" came on next, she was out of here.

Rob pulled his wallet from his back pocket. "What do you want to drink?"

"Cherry Coke. But we're going dutch, remember?" She fished in her purse for change. She knew good and well there were no bills in her purse, but surely she could scrounge up fifty cents. But her frantic search produced only a nickel and two pennies.

"Don't worry," Rob said. "I've got it. This is a business meeting, remember? I can take it out of petty cash."

"Thanks." She couldn't meet his eyes, even though she suspected they held nothing but kindness.

While the high-school kid behind the counter poured cherry Cokes in shapely glasses, Rob took two straws from the dispenser and handed her one. "Booth or counter?"

"Booth, please." Less likely someone would see them together. She chose a booth at the back of the drugstore and settled in as far as she could without actually hugging the wall.

Rob slid in across from her and took a long draw on his straw. She did the same, enjoying the sweet cherry-flavored concoction, thankful for the distraction.

"So what is it you wanted to talk about?"

"Well, first . . . I'm not sure if you're aware of this, but I have instructions to keep our relationship strictly professional."

"Our relationship?" He motioned between them. "Yours and mine?" She nodded.

"Instructions from whom?" His surprise seemed genuine.

"From your father."

"What? You're kidding, right?"

"Would I kid about something like that?"

"I don't know. I've only known you for two weeks. Would you?"

"No. I would not."

"What did he say, exactly?"

She repeated Mr. Merrick's words as accurately as she could remember.

He looked shocked. "Did you say something that made him think you—?"

"Oh, right. I told him I had designs on you, which was why I took the job in the first place, and that I intended to marry you before the year was up." She glared at him. "No, I didn't say anything! What do you think I am, stupid?"

"Sorry. That was a dumb question." His eyes narrowed and a far-away look shadowed his pale-blue irises. "But this explains a lot."

"What do you mean?"

He shook his head. "Never mind. I don't need to drag you into this. But I am sorry, Michelle. My dad can be a real pain sometimes."

"It can't be easy, working for your dad." She suddenly understood why Allen griped so much about working on the farm. And her brother only worked on weekends now that he was away at college. He had a lot more freedom than Rob Merrick did.

"We make it work," Rob said. "But then, I didn't know Dad was warning all the pretty employees away from me."

She laughed—and tucked away that "pretty" to ponder later. "I got the impression he was trying to protect you from *me*, not the other way around."

"Doesn't matter. I don't need that. I'll talk to him about it. And I apologize. That was about as unprofessional as it gets."

"*Please* don't say anything to him, Rob." She hadn't meant it to come out sounding so desperate, but she was serious. "I could lose my job if he knew I told you."

"I won't let that happen." He slid the straw up and down in his Coke. "So what else did you want to talk about?"

"Huh?" Why hadn't she just kept her big mouth shut altogether? *Because, admit it, Penn—you wanted to spend time with the guy.* The thought startled her. And made her wonder whether it was so obvious that Mr. Merrick had deemed his warning justified. The room grew overly warm.

"You said you had several things you wanted to talk to me about."

She had no desire to spill her guts to this man, especially if he was just going to go back to daddy and relay all her complaints. "No, that's pretty much it." She took a sip of her Coke, but the glass was empty and her straw made a loud slurping sound. "I just . . . wanted you to know why I hesitated when you said this was a date."

"Well, again . . . I'm sorry. By the way, good job on the story in last week's edition."

"Yeah, well, speaking of fathers who are a pain . . . "

He cocked a questioning eyebrow at her.

She sighed. Another can of worms she probably shouldn't have opened. "My dad wasn't too thrilled with the story. My *parents*, I should say—except that my mom rarely has an opinion of her own. She just pretty much agrees with whatever my dad thinks."

"Why wasn't your dad thrilled?"

"He doesn't think that kind of news should be in the paper."

"What kind of news?"

"Negative news. He thinks a small-town newspaper should be all rainbows and smiley faces and fluffy kittens."

He laughed. "Well, yeah, we probably would sell more subscriptions that way."

She shrugged. "Maybe. And after all, that *is* what it's all about, right? Selling more papers?"

He ignored her sarcasm. "So what did *you* think about the story?"

Her jaw dropped. "That's *exactly* the question my dad asked me. Except that was his 'diplomatic' way"—she chalked quote marks in the air—"of saying he didn't think much of it." She told him about the conversation she'd had with her parents. "Dad didn't like the photo either—no offense. Did you realize the house number was showing in that photo?"

"So?"

She shrugged. "It just seems like if we weren't going to use names, we probably shouldn't have put the woman's address, either."

"It's a number, Michelle. There are probably at least fifty other houses in town with that same number. Besides, it's public record. Anybody who's dying to know who those people are can walk into the police station and ask to see the report."

"I hate to guess what they would have thought about the one *you* wanted to run."

"Do you care?"

"What do you mean?"

"Do you really care what your parents think about the article?"

"Of course I care. They're my parents." She studied him. "Don't you? Care what your dad thinks, I mean?"

He shrugged, looking uncomfortable that the subject he'd brought up had backfired on him.

She didn't know what to say after that, and Rob suddenly seemed in a hurry to leave. "Well . . . " He pushed his Coke glass aside and started a slow slide out of the booth. "I'd probably better go. I've got . . . stuff to do. Have a good weekend."

"Okay. You too. See you Monday."

"Right."

He dug his hands into the pockets of his khaki pants. "Shall I walk you to your car?"

"Thanks, but I have some shopping to do first." As if to prove it, she walked to a nearby display of sunglasses, popped on a pair, and studied herself in the mirror. But through the dark green lenses, she watched his reflection in the tiny rectangular mirror as he left the drugstore. And for the thousandth time, she determined to get a grip on her big mouth.

CHAPTER EIGHT

Rob knocked on the door jamb and waited for his father to look up from his desk. "Sir? Are you busy?"

"I'm always busy, Robert. And you know what Mondays are like. But come in. What's up?"

"Mind if I sit?" Moving a pile of newspapers and magazines from the chair in front of his father's desk, he plopped into the seat without waiting for an answer.

"Sure . . . What's up?" his father said again, still shuffling papers around on the desktop.

"I need you to promise me something first."

He had Robert Merrick Sr.'s attention now. "Well, now, you know how I feel about promises."

Did he ever. He bit his tongue. "I'm serious, Dad. I need your assurance that what I ask you won't—affect anybody's job here."

His father took off his glasses and rubbed the bridge of his nose. "What's going on? You can talk to me, Rob."

It wasn't a promise, but it would have to do. He looked into his father's eyes—ice-blue eyes he'd been told were identical to his own. "Did you tell a certain employee to stay away from me?"

His dad actually laughed. "I have a pretty good idea what this is about—*who* this is about. But for your information, I tell all our employees of a certain gender to stay away from you."

"Dad!"

"Robert, do you have any idea how many women come in here to apply for a job just so they can get a glimpse of you?"

Had the man lost his last marble? "What are you talking about?"

"Surely I don't have to tell you that half the women in this town would give their two front teeth for a chance to go on a date with Rob Merrick. I'm just trying to ensure that the ones I actually hire are here to do their job, not to make goo-goo eyes at the second-in-command."

"Not to change the subject, but since when am I second-in-command? If I'd known that, I would have given myself a longer vacation. And a hefty raise . . . "

His attempt at humor fell flat.

"I use that term only because someday you'll be running this company. For now, you work your way up the ladder like I did. But back to the subject at hand—if my guess is correct and Miss Penn is the tattletale, that would indicate that she's chosen to ignore the conditions of her employment. Perhaps I should have a word with—"

"No, Dad! She didn't do anything wrong. In fact, the only reason she said anything is because I asked her for a date." It wasn't exactly a lie. "And she turned me down."

"You asked her for a date? Now, why would you go and do that? You know how I feel about that sort of thing. We have a policy. Surely that thing with Joy Swanson should have been enough to—"

"Dad. I didn't want to come back to work here in the first place, but I did, and I admit, I've enjoyed it. A lot. I appreciate your giving me a great job right out of college, and I know I'm getting training that will serve me well for the rest of my career no matter where I go." He was trying to cover all the arguments they'd been through a hundred times so his father wouldn't have to make them again. "But if working here means I can't date who I want to date, or that you're going to make my friends feel threatened for even being seen in public with me, then I think it's time I found something else to—"

"Now, hang on, hang on." His father raised a hand. "There's nothing that says you can't fraternize with the employees. But it wouldn't matter whether I was your father or your boss—nothing good can come of having an interoffice fling."

"What if it was more than a fling?"

The look on Dad's face told him he'd given the wrong impression. *Fling* must mean something more to his father's generation. "That didn't come out right. I just meant, what if I really cared about one of the employees? What if I thought she might be someone I wanted to get to know better?"

"That's exactly my point, Robert. You can't possibly know Michelle Penn well enough to have made that kind of a decision."

"How long did you know Mom before you asked her out?" Rob wasn't playing fair. He knew the answer to that question.

"You know very well how long. But we're not talking about that."

No, Dad, God forbid we should ever talk about Mom. "Still, do you see my point?"

"And do you see mine?"

"No. I don't. I'm twenty-four years old. I really don't think I need my old man telling me—"

"Robert. That's disrespectful."

"Sorry." He backtracked before his dad could launch into a lecture. "I don't need my *father* telling me who I can and cannot ask out on a perfectly innocent date."

"Perfectly innocent until one of you falls in love. Not to beat a dead horse, but let's not forget the Joy Swanson incident."

"You won't let me forget. Besides, that turned out fine."

"Says you. Joy may have a different opinion."

"She still works here, doesn't she? And so do I. And we get along just fine."

His dad's features softened. "Believe me, son, I know what I'm talking about. And not just because of the thing with Joy. There's a reason for these rules. Things can get extremely complicated. Even your mother would have admitted to that."

"Well, she would have known." His parents had met when they worked for the same news agency back in the forties, though his father never talked about it.

"And she would have given you the same advice I'm giving you."

Rob swallowed hard. It was the closest his father had come to talking about Mom since . . . since a day he suspected they both wanted to wipe off the face of the calendar.

* * * * *

Michelle pulled out her calculator and did a quick tally of the groceries in her cart. If she put the cookies back, she'd have enough. She ate too many sweets anyway. And if she really got hungry for cookies, she could go out to the farm and bake some with Mom.

She sighed at the thought of the farm. She'd talked to her mom on the phone a couple of times, but she hadn't been out to see her folks since the night they'd raked her over the coals about her first byline. Well, maybe "raked over the coals" was a bit of an exaggeration, but she sure hadn't received the praise she'd expected.

When she'd called her mother about mailing her Social Security card, Mom acted as if nothing had happened. Her mother had enclosed a short note in the envelope with the card and had made no mention of their discussion about the article in the paper.

This week's edition of the *Beacon* had nothing controversial in it as far as Michelle knew, and being the opening-game football issue, there wasn't room for any real news anyway. She smiled to herself, filing away that line to use on Rob Merrick the first chance she got.

She replaced the package of cookies on the shelf and headed for the produce section. Two heads of lettuce, a bag of apples, and a bunch of seedless grapes later, she inventoried her cart with satisfaction. Mom would be proud of her choices. Now, if she could just remember to eat all this healthy food before it went bad.

She was finding it challenging to cook for one. She was a good cook, but she'd grown up cooking for her family, a crew of Dad's hired men, and her 4-H club. With math not being her strong suit, it was hard to divide a recipe into sixths.

She put one head of lettuce back in the produce bin and started for the checkout. Rounding the corner, she almost ran into a woman with a shopping basket over one arm and a toddler in the other.

She took in a sharp breath. It was the little jet-haired girl from Rob's photographs. The battered woman from her news story.

"I'm so sorry," Michelle said, wondering if the woman would recognize her.

The woman gave her an anemic smile. "It's okay." Her face was no longer swollen, but her fair skin still bore the green-and-yellow mottling of fading bruises. She dipped her head, letting her straight, mousy-brown hair conceal her face, as if she could hide the evidence.

"I should watch where I'm going. Sorry," Michelle said again.

The woman hitched the little girl up on her hip and eyed Michelle. "You don't remember me, do you?"

"Yes . . . I do remember." Michelle absently rubbed her own eyebrow in sympathy. "I was there with the *Beacon*."

"No, I mean before that."

"I don't understand."

"I was Becky Brannon. Before I became Becky Preston. I was a year behind you in school, but I sat right behind you in choir my junior year. With the altos . . . ? You're Dan and Beth Penn's daughter, right?"

"Yes. But I—" Michelle squinted and studied her, trying—and failing—to see the Becky she remembered only vaguely from high school. "I'm sorry. That day . . . I didn't realize we knew each other from before."

"It's okay. You were one of the popular girls. I wouldn't expect you to remember. But you were always nice to me. Not everyone was." She looked away, as if the memory embarrassed her.

Trying to ease the awkward moment, Michelle reached out and tugged at the hem of the little girl's sundress. "That's a pretty pink dress you're wearing, sweetie."

The toddler stuck a thumb in her mouth and buried her head in her mother's shoulder. But Becky smiled. "Can you tell Michelle 'Thank you'?"

The tiny girl mumbled something that her mother let pass as "Thanks."

"What's her name? She's beautiful."

"Eden Crystal." Pride swelled Becky's voice. "She just turned two."

"She's adorable. Well . . . " Michelle gave her cart a little push. "I'd better finish my shopping." But before she'd gone ten feet, something made her turn back.

Becky was still standing there, watching her.

Michelle rolled the cart back to where she was standing. "Are you doing okay? Since . . . the other day?"

"We're all right." Becky looked at the floor. "He—He's still in jail."

"I'm sorry." She looked at the same tile on the floor that Becky's eyes seemed glued to. "Do you need anything? Money or . . . anything?" Why was she even asking a question like that? She'd be doing well to pay her own rent this month. Still, something made her ask.

"We get by. His mother helps a little."

"Do I know him? Your husband, I mean?" She couldn't remember anyone named Preston at Bristol High. But then, she hadn't remembered Becky Brannon either. Not really. Had she really been that isolated and self-centered in high school? How had she not been aware that this kind of stuff was happening—even in tiny Bristol?

Becky shook her head. "I met him in Florida. One of those spring-break flings. Big mistake."

Colossal mistake. But Michelle only said, again, "I'm sorry."

"Listen, there is something you could do."

"Okay . . . " Michelle was suddenly sorry she'd offered. It would be just like God to see that she made good on it.

"That guy from the paper—the one who took all the pictures?"

"Rob."

She shrugged. "I guess. I don't remember that day too good, but I think maybe he got pictures of Eden."

Michelle held her breath.

"I don't want those floating around," Becky said. "Or . . . coming back to haunt Eden. Can you tell him? The photographer? Or maybe get the pictures back from him?"

"Do you want the pictures?" She regretted giving her the option as soon as the words were out.

Becky closed her eyes, and Michelle could almost see her remembering the pain of that day. "No," she said finally. "I just don't want anybody else to see them."

Michelle touched the soft cotton of Eden Crystal's dress, feeling somehow that she was touching Becky when she did. "I'll see what I can do. I've only worked at the paper a couple of weeks, but I'll do my best."

"Thanks."

She nodded and turned to go.

"Michelle?" Becky spoke her name.

She turned back yet again. "Yes?"

"What you wrote—in the newspaper?"

"Yes?" She held her breath.

"That's exactly how it feels. It almost seemed like . . . like you knew. If you do, I'm sorry."

"Oh. No, I don't—"

But this time it was Becky who turned away before she could answer.

She watched Becky trudge away, the sweet child's arms wrapped about her neck. And stronger than pity, stronger than compassion, the emotion Michelle felt was envy.

CHAPTER NINE

Rob spiraled the football harder than he intended, and it hit Doug Jensen's open hand hard before bouncing onto the turf.

"Ouch! You trying to kill me, Merrick?"

"Sorry, man. Don't know my own strength, I guess."

The high school field was lush and green, and only because Bristol High was playing out of town later tonight had he and Doug been able to get onto the field. They'd come to jog on the asphalt track that circled the field, but Doug had found a scuffed football abandoned on the sidelines, and now they were horsing around, reliving their own glory days as small-town football stars. They'd played for rival teams, though, so there were as many good-natured barbs being tossed between them as pigskin passes.

He threw another too-hard pass. Doug caught the ball but held it, studying him from the twenty-yard line. "Something eating you?"

"No." He waited for his buddy to lob the ball back and this time took care with his pass. "My old man's on my case."

"What did I tell you about moving back home?" Doug shook his head. "Not a good idea, man."

"It's only temporary. Till I find a place."

Doug looked skeptical, but Rob didn't try to defend himself. Dad's house was plenty big. Rob had the whole second story to himself, and the two of them rarely bumped into each other once supper was over. It was the working hours that were the problem, and there was no office big enough.

Doug threw a nice spiral pass. "So what's he on your case about?"

"A chick." Rob caught the ball, then snapped it back.

"I should've known. Man, I told you the women would get you in trouble."

He laughed, catching another toss. "You're a good one to talk . . . since you went and married one."

"Yeah, well, that's different. Once you marry 'em, they're fine."

Rob grinned and nailed him with the ball.

"So what's the problem?"

"There's a girl at work I wouldn't mind asking out. Dad says no way."

"As in, 'No way or you're fired'?"

"Well, he hasn't exactly said that. Probably more like, 'No way or *she's* fired.' Or 'No way or I'll make your life miserable.'"

Doug cocked his head. "Is she worth it?"

"I wouldn't be talking to you about it if she wasn't."

His friend let out a low whistle. "That says a lot, coming from you. Maybe you ought to let me take her off your hands."

"Excuse me?" He shot Doug a look. "I doubt Denise would appreciate that."

"Oh, yeah. I forgot I was married, for a minute there." His laugh turned to a wince. "I shouldn't have said that. Not cool."

"No regrets though, right?"

"Huh? About Denise?"

"About marriage."

Doug didn't hesitate. "Not one. Not ever."

"So married life's treating you okay, huh?"

"It's good." The way Doug grinned made Rob think it was *very* good.

Rob checked his watch. "I need to get home and shower. You sure you don't want to ride to the game with me?"

"Wish I could, man, but I promised Denise I'd take her to a movie in Wichita tonight." He wiped his palms on the grass and handed Rob the ball. "Here. Don't say I never gave you anything. Have fun at the game."

An idea popped into his head and began to germinate. "Maybe I will," he muttered under his breath. "Just maybe."

He ignored his buddy's quizzical look and jogged to his car. He had to act fast if he was going to pull this off.

* * * * *

The phone was ringing when Michelle unlocked the door to her apartment. She dove over the back of the sofa to grab the receiver then nearly strangled herself, trying to make the cord reach. "Hello?"

"Michelle, it's Rob."

"Yes?" Against her best efforts to stop it, her voice trembled a little. He'd better not be asking her to come in to work when he'd cut out of work early this afternoon—as he had every Friday since she'd started working at the *Beacon*.

"Listen, I'm covering the game tonight—the Bears are playing over in Pretty Prairie—and I wondered if you'd want to come along. To help out, I mean. I need to take photos, and I could use some help keeping stats and hauling equipment."

"Tonight?"

"Um, yes, tonight. If you'd read a little newspaper called the *Beacon*, you'd know that Friday night is when the football games are usually played around here."

She mimicked his sarcasm. "And if you ever conversed with your employees, you'd know that Friday night is when I wash my hair."

His silence told her that either he was laughing so hard it rendered him speechless or he thought she was serious.

"You know I'm kidding, right?"

"Oh. I thought—"

"I only wash my hair the first Friday of the month. Lucky for you, that was last Friday, so I suppose I could come with you." If the phone cord would have reached, she would already be in her closet deciding what to wear.

"Oh. Okay, then."

"You sound surprised."

"Well, I thought—"

"This is for work, right? Strictly professional?"

"Yes. Yes, of course."

"Well, then, I don't see a problem."

"Great. Can you be ready by five thirty?"

She untangled the cord and picked up the phone, carrying it around the corner into the kitchen. The clock on the stove said it was already almost five. "That's cutting it pretty close, but I'll see what I can do."

"Okay, great. See you then."

She slammed down the phone and raced down the hall to her bedroom. Thank goodness she'd done all her ironing last night and her favorite hip-hugger jeans were fresh out of the dryer. She dressed in record time and was waiting in front of her apartment when his car pulled into the lot.

He reached across the front seat and opened her door. "Hi there. Ready for the big game?"

She made a face. "Ready as I'll ever be. You are aware, aren't you, that I know next to nothing about football?"

"Not a problem. I can teach you as we go." He looked down at her feet. "Are those comfortable shoes? We'll be on the sidelines all night."

"You mean, like, down on the field?"

"Yep."

"Hang on. Maybe I'd better change into tennies."

"Okay. I'll wait."

She jumped out of the car, charged into the house, and changed into tennis shoes. It wasn't the look she'd really wanted for tonight, but it would have to do. Back in the car, she tucked her purse between them on the seat and checked to make sure she had her notebook and pen. "Okay. Ready."

Rob headed out of town, tuning the radio to KGRV. Karen Carpenter's mellow voice filled the air, a new song the radio had been playing ten times a day by listeners' requests. "We've only just begun . . ." crooned the rich alto voice. Michelle sang along under her breath. Something about the song—and the crisp autumn evening, and the cute guy in the driver's seat beside her—made her feel happy. And hopeful. In fact, she couldn't remember the last time she'd felt this way.

Well, yes . . . she could. She felt her happy mood dissipate as she realized that this whole night was uncannily like the last time she and Kevin had been together. Kevin Ferris was the last person she wanted to think about tonight. Wasn't it enough that every morning she still woke up and said a quick prayer for his safety while he was in Nam? And every morning, she disciplined herself to let that prayer be her last thought of Kevin for the day.

Because he had made his feelings clear . . . he didn't want her waiting for him. He didn't feel any commitment to her. "I don't even know if I'll come back," he'd told her the night they broke up. "We've had a good run, babe, but it's time to go our separate ways. I don't want you waiting for me."

"What if I *want* to wait for you? Can I write you?"

Kevin had looked at the floor of her front porch where they'd stood together for the last time. And when he looked up again, she somehow knew. He wasn't breaking up for her sake. He wanted out.

She still got a sick feeling in the pit of her stomach when she let herself think about it. It was pretty bad when your boyfriend would rather go to Vietnam than marry you.

"Sorry to interrupt your concert . . . " Rob's voice canceled her trip down memory lane.

She clapped a hand over her mouth, thoroughly embarrassed to realize her sing-along had grown loud enough for him to hear. "Sorry . . . "

"No, you've got a great voice. For a minute, I thought I had Karen Carpenter right here in the car with me."

She rolled her eyes, blushing.

Rob seemed not to notice. He pointed through the windshield at an expansive grain elevator. The Hutchinson landmark loomed in the distance. "I just needed to ask whether you want to stop up here and grab something to eat on the way. There'll be a concession stand at the game, but there's a Dairy Queen in Hutchinson, and frankly, I'd prefer that to a soggy hot dog."

"Sure. That'd be fine." She quickly calculated whether she had enough money to buy a burger and get into the stadium too. Rob ought to pay her way at the game since this was work-related, but just in case, she'd order light.

"Okay"—Rob turned the radio up—"carry on with the concert."

She laughed but decided it might be awkward to join Stevie Wonder singing "Signed, Sealed, Delivered, I'm Yours." But when "Hitchin' a Ride" came on next, she was back "in concert" and amused to realize that she was, indeed, hitchin' a ride with Rob Merrick.

Maybe he was just being polite, but she silently soaked up Rob's offhand compliment about her voice. She didn't know how great her voice was, but she did love to sing, and she did a pretty fair Karen Carpenter imitation. Besides, she couldn't seem to help singing along. That was half the fun of listening to the radio.

They'd just passed the sign that said Hutchinson was the next exit when the car lurched and began to rumble as if they'd hit one of those country roads her dad dubbed Washboard Lane.

Rob hit the brakes and grabbed the steering wheel with both hands. "Uh-oh." He coasted to the side of the road and crept along the shoulder until they were halfway down the exit ramp.

CHAPTER TEN

Michelle stood beside Rob on the shoulder of the off-ramp, staring at the rear tire on the driver's side. Or what used to be a tire. Now it was a puddle of rubber and tattered tread.

She frowned. "We must have run over a nail."

"Yep." He looked at his watch and ran a hand through his hair, making it stand up in an Elvis Presley pompadour. "We'll have to walk into town and call somebody."

"What do you mean, *we*? You have a frog in your pocket?"

"Oh. Right. *You'll* have to walk into town and call somebody. I'll stay here and guard the car."

She stuck her tongue out at him. "Ha ha. Very funny."

"Okay . . . I'll go."

She studied him, trying to figure out whether he was still joking around. He didn't look like it. "Why don't you just change the tire?"

"You know how?"

She stared at him. "Of course I know how. You don't?" She opened her car door.

"I seem to remember I had to change one to pass driver's ed, but that was almost ten years ago. I don't think I'd remember if my life depended on it."

"Come on, I'll show you. Set the emergency brake, okay?" She motioned for him to follow her.

"You seriously remember how to change a flat tire?"

"You forget, I'm a farm girl."

"Oh, right. The ol' farm-girl thing." But the look he gave her said he was impressed.

He opened the trunk, and they unearthed the spare tire from under a mountain of sports equipment. "Good grief. You could open a YMCA with all this stuff."

"I was a Boy Scout. Our motto is 'Be prepared.'" He gave her a three-fingered salute.

" 'Be prepared'? Are you kidding?" She propped a hand on her hip. "Prepared to organize a football game or a tennis match, maybe. Not to change a flat tire."

He looked at the asphalt, obviously trying to appear sheepish. "Okay, tell me what to do."

She grabbed the jack and tire iron, popped off the hubcap, and handed the tire iron to him. "Loosen those lug nuts and I'll get it jacked up."

He looked at her like she was kidding.

"What's wrong? You've never seen a woman who knew how to work a jack?"

"Um"—he puffed out one cheek with his tongue—"I've never seen a lug nut. At least not that I know of."

"You're kidding, right?"

"Sadly, not kidding. I assume it would be these little screw thing-amajigs?" He tapped a lug nut with the wrong end of the tire iron.

She stared at him, incredulous. "Were you born in a cave?"

"Were you born in a barn?" he shot back.

"Hey, don't make fun. I'm proud to be a farmer's daugh—"

"No, not that . . . " He looked past her, pointedly eyeing the passenger door, which she'd left hanging open.

"Oh." She dropped the jack near the rear tire, walked around the back of the car, and gave the door a shove. "There. You happy?"

He looked at his watch. "I'll be happy when we're standing on the sideline, getting our story. How do you do this, anyway?"

She took the tire iron from him, fit the wrench end on the first lug nut, and gave it a crank. "Like that. You get those loosened, and I'm going to find something to block the tire with."

Heat radiated off the highway as she searched the side of the road for a rock large enough to serve as a block. A few yards down the exit ramp she found a couple of hunks of asphalt that would work. She lugged them back to the car and wedged them behind the rear tire.

On the other side of the car, Rob was huffing and grunting as if he were single-handedly lifting the car.

"You finished with that yet, Mr. Handyman?"

Still squatting beside the tire, he wiped his forehead on his sleeve. "No, I'm not finished. Those things are on there *tight*."

She knelt beside him. "Let me see."

He gave the lug wrench another crank.

"Well, no wonder, Einstein. You're turning it the wrong way. They unscrew counterclockwise."

He shot her a look. "You might have mentioned that before I got them all tightened."

She manhandled the lug wrench to no avail. "Great. Now you have them so torqued I can't get them off."

"Here"—he took the wrench back from her—"let me try."

He turned the opposite way and easily loosened the first lug nut. He turned to her as if he'd just climbed Mount Everest.

"Oh, yeah. Take all the credit *now*."

He chuckled, but when he checked his watch again, he frowned. "They're probably kicking off right about now."

"It's not like you're going to get fired if you miss a few minutes of the game."

"Don't be so sure," he huffed.

She couldn't tell whether he was serious or not but decided it would be best not to broach the subject right now.

She talked him through changing the rest of the tire and stood watching while he did the muscle work. He looked up at her from his position on the side of the road. "Don't work too hard there."

"You're doing fine. Besides, you'll thank me someday for your new-found skill. I'd hate for you to be stranded next time you have a flat."

He only snorted in reply.

Ten minutes later they were crawling down the exit ramp on the spare tire. Rob turned on his left blinker as if heading back onto the highway.

"Hey, what about that Dairy Queen?" She pointed back toward town.

"We don't have time. We're going to miss the first quarter as it is."

She watched the exit sail by outside her window. "That's really not very nice, you know. My mouth was watering."

He shrugged, intent on the road.

"You'd better stop on the way home," she said, pouting.

"Oh, you poor baby."

"Don't make fun of me."

"I'm not making fun of you. I'm saying you might be a little spoiled."

"*Me*, spoiled? You're the one who's spoiled." She was teasing, trying to get a rise out of him, but he'd mentioned that he was an only child and she had a feeling the *spoiled* label wasn't far from the truth. "I bet you had your mama wrapped around your little finger."

"Are you going to talk all the way to the game?" His expression said he was joking, but he kept his eyes trained on the road, and she sensed she'd hit a sore spot.

Feeling strangely chided, she worked to keep her tone light. "Sorry. I'll keep my mouth shut."

He turned up the radio, and Diana Ross's smooth vocals buttered the space between them. "How about you make yourself useful and serenade me."

"Huh-uh. I can't sing on command."

"You were doing fine a few minutes ago. Just pretend I'm not here."

"Then who's driving the car?"

"Real funny. Come on. Don't be shy. You know you're dying to belt it out." He reached for thin air and pulled down a convincing, though invisible, "microphone." He leaned toward her, singing into his fist in a tone she knew was meant to mimic her. "Ain't no mountain high enough . . . "

"Ha ha. Very funny."

He studied her briefly. "You know I'm just kidding, right? You've got a really great voice."

Heat crept up her neck and flushed her cheeks.

He gave the volume knob another twist to the right and they rode without speaking for the next few minutes. But when Neil Diamond's "Cracklin' Rosie" came on, she couldn't help it. She had to sing along.

He gave her an I-told-you-so look, which she ignored.

The song ended as they pulled into the small stadium's parking lot. Suddenly her nerves kicked in. "Now what exactly is it I'm supposed to help you with?" she said.

"You can keep stats while I take pictures."

"You do remember that I know next to nothing about football."

"Okay, then you can haul equipment while I keep stats and take pictures and if I decide I need the tripod for a few shots, you can come back to the car and get that for me."

"So basically I'm a pack mule."

"You said it, not me." Laughing, he jumped out of the car before she could smack him.

She was relieved they'd found their easy way with each other again. But her mind was working to come up with a way to find out why he'd reacted like that when she'd teased him about being spoiled.

And she wasn't altogether sure she wanted to know.

Chapter Eleven

Rob could read the scoreboard from the parking lot. Six minutes left in the first half and Bristol was up 14–7. *Great.* He shook his head. He'd already missed two touchdown photos.

He'd parked as close as he could in the already-crowded parking lot, but they had a hike to get to the sidelines. He grabbed his camera bag from the backseat. "Come on. Follow me!"

He heard Michelle huffing to keep up with him as they scrambled up the berm near the visitors' goal. The breeze held the faintest hint of fall, and the air was charged with the freshness of a new school year. He remembered and wondered how it was possible that six autumns had passed since he was on the field in pads and helmet.

"Are you sneaking in?"

He looked over his shoulder at her. "What do you mean?"

She pointed down to the stadium entrance. "Don't we need tickets?"

He patted his hip pocket where his wallet was. "What do you think your press pass is for? If anyone says anything, just show them."

"I don't have a press pass. No one ever gave me one."

He rolled his eyes. "I'll talk to Dad on Monday. You should have one. But don't worry. I don't think they're going to throw us in jail in the big city of Pretty Prairie. If anyone says anything, let me do the talking."

He walked along the sideline and staked out a spot near the Bears' bench where he could get some candid shots. But when he saw quarterback J. D. Baker sitting lengthwise on the bench, his right leg stretched out and the trainer working it over, his hopes fled. A photo of the senior quarterback icing an injury instead of tossing a touchdown pass in the season opener would be enough for some Bristol fans to cancel subscriptions.

Maybe he'd luck out and the Bears would make another touchdown . . . but he wouldn't hold his breath.

He handed Michelle his backpack. She took it, looking as nervous as she had that day they'd covered the domestic altercation at the house on Donner Avenue. "You okay?"

She nodded. "Just tell me what to do."

"Stick with me. You'll be fine. I just hope we get something we can use."

Rob uncapped his camera lens and focused on the field. If the injury shut them out and he didn't have one touchdown pass to plaster on the front page, his name was going to be mud. With the whole town—but more importantly, with his boss.

More and more he was having second thoughts about working for his father. Dad had promised they'd have a "professional relationship" inside the walls of the *Beacon*. But that was easier said than done. The fact that he'd had to finagle a way to invite Michelle to the game that would meet with dear old Dad's approval should have told him something.

He snapped a couple of boring shots and sent up a prayer that God could grant him one front-page-worthy photo before the night was over. *Just one good shot, Lord . . . please.* He felt a little guilty, praying about something so trivial, when soldiers were dying in Nam and children were starving in China.

A memory came suddenly. He was five or six and he'd come upon a fallen nest on the lawn. A pathetic, featherless fledgling had spilled out of it. He could still remember how he'd felt, watching that bird struggle. He'd run into the house crying and dragged his mother outside to show her. "Pray for him, Mama. Pray."

His mother had knelt right there and prayed, then she'd scooped the little bird back into its nest and propped the nest into a crook of a limb, far enough out that Bitsy, their cat, couldn't get to it. His mom had taken Rob into her arms and sung a song about a sparrow and God's eye watching that little bird, just as it watched Robbie Merrick.

He realized now that the bird hadn't stood a chance. And he'd always wondered whether Mom really believed God cared about some stupid bird.

He shook off the disturbing thought, angry that he seemed to have no control over the way such thoughts rammed into him at random moments and always left him feeling a little disoriented.

"Am I supposed to be writing something down?" Michelle stood at his shoulder with her notepad and pen in hand, unaware that she'd rescued him.

"Don't worry about it. I can get the stats from the press box after the game." It was the way he'd always written sports stories. His memory provided the play-by-play. The stats just confirmed that he'd remembered accurately.

"Wait a minute . . . " She propped her free hand on her hip. "I thought that's why you dragged me along."

"No, remember? I dragged you along to be my pack mule."

"Oh, yeah. How soon I forget."

He laughed, happy she was here with him. Happy he'd have such a pleasant distraction on the drive home.

* * * * *

By the time the game was over, the air had grown crisp. They stopped by the concession stand on the way back to the parking lot, taking advantage of half-price hot dogs.

Michelle paid while Rob was in the restroom. If he didn't offer to reimburse her, she'd put it on her expense report.

They downed hot dogs and Cokes as they wound their way through the parking lot to Rob's car. By the time they were on the road toward home, she was happy for the warmth of the heater. She rubbed her hands in front of the vent, laughing at Rob's lament over the Bears' loss.

"Laugh all you want, but when I put a photo of the guys lined up on the sidelines, it won't be funny."

"Maybe you'll have to break down and publish a photo people will actually be interested in seeing on the front page."

"You just wait till the letters to the editor start flooding in. Then you'll see how much people love seeing sports on the front page."

"People? Don't you mean men?"

"That's what I said. People."

She glared at him, but she couldn't actually be annoyed when he looked so cute with that scowl on his handsome face.

He gripped the steering wheel with his left hand and looked over at her. "You're a hard one to figure out, you know that?"

"What do you mean?"

"You don't like hard-hitting social issues on the front page, but you don't like fast-paced sports on the front page either. Just what *would* you like to see there?"

"I'll tell you exactly what. A picture of kids playing in the park or a story about Mrs. Beakman or maybe a—"

"Who?"

"Harriet Beakman. She's been the head librarian at the public library for as long as anyone can remember. Or how about the new slide at the swimming pool? But not just a picture of the slide. Make sure somebody's kids are on it. Smiling."

He laughed. "So in other words, rainbows and smiley faces and fluffy kittens?"

She stopped short, recognizing the exact phrase she'd used when she told him how unhappy her parents were with the story about Becky Preston being on the front page. But they were right, and suddenly an idea came. "Tell you what, Rob Merrick. I'll make you a deal."

"What kind of deal?"

"You get to decide what goes on the front page, right?"

"Within reason." He cocked his head, looking wary.

"Okay . . . you let me choose the front-page photo and story every week for the next month, and if you don't get at least twenty new subscriptions during that time, I'll . . . " She scrambled to think of a fitting punishment.

"I know. You'll go to dinner with me without my having to pretend it's for work."

"What?" Was he implying what she thought he was implying? This was *not* what she considered punishment, but she wasn't about to tell him that.

"Yes. I confess, I didn't really *need* you tonight. I just knew it was the only way to get you to go out with me."

"Excuse me, but you might want to rethink what you just said."

"You don't believe me?"

"I believe it was the only way to get me to go out with you. But you most certainly *did* need me tonight."

"Huh?"

"You'd still be sitting on the side of the road if I hadn't been along to change that tire." She looked out the window just as they passed the exit sign for Hutchinson. She pointed behind her. "And, hey, don't miss your turn. You owe me Dairy Queen."

"What? You just ate!"

"I didn't have dessert."

"You're sitting over there shivering and you want ice cream?"

"You can turn up the heater."

He snickered, but he pumped the brakes and eased onto the exit ramp as if that had been his intention all along.

Chapter Twelve

"I'm waiting on that front page, Penn." Rob's head bobbed over the wall that separated their cubicles. "Don't disappoint me."

"Don't you worry, Merrick. I've got everything under control. You just save me a three-by-five spot above the fold and mind your own business."

It was Monday afternoon and Michelle still hadn't come up with a front-page photo she could be certain would garner new subscribers. The front page was typically the last one they laid out on Wednesday before they sent the paper to the printer, so she still had a little time. She'd heard Rob tell his father he had it under control, but she was starting to get nervous. This was going to be harder than she'd thought.

She'd spent the weekend wandering around town looking for subject matter, and she did end up with some cute photographs of kids playing at the park and one of the final day the public swimming pool was open. But those were both pretty cliché. And cliché was the last thing she wanted. She didn't just want to wow *Beacon* subscribers— she wanted to wow Rob Merrick. If by some miracle she could wow his father too, so much the better.

On Friday night, she and Rob had sat in the Dairy Queen for two hours, talking and laughing over ice cream cones and giving each other a hard time over the flat tire and missed photos. She liked the guy. A lot. And if she could find a way around his father's stupid rule about "fraternizing," she would go out with Rob in a heartbeat.

I need an idea, Lord, and time's running out. She'd taken to shooting up little prayers whenever work presented a challenge—which was turning out to be several times a day. After three weeks, she was feeling more comfortable in her job, but it seemed there was always something new she had yet to learn.

A familiar cacophony on the street outside the office drew her from her cubicle to the front windows. The ice cream truck was still running its route? She looked at the clock. Of course. School was just getting out. Smart driver. And maybe an answer to the prayer that had barely left her lips.

She ran back to her desk, grabbed her camera, and looped the strap over her neck. She just might have her front-page photo. *Thank You, Lord.*

Rob came to the doorway of his cubicle. "Where are you going?"

"I'll be right back." She felt his eyes on her, but she wasn't about to tell him her idea.

She went out the back door and trotted down the alley to the side street, where the ice cream truck had just pulled over. Already, schoolchildren with backpacks were gathering, and doors of houses flew open up and down the street as the ice cream truck parked and set up shop along the brick avenue in the old Brunswick development. That thought gave her an idea for a caption, and she began composing in her head even as she tweaked the camera's settings and put it to her eye. She loved what she saw through the viewfinder and fired off a dozen shots in succession. If only the paper printed in color.

A little girl in line with her big sister reminded Michelle of Eden, Becky Preston's daughter. Did Eden ever get to enjoy treats like ice cream from the truck on a hot summer's day? She had a feeling three square meals were a treat at their house. She'd thought of Becky and Eden often since that day she'd run into them in the grocery store and wondered if Eden's father was still in the picture.

When the line of children and mothers with babies in tow thinned, she took a few close-ups and jotted down names. One of the young mothers offered her phone number in case they needed to clarify any information. Michelle thanked her, but if the first few shots she'd taken from down the street turned out, she wouldn't need names.

The September air had grown warm. Watching the driver hand out frozen treats, she wished she'd brought her purse. Remembering that she'd worn the same sweater to the game on Friday night with Rob, she dug into the pocket. Sure enough, her change from the concession stand was there. She retrieved two dollar bills and smoothed them out.

"Two Eskimo Pies, please," she told the elderly driver. While he made change, she asked him a few questions about his route and found out he'd be making his rounds in surrounding towns for a few more days before cooler weather shut him down.

He handed her the foil-wrapped delicacies and she thanked him. Tucking her camera inside her jacket, she jogged back to the office, hoping the pies weren't a leaky mess by the time she got there.

Curbing a smile, she went back to her cubicle but handed an Eskimo Pie to Rob over the partition. "Not only do I have your front-page photo, but I got you a little treat besides."

His eyes lit up. "Hey, my favorite. How'd you know?"

"Lucky guess."

He tore open the wrapper and took a huge bite. Satisfied, she went to her desk and did the same. While she ate, she worked hunt-and-peck style on the Selectric to type out the caption she'd come up with. She read it several times, tweaking the wording as she went: "*Children line up along Hamlin Street in Bristol's Brunswick development Monday afternoon for the 'Pied Piper' of ice cream. The neighborhood near Main Street hosted an impromptu end-of-summer celebration when the ice cream truck made what will no doubt be one of it's last rounds of the season.*"

She read the caption and smiled. It was a small blurb, but people probably had no idea how long it sometimes took writers to come up with something clever and unique. She was proud of her caption. Now to hit the darkroom and see if she'd gotten a photo worthy of it.

She got a Coke from the vending machine in the break room then took her camera to the darkroom. The smell of the developer chemicals had become as familiar as the cleaning supplies she used in her apartment. She was just getting everything lined up and measuring chemicals into the trays when someone knocked on the door.

"Michelle?" It was Rob.

"You big snoop! What do you want?" But she couldn't help but laugh.

"You need help?"

"I think I can figure it out." She'd watched him develop film each week now, and last week he'd let her do most of it herself. But since she hadn't taken the film out of her camera yet, she decided to let him in. It wouldn't be good to ruin her first shot at the front page just because she was too stubborn to accept his help. Besides, as much as she tried not to think about it, the guy was growing on her.

She opened the door a crack and peeked out.

His eyes grew round. "You didn't take the film out yet, did you?"

"I'm not that stupid."

"Don't forget to rewind it."

She narrowed her eyes. "Thanks for reminding me." A few days ago she'd forgotten to rewind the film before taking it out of the camera and ruined a whole roll.

Poking her head out into the newsroom where he stood, she flipped the switch that turned on the red light over the door, signaling that film was being developed and no one was to open the door. She flashed a smile. "Come in if you want. And prepare to be impressed."

* * * * *

Rob rolled his eyes but took Michelle up on the invitation and stepped into the darkroom with her. The scent of her filled the room—a heavenly baby-powder-and-lemonade fragrance that made him want to nuzzle her neck.

He blew out a breath and tried to gather his wits. It didn't help that the room was dark and she was so close he could almost feel her steady breathing.

She closed the door, went to the counter, and opened her camera. "Okay, do not open that door. I'm taking out what may very well be a masterpiece."

"What'd you do, shoot a tornado?"

"Is that what it would take to make you think I scooped your quarterback photo?"

He smiled in the dark at her use of the word "scooped" but let it go and leaned against the counter behind her, watching her work. He felt a little guilty, knowing she didn't really need his help in the darkroom any more. But he was curious to get a glimpse of the photos she was bragging on before she'd even seen them.

She developed the negatives, and a few minutes later she pulled a contact sheet from the chemical bath. She hung the print on the line to dry, flipped on the light, and took a loupe from the shelf. Peering through the magnifier, she inspected several tiny images on the sheet. "Oh. Wow." There was genuine awe in her voice, and he moved closer to look over her shoulder.

She handed him the loupe. "Take a look. Especially the first few shots." She moved aside so he could see.

They were nice shots . . . . If you liked small-town, everyday, ordinary photos on the front page. He cleared his throat. "So this is what you want on the front?"

Even in the dim light he could see her stiffen.

"I'm just asking. It's your call."

She opened her mouth as if to say something then seemed to think better of it. Finally she turned to face him, her shoulders squared and her head high. "Yes. This is what I want on the front page. Probably this one." She pointed to the second photo on the sheet.

"Okay," he said. It was her funeral. "Do you want to make the print, or shall I?"

"I'll do it."

"Okay." He felt awkward and regretted not being more encouraging about her photo. But it was too late to backpedal and gush now. Besides, he probably needed to leave an opening to tell her "I told you so" later.

Chapter Thirteen

"Uh-oh."

Michelle heard Rob over the cubicle wall and knew he expected her to ask what he was *uh-oh*-ing about. She was still a little peeved at him for his lackluster reaction to her photos on Monday, but she was trying not to let it bug her. He was just mad because he'd missed his football pic.

Finally her curiosity got the best of her, and she went to his doorway. "What's wrong?"

He wrinkled his nose. "Typo." Without looking at her, he held up the hot-off-the-press copy of the *Beacon* he was reading. "Front page."

"Hey, where'd you get that?" She hadn't seen the paper come back from the printer. She could hardly wait to see how her photo had turned out. "Where's a typo?"

He pointed to the caption beneath her three-column picture. "It should be '*its*.' I–T–S, no apostrophe."

"Let me see that." She knew the difference between *it's* and *its*. The possessive didn't take an apostrophe. But she'd typed her own caption, so if it was wrong she had no one to blame but herself.

She looked over his shoulder. Sure enough, it was wrong. "Rats! I can't believe I did that." But the photo was crisp and sharp and made an eye-catching splash on the front page. Why couldn't he say something about *that*?

"We all do it. It's just too bad when it happens on the front page. You watch; we'll get letters."

"Are you serious? Because of one stupid little apostrophe?"

He nodded.

"Great. And I suppose next you'll tell me I spelled Hamlin wrong."

"Huh?" He looked at the caption again, as if trying to figure out what she meant.

She rolled her eyes. "You don't even get it, do you?"

"Get what?"

She struck an orator's pose and reeled off the first verse of Robert Browning's poem. "'Hamelin Town's in Brunswick, by famous Hanover city. The river Weser, deep and wide, washes its wall on the southern side. A pleasanter spot you've never spied, but when begins my ditty, almost—'"

"What are you talking about?" Rob looked at her as if she'd lost her last marble.

"The Pied Piper of Hamelin. Browning. I had to memorize it in fourth grade." She was actually pretty impressed with herself that it had tripped off her tongue so easily. Fourth grade was a long time ago.

But Rob's eyes glazed over.

"I noticed the ice cream truck was on Hamlin Street—even if somebody did misspell *Hamelin*—"

"Oh, you're a good one to talk about misspellings," he gloated.

She ignored him and rambled on. "Then there's a Browning Avenue, and the neighborhood is Brunswick. They had to be thinking about the Pied Piper when they named the streets. This is a good German town, right?"

"I don't have a clue what you're talking about, but why don't you do some research on that. Maybe there's a story there."

"You seriously don't know the Pied Piper?"

"I know 'pay the piper.' And Peter Piper. Do those count?" He struck a pose, mimicking her. "'Peter Piper picked a peck of pickled peppers. How many pickled peppers did Peter Pi—'"

She backhanded him on the shoulder. *What a dolt!* The thought made her giggle. Now she was even thinking in Old English. And Rob Merrick was impossible to stay mad at for more than five minutes.

They joked around until she noticed the clock on his desk showed it was almost five o'clock. "You can stay all night if you want to, but it's almost closing time and I need to take care of a couple things before I leave."

He glanced at the clock. "Wow, is it already five?"

"Time flies when you're having fun," she quipped, backing out of Rob's cubicle.

"See you tomorrow, Penn. Have a good night."

"You too."

She made a few notes for a story she was working on, shut down her Selectric, and started out the front door.

She had her hand on the latch when Mr. Merrick appeared behind her. "I'd like to talk to you for a minute before you go, please."

She checked Myrtle's clock to make sure she wasn't leaving too early. Nope. It was five after five. The man had been in the office all afternoon. Why had he waited till she was walking out the door to call a meeting? But she followed him into his office.

"Sit down for a minute, please, Michelle." At least he'd quit calling her *Miss Penn*. "Close the door behind you."

Uh-oh. She sat on the edge of the armless chair in front of his desk. "Yes, sir?"

He rested his elbows on the tidy desktop and steepled his hands. "I have several matters I'd like to talk to you about."

"Okay . . . " It sounded like she'd be here for a while. She scooted back in the chair and crossed her legs.

He reached behind him to the credenza and produced a copy of the day's paper. "Robert said you're responsible for this?" He jabbed a manicured finger at her ice cream truck photograph.

"Yes, sir. And I'm aware of the typo. I—"

"Typo?"

She hesitated. "Yes . . . in the caption. I don't know how it slipped by me, but I'll do my best to see that it doesn't happen again."

He slipped a pair of reading glasses from the pocket of his dress shirt and used them like a magnifying glass to read the caption. "Ah, yes. I see it now. Well, that's not why I wanted to talk to you, but it certainly does hammer home the point." He looked at her as though she should know what he was talking about.

She didn't have a clue. "I'm sorry, I'm not sure what—"

He put his glasses back in his pocket and cleared his throat. "It seems you have a distraction here that is keeping you from doing your job as well as you might."

She stared at him. "Excuse me? In what way am I not doing my job well?"

He jabbed at her photo caption. "You pointed it out yourself."

"But, Mr. Merrick—" She tried not to let him see how flustered he had her. "You called me in here before you even knew about the typo. So there must be something else. What is it that I need to improve upon? Tell me, and I'll do my best to correct it."

"I think you know very well what it is that needs correcting, Miss Penn. I laid out the guidelines when I hired you, and you are apparently unable to follow them. Consider this a warning. If you force me to address the issue again, I'll have to let you go."

She felt as if he'd slapped her. The only thing he could be talking about was Rob. Yes, they talked to each other. A lot. In the break room, in the darkroom, and over the partition between their cubicles. But most of the time they were talking about work. Or at least they were working while they talked. Surely Mr. Merrick didn't expect her to completely ignore the people she worked with.

Maybe he'd found out that Rob had taken her along to the football game. Still, she'd done nothing wrong, and if she had to play dumb to force him to say what he was only hinting at, so be it. She squared her shoulders. "I have done my job to the very best of my ability. I've turned in every story on time. I've even put in extra hours without pay."

"I'm not aware that you've been asked to put in extra hours. When was this?"

"I went to the game with Rob—Robert III—and helped him shoot pictures of the game."

"And that would likely explain why—despite the Bears' two touchdowns—we don't seem to have one shot of the first quarter. Instead our front-page features the ice cream man? Robert said that was your doing."

She glanced back toward Rob's cubicle, wondering if he knew she'd gotten called in to his father's office. And if so, why he wasn't coming to her defense. "Mr. Merrick, I don't know what Rob told you, but the reason there are no pictures of the first half of that game is because Rob had a flat tire. I changed the tire, or we'd probably still be sitting on the side of the highway."

"It's my understanding that there was plenty of time for the two of you to stop at the Dairy Queen after the game."

"I don't see what that has to do with anything."

"I consider that a breach of the job expectations laid out for you when you were hired."

"Are you serious?" Her words came out harsher than she'd intended, but she could not believe the gall of this man. This wasn't a kindergarten he was running. She and Rob were adults. If they wanted to go to Dairy Queen on their off-hours—as coworkers or even as friends—who did Merrick think he was to stop them? This was a lawsuit waiting to happen, and she had half a mind to let him know it.

But she thought better of it. At least until she had a chance to talk to Rob. If he knew about this and hadn't said anything, he was going to hear about it from her.

"I am quite serious, Miss Penn. I made it perfectly clear that you were to keep your relationship with my son strictly professional. I have not changed my mind, and if it wouldn't leave us so short-staffed, I'd let you go right now. But I'm going to give you another opportunity to demonstrate that you understand what I mean."

"Mr. Merrick, if you're referring to the fact that Rob and I went to the game together, I can assure you that it was work-related." She explained again about the flat tire and told him what duties she'd performed at the game. "Let me be sure I understand. As long as it's work-related, Rob and I can speak to each other, right?"

His expression said he got how ridiculous his rules sounded when they came from someone else's perspective. Score one for Miss Penn.

"And," she continued, "we can travel together for a work event?"

"I don't think you're quite as dense as you'd like me to think. I made myself quite clear: the *Beacon* does not allow employees to have a dating relationship."

She stifled a gasp. "There's nothing even close to that happening with your son and me. I don't know why you're making these accusations. I—" If she didn't get hold of her emotions, she was going to say something they'd all regret. "I understand what you're saying. You don't need to worry," she finished in a whisper.

"Then you're free to go."

Gritting her teeth, she rose slowly and left the room. She knew she should just go on out the door and go home, as she'd been trying to do when Mr. Merrick called her into the office. But something made her turn on her heel and head back to Rob's cubicle, where only moments ago, he'd told her—as if everything was just hunky-dory—to have a great evening.

Maybe he was innocent. Maybe. But if not, she had a few choice words for him. And she wouldn't sleep until she'd delivered them— or made sure he didn't deserve them.

Chapter Fourteen

Rob finished clearing off his desk, hoping his old man had already left for the night. He flipped off the light, turned to leave, and almost crashed into Michelle just outside his door.

"What are you doing here? I thought you went home."

She rolled her eyes. "I tried to go home."

"What's wrong? You have a flat tire? I can fix that for you." He flexed his biceps.

That didn't even get a grin out of her.

He frowned. "What's going on?"

"I got called in to the principal's office." She nodded toward his dad's office.

"Why?" He held up his hands in surrender. "I didn't tell him about the typo. I swear."

She narrowed her eyes at him. "You really don't know why he wanted to talk to me?"

"I try to stay out of my old man's business as much as possible. You know that." Maybe she didn't know it, but it was true. If he had to work for his father, he was going to be like any other employee. "So what did he want?"

"He wanted to make it perfectly clear—again—that we are not to see each other outside of work. If we're ever allowed to travel in the same vehicle, it apparently does not include the right to stop at a Dairy Queen on the way home."

"You have got to be kidding me." He was going to have words with his father. Strong words. "Why didn't he talk to me? It was my idea."

"That's what *I* was wondering. You'll be happy to know that I saved your hide. I didn't tell him the whole thing was your idea."

"Well, you should have." He brushed past her and started for his dad's office.

"No. Don't, Rob." Michelle came after him and grabbed his arm. "He'll fire me for sure if you say anything."

"What do you mean, he'll fire you?"

"He told me—just now—that if it wouldn't leave the office so short-handed, he'd let me go now. I got away with a warning."

"Mish . . . I'm sorry."

She tilted her head. "What did you just call me?"

"Mish. You know, Mish–Elle. Michelle. Why?"

She shook her head. "That's what my dad calls me." The warmth in her voice left no doubt that it was a good thing. He made a mental note. And wished he could muster the same attitude toward his own father.

He slumped into the chair. He wanted to respect his father. He really did. And, actually, it wasn't respect that was the problem. It was affection for the man that was missing. Was it so wrong to want to look forward to seeing his dad rather than feeling a sense of dread or misplaced guilt every time he knew the man was in the building? He was beginning to understand the saying "Familiarity breeds contempt." And yet that didn't seem to be the case with a lot of people he knew.

Certainly not with Michelle Penn. The longer they shared cubicles next to each other, the more he liked her. There was something so unassuming and straightforward about her. Something that made him want to defend her.

"Is the boss still in his office?"

She narrowed her eyes at him. "Why?" She only looked cuter when she got all serious like that.

"Because I'm going to go talk to him." He pushed back his chair, trying to look more confident than he felt. "I'm not under any illusions that he's going to change office policy. In fact I can pretty much guarantee he won't. But you shouldn't be punished because of me. That wasn't fair—"

"I wasn't punished, Rob. You act like he called me in for a flogging or something."

"No, but he threatened you. That's worse."

"Depends on the punishment."

"You don't act like this bothers you all that much."

"It bothers me. I was fuming when I walked out of his office two minutes ago," she admitted.

"I don't blame you."

"But there's not a thing I can do about it."

"Do you want me to talk to him?" He hated that he hoped she said no.

"What am I supposed to say to that, Rob? Talk about not fair . . . "

"Okay. That does it. I'm talking to him."

This time she didn't try to stop him.

* * * * *

The temperature was already in the upper eighties when Michelle drove past the bank marquee on the way to work on Monday morning. She couldn't remember when it had been this hot so late in September.

She hadn't heard a word from Rob all weekend—not that she expected to. But she'd spent the whole weekend wondering how his talk with his father had gone. Or if he'd even followed through with it.

She wasn't going to ask Rob either. She planned to ignore him and let him volunteer any information about how "the talk" went if he so chose. Fortunately Monday mornings were always busy, and it wouldn't be difficult to hole up in her cubicle and ignore everyone. She had two stories to write, and Rob had asked her to get some shots of the new flower shop's grand opening at ten o'clock. It wouldn't be a front-page photo, but it would be an easy assignment.

Through the blinds, she saw Mr. Merrick in his office. To her relief, he was on the phone and didn't seem to notice her. Rob apparently wasn't in yet, but Joy Swanson was at her desk—unusual for a Monday morning, since the deadline for ad sales was noon every Monday.

"Good morning!" Michelle put on her perkiest smile. "Are all the ads in already?"

Joy looked up and leveled a cool gaze at her before turning back to her work. Her expression remained unchanged, as if Michelle were invisible.

Michelle's face grew warm, and she hurried to her cubicle. She'd gone out of her way to be friendly to Joy, but the woman had yet to thaw one degree.

Michelle turned on her Selectric and settled in to work, wishing Joy's brush-off didn't sting so much. One of these days she'd get up the nerve to ask Ms. Swanson what her problem was, but for now the woman intimidated her too much.

She was trying to decipher a news release when Myrtle stepped into her cubicle. "Mr. Merrick wants to see you."

"Now?" Rob must have talked to him. This was not good.

The receptionist rolled her eyes. "Well, I didn't walk all the way back here to tell you he wants to see you *yesterday.*"

"Okay. Thanks, Myrtle." She'd learned quickly that the best way to handle Myrtle Dressler was to ignore her gruff comments. Michelle smoothed her skirt and tried to check her reflection in the glass of the framed map that hung behind her desk. Not that looking good was going to help her now. This was it. She was going to get fired. She tried to imagine how she would tell her parents. How disappointed they would be in her—even though they'd no doubt be secretly happy that she'd be forced to move back home.

Myrtle was waiting, so Michelle typed a quick note to herself about the story she'd been working on and followed the older woman to the front of the building. Myrtle abandoned her as soon as they got to the reception desk.

Michelle wiped her palms on her skirt and knocked on Mr. Merrick's open door.

He looked up.

"Myrtle said you wanted to see me?"

"Yes. Come in, Michelle."

He didn't ask her to close the door. That was a good sign. Either that or he intended to make an example of her in front of the whole office. She could see Joy Swanson still at her desk—no doubt pretending to type while she bent an ear. Myrtle likely had her neck craned toward the boss's office too.

Mr. Merrick shuffled some papers on his desk before handing a couple of them to her. They were letters to the editor. She skimmed them then worked to curb the smile that wanted to come. "This is great. . . ." It came out sounding more like a question, but she couldn't tell whether he agreed, by his stony face.

"We've also gotten half a dozen phone calls saying pretty much the same thing."

"Really?" The letters complimented the *Beacon* for using pictures of local children and for publishing something besides sports or national news on the front page. She glanced at one of the comments again.

"It's wonderful to see a photograph that actually captures the charm of Bristol—the reason so many of us chose to live in this small town. I hope we can count on seeing more of the same in the future."

Mr. Merrick drummed his ball-point pen on the desktop. "I probably shouldn't tell you that this smacks of a campaign to keep Michelle Penn employed."

"I don't understand."

"Do you know the people who wrote those letters?"

Did he seriously think she'd *solicited* the letters? She looked at the names on the letters again. "Mary Genevieve teaches at the elementary school—at least she used to. I think I know who Beatrice Goodman is. A Goodman family used to attend our church."

"These aren't, by chance, your mother's friends, are they? Or *your* friends?"

"You think I asked these people to write letters? Or that I'd ask my parents to?" For the first time, she wondered if Mom and Dad *had* done something so crazy as to organize a write-in campaign. But she was pretty sure they didn't know the two women who'd written the letters—at least not well enough to make such a bold request.

"I didn't say that," Mr. Merrick said. "But it does look a bit suspicious. We average maybe three letters to the editor a week—rarely all on the same topic. And the phone calls . . . " He waved a hand as if dismissing the very idea that the phone calls could have been legitimate.

"I promise you—I had nothing to do with any of it."

"It doesn't matter," he said. "The only thing that does matter is that the ice cream truck franchise called and placed an ad. I seriously doubt you had anything to do with that."

"Well . . . except for my front-page photo," she blurted.

He merely nodded, which she chose to take as an acknowledgment that she was right. Otherwise she might say something she'd regret.

"Just so you know," he said, "this does not change what we talked about last week. But I told Robert I'd like you to be responsible for the front-page photos for the next couple of issues. Something in the same sappy vein as your ice cream truck. We'll see if people continue to respond positively."

She bit the inside of her cheek to keep from smiling. "I–I'd like that. Thank you." She laid the letters back on his desk.

"Nothing to thank me for." He tapped the letters on his desktop, placed them in a desk drawer, and gave her a why-are-you-still-here? look. "That will be all."

She turned on her heel and went back to her desk. Robert III had been on the gruff side when she first met him. It had taken a while before she saw his gentler side, but she was starting to believe that anything kind or sweet about him had come from his mother. It certainly hadn't come from this jerk.

Chapter Fifteen

Rob had just started working on the week's front-page stories when he heard Michelle in her cubicle. He pushed back his chair, rose, and peered over the divider. "Did you talk to the boss yet this morning?"

"Just now." She seemed to be biting back a smile.

"You don't have to be so smug about it."

"I'm not being smug. Can I help it if I was right?" She made no effort to hide her smile now.

"Show-off."

"Don't be mad. I'm sure you'll get to go back to putting athletics on the front page as soon as basketball season starts."

"Don't forget softball."

She smirked.

"I don't like being shown up, Penn, but I can be man enough to give congratulations. My old man was pretty impressed about the ad. They've never advertised in the *Beacon* before."

"They probably just want to be sure people know they're still making their runs, since we've had such a warm fall."

He eyed her, trying to decide whether she was just being magnanimous. "He didn't tell you, did he?"

"Who? Tell me what?"

"According to Joy, the guy said he sold out the truck on Friday."

"Sold out?"

"Of ice cream. Sold everything he had on the truck. He said the customers told him they saw in the paper that he was still running his routes. Convinced him of the power of advertising."

"Ohh . . . " Understanding dawned in her eyes. "No, your dad didn't mention that part. Maybe Joy didn't tell him."

"Oh, she told him all right." He came around to stand in Michelle's doorway. "That turkey! He owes you an apology."

"Don't worry about it, Rob. You already talked to him once." She looked at him with a question mark in her expression. "Didn't you?"

"Yes. I did."

"Well, then, there's no sense in jeopardizing your job too."

"Too? He didn't threaten to fire you again, did he?"

"Not this time."

"I'm sorry, Michelle." He shook his head. "I don't know how many times I can apologize for the man when I seriously doubt he's going to change, but—"

"You don't owe me apologies on his account."

"Well, I am sorry."

She waved him off then tilted her head and swallowed hard. "So you're not mad about the front-page thing?"

"I'm not mad at you." That was all he could say without fibbing. "Like the boss says, you can't argue with subscribers."

A commotion outside his cubicle made them both turn. Two good-looking women were making their way down the corridor toward the cubicles. "May I help you ladies?"

"We're looking for Michelle Penn. The receptionist said we'd find her back here."

Rob stepped aside so they could see Michelle at her desk. When she spotted the women, her hazel eyes lit up like sparklers and she jumped up to embrace both of her visitors. Rob watched over the partition while the squeal-fest that ensued made everyone else in the office stare.

Afraid his father might intervene and embarrass her, he whispered to Michelle, "Why don't you take your coffee break now. You can take your friends to the break room . . . or if you want to take a little longer break and go down to the drugstore, I'll tell the boss you'll be right back."

"Thanks, Rob. Oh—sorry." She stopped beaming long enough to introduce him. "These are my friends, Kathy Parks and Carol Vohlmer. We were best friends in high school and roomies at K-State."

"Yeah," Carol said, giggling, "until you took her away from us."

He wondered if Michelle picked up on her friend's unintended meaning.

The blush that crept up her neck answered that question.

He pretended not to notice and shook the girls' hands in turn, submitting to their frank appraisal. "Nice to meet you, ladies. Michelle can show you the break room," he said, hoping she'd take his hint. His father did not take kindly to such disruptions in the office—especially not on a Monday morning.

"Well, we can't stay long," said Carol. "We're on our way back to school, but we just had to see Michelle before we left town."

"You'll have to show them the microwave oven. Now, there's a story."

Michelle gave him a ha-ha-very-funny smirk and brushed past him. "Come on, girls. Wait'll you see this."

They left him in a wake of giggles and girl-talk, making him grateful they were leaving the newsroom. But, oh, he would have loved to be a fly on the wall in that break room.

* * * * *

"You work with Rob Merrick? You never said anything!" Kathy's eyes were as round as quarters and twice as shiny. She had cut her hair and bleached it platinum blond. She looked hip—and maybe just a little cheap. Michelle wondered if something was going on with her.

Carol narrowed her eyes at Michelle. "What is your problem? You've been holding out on us!"

"I have not." She laughed. "The first letter I sent you said I was working with Rob Merrick."

"We thought you meant the old man." Carol clutched her heart. "He is such a hunk!"

"The old man?" she deadpanned.

"No, you goose! The son!"

"Shh! He'll hear you!" But she joined the giggling, loving that her friends had stopped by to see her here. She showed them to the small table in the corner of the break room and filled three Styrofoam cups with coffee.

"Rob is super nice too." Under her breath she added, "Unlike his father."

"My mom couldn't believe it when she heard you were working here." Kathy looked toward the door and lowered her voice. "She said Mr. Merrick has chased off half the people who've ever worked for him."

"I believe it. He's practically fired me twice already."

"You're kidding."

"Not kidding." She pointed at the microwave oven on the counter. "If your coffee needs warming, just let me know."

"Hey"—Carol punched her arm—"what was Rob talking about? Something about a microwave-oven story?"

Michelle laughed and gave them a comical version of her first day on the job when she'd practically burned the place down, trying to warm up a cookie. "Rob hasn't let me hear the end of it since."

Kathy gave her a knowing look. "Sounds like you two know each other pretty well."

"We do, but—" She stopped, unsure whether she wanted to reveal how she felt about Rob. Knowing Carol, it wouldn't stay secret for very long, and if it got back to Rob . . . She held up her coffee cup. "I'm going to heat this up. Anybody else? I promise I won't scorch it."

She carried her cup over to the oven, put it inside, and casually turned the dial to fifteen seconds. Carol gave the same reaction as Michelle had the first time she'd heard the oven start, jumping out of her skin. When Carol and Kathy quit laughing, they each took a turn trying out the microwave to heat their coffee.

"A girl in my sociology class said they have one of those," Kathy said. "She says in five years every household in America will have one. But then, they're filthy rich. They've got all the latest gadgets."

"Back to the subject," Carol said, when they'd settled back at the table. "What about Rob? Does he have a girlfriend?"

"No," she said quickly. "We sort of went out once—"

"What?" Carol squealed. "You never said anything."

"Let me finish. It was just to a ball game. It was sort of for work, but his dad had a fit. Employees aren't supposed to date each other, so we're playing it cool."

"Michelle! I'd be looking for another job so fast, your head would spin." Kathy had a dreamy look in her eyes, and for the first time since she'd left college, Michelle didn't feel jealous of her friends.

"There's nothing that pays as well, at least not in Bristol. And if I worked out of town, then I'd eat up everything I made, paying for gas."

"Do you ever hear from Kevin?"

The question hung in the air between them. The truth was, she hadn't thought about Kevin Ferris for days. Her breath caught. She'd even forgotten to pray for him recently. If he got killed . . . how would she ever forgive herself? She shot up a prayer right then. "No. I haven't heard from him, and I don't expect to."

"The man is a fool. I still don't know what he was thinking."

"Me neither," Carol echoed.

"Forget about it." Michelle waved away their sympathy. "It was his choice. He didn't owe me anything."

"Still . . . "

She glanced at the clock over the refrigerator. "Hey, guys, I hate to run you off, but I'd really better get back to work. Monday is one of our busiest days, and Rob and I have to develop some pictures."

"You develop them here?"

"Yes, in the darkroom."

That sent the girls into another frenzied swoon.

"Penn, you have got to be the luckiest woman I've ever met," Carol said. "Who else gets paid to spend time in the darkroom with Rob Merrick?"

"Cut it out, you two." But she soaked up their fawning. "I'm so glad you stopped by. Maybe some weekend I can come up to K-State and spend—"

The door to the break room opened and Mr. Merrick stuck his head in.

Michelle jumped up. "Mr. Merrick . . . "

Kathy hiked her purse over her shoulder and rose. "We'd better hit the road, Carol."

Michelle started to introduce her friends, but almost before she opened her mouth, her boss left. He was no doubt waiting to pounce on her once her friends left. At least he hadn't embarrassed her in front of them.

Yet.

Chapter Sixteen

Rob heard Michelle's friends in the hallway—trying, but failing miserably, to be quiet. When she finally came back to her desk, he breathed a sigh of relief. He couldn't believe his father hadn't called her down for having friends in the office. It would no doubt come up in the staff meeting on Friday.

Not two minutes later, Michelle's head popped over the partition. "Am I in trouble? Having my friends here . . . ?"

He gave a little grimace. "I wouldn't let it happen too often. But nobody's said anything yet."

She let out a breath. "Sorry, but I just hated to ignore them. I haven't seen Carol or Kathy since school started."

"I'm kind of surprised Myrtle let them back here."

"You obviously don't know Carol. She could talk a polar bear into moving to the Sahara."

He laughed. "So, you were friends in high school?"

"All four years. You don't remember any of us, do you? We were lowly freshmen." She smirked. "Not even a blip on your radar."

"Sorry. I guess I was distracted. By all the studying and academics, of course," he added quickly.

"Oh, right. More likely by some cute senior girl."

"I plead the fifth. But don't tell me you weren't sweet on some guy back then."

"Also pleading the fifth."

"I'll tell if you will."

She grinned. "You go first."

"Oh, no you don't. I pled the fifth first."

"Fine. Okay, there may have been someone. But that's ancient history."

"How ancient?"

He thought she hesitated a second too long. But she seemed to recover. "Pretty ancient. Like, back in the sixties."

He laughed. "That long ago, huh? So was it pretty serious?"

She shook her head. "Oh, no you don't. Your turn."

He shrugged. "Never really had a girlfriend."

"You have got to be kidding. I spilled all for *that*?"

He smirked. "You call that 'spilling all'?"

"Well, that's all you're getting now, for sure."

"Oh, no. I'll get it out of you." He affected a heavy German accent, attempting a *Hogan's Heroes* Colonel Klink impersonation. "I varn you—ve haff ways to make you talk."

"Very funny."

"You wait and see. I'll get it out of you," he said again.

"Will not."

"Will too."

"Will not, Kevin. How much you want to bet?"

He grinned knowingly. "So his name was Kevin?"

Her eyebrows went up. "How'd you know that?"

He cracked up. "You just called me *Kevin*."

"Did not."

"Did too."

He could see her replaying their conversation in her mind, and she apparently realized her faux pas, because her hands went to her mouth and her cheeks flushed pink. Without another word she slinked below the partition, and a minute later, he heard the furious clatter of her Selectric.

He was tempted to go to her cubicle and tease her out of her embarrassment, but something told him it was more than embarrassment. Just how serious had this Kevin person been? Bristol High was a small school with only about a hundred students in each class, but he truly didn't remember Michelle or her friends. He'd admittedly been a hotshot athlete and the new kid on the block, having moved to Bristol from Kansas City during his sophomore year. And while there had been a couple of girls in the class below him that he'd been interested in, he hadn't given the frosh girls a first glance, let alone a second.

He found it difficult to concentrate on the story he was working on—a boring school board meeting. His mind kept going to Michelle's reaction when he'd said Kevin's name. He'd just assumed she wasn't going steady with anyone. But maybe that had been wishful thinking.

Still, if she did have a boyfriend, it cast her flirting in a whole new—and not very attractive—light. He shoved aside the notes he was working from and raked a hand through his hair. As if he didn't have enough going against him and Michelle with his dad's stupid office policies.

One thing was sure. He had to get out of here. If Michelle was available, he had to be free to go after her. And if she wasn't, he couldn't torture himself by being around her every day.

* * * * *

Michelle stared at her keyboard, the numbers blurring. She'd had two years to get over Kevin. And she *was* over him. She was. But why did it still hurt to think about what had happened between them?

When she thought about Rob questioning her, about having to try to explain it to him, she felt sick to her stomach. It wasn't like she was the first woman who'd ever been dumped. But being dumped for Vietnam? That might be a first.

Against her will, memories came flooding in. Kevin had looked so handsome that night. A year older than she, he'd been working on his father's farm for the past year. He'd always wanted to farm, and even though Michelle wasn't sure she wanted the life her mother had lived, she *was* sure she wanted Kevin. And if that meant being a farmer's wife, she was okay with that.

He'd invited her to go out to Mercer Lake with him for a picnic. She was sure—more sure than she'd ever been about anything—that Kevin was going to ask her to marry him. Kathy had been sure of it too, and she and Carol had been waiting with bated breath to hear all about it.

As it turned out, Kevin's "romantic" picnic had been planned to soften the news that he'd enlisted in the army. He was headed for boot camp in two weeks and likely to Vietnam as soon as he finished basic training.

She stared at the Selectric keyboard, her cheeks heating. She still felt the humiliation when she remembered how long it took her to realize that Kevin was not just telling her he was headed for Nam. He was breaking up with her. For good.

The next weeks had been the most painful of her life. She'd had to figure out how to tell all her friends that instead of an engagement ring, she'd gotten the rules of engagement. Kevin Ferris's rules of engagement.

She'd been in mourning the rest of that summer, feeling as bereft as though she'd lost Kevin to death. Her parents had indulged her the hours spent holed up in her room, reading sad novels and soaking through box after box of Kleenex. But when she'd finally let her mother in long enough to reason with her, Mom had gently pointed out that while it was normal to grieve the loss of a boy who'd been her steady for almost three years, it was perhaps more a dream she was grieving than the boy himself.

"What do you mean?" Michelle had asked, sniffling.

"Oh, honey . . . " Mom wrapped her in a hug. "I know you miss Kevin, but I think you're mostly sad that you didn't get to have the wedding you dreamed of and the charming little house in the country to fix up."

"And the babies. Don't forget the babies."

Mom laughed softly, but Michelle heard the deep relief in her voice. "Sweetie, you have your whole life to make that dream come true. You're still young. There will be a husband, and there will be babies. I know it's hard to be patient, but I have no doubt that God has everything planned out better than you or I could ever imagine."

Well, she wasn't so young anymore. She would turn twenty-two in December and the family-shaped hole in her heart was still empty. She felt like she'd wasted the last two years, wasted the money Dad had paid for tuition. And now she was wasting her time at a job she wasn't gifted for, that she saw no future in.

She was trying her best to be patient, but if Mom was right about God, she sure wished He'd hurry up and start letting her in on His plans for her life.

CHAPTER SEVENTEEN

Michelle rubbed her arms briskly and walked faster. It was chilly even for October, but in spite of her mother's claims that she was anorexic, she'd actually gained six pounds since she started working at the newspaper. She was determined to get the weight off before she had to buy a new wardrobe. She hadn't realized how crucial those walks across campus had been at keeping her as thin as she'd been while she was on the cross-country team in high school.

She had recently started taking brisk walks around the block over her lunch hour. It wasn't a vigorous workout, but already she could tell that her clothes weren't fitting quite as tight. She headed east across Main, taking a different route than she normally did and trying to walk with the wind. She smiled, imagining Rob giving her a hard time about that. "You're going to have to walk against the wind one way or another, babe," he'd say.

She'd walked about five blocks when she looked up at a street sign and realized she was on Donner Avenue. Glancing farther down the street, she recognized the house. Three-fifty-eight Donner. . . . where she and Rob had witnessed Becky Preston's husband being hauled off in a police cruiser.

In its drab surroundings, the house looked even more barren now than it had last summer. The paint was chipped, and the shutters hung crooked or were missing altogether. Even the leaves still clinging to the trees were brown and shriveled. Looking up at the front porch, Michelle could still recall how helpless she'd felt to see that sweet little girl, so terrified and confused, clutching her mother's knees. The yard was devoid of toys, and Michelle wondered whether Becky and Eden even lived there anymore. And whether the husband was out of jail yet. She hoped not.

She walked on by, trying to ignore the twinge of guilt she felt. It had been weeks since she'd run into Becky at the grocery store. She'd thought of the poor woman many times since then, and she felt bad that she hadn't done the one thing Becky asked her to do—destroy the photos Rob had taken that day. She truly didn't think Rob would ever do anything harmful with them. The incident was old news by now. And she hadn't exactly promised Becky . . . . Still, she'd said she would do her best to get the pictures back, and she hadn't even tried.

Stretching out her stride as she walked past the house, she made a mental note to ask Rob if she could have the photos. She hesitated at the thought. He'd seemed a little preoccupied lately. They talked shop over the partition between their desks several times a day and he still teased her every chance he got, but he seemed more distant than he had at first and she wasn't sure why.

Maybe he was as afraid of his father as she was. If she couldn't afford to lose her job, how much more could he not afford to lose his? But none of that changed the fact that she still found herself wishing for a chance to be alone with him, like when they'd ridden to the game together or chatted over coffee in the break room. She didn't think it was an accident that, recently, he'd waited to take his break until after she'd come back from hers.

She checked her watch. If she was going to have time for a sandwich, she needed to start back. She made a U-turn and walked back by the house on Donner. As she crossed the gravel drive, a car pulled in off the street. The driver slowed to let her cross and Michelle realized it was Becky. She gave a little wave, feeling trapped yet glad to see her at the same time.

She stopped and waited for Becky to roll down her window. Eden was in an infant seat on the front passenger seat. Michelle's heart did the little flip-flop it always did when she saw a baby. Bending to look through the window, she smiled and waved, earning a sparkly smile from the toddler in return.

She took a step back and spoke to the child's mother. "Hi, Becky. Do you remem—"

"Sure. I remember . . . " Her eyes held a question, as if she wondered why Michelle had come to visit her.

"I was just out walking," she explained. "Trying to lose a little weight." She gave an awkward laugh and felt badly as soon as she said it, since Becky looked as though she could stand to gain a few pounds. Her cheeks had that sunken "Twiggy" look, and her blouse hung loosely on her. But when Becky turned off the ignition and crawled out of the car, Michelle saw why. It was a maternity blouse, and from what Michelle knew of those things, it looked like Becky might be five or six months along.

"Yeah, I've got another bun in the oven."

"Oh!" She hadn't realized she was staring. "That–that's great. Congratulations."

"It happened before . . . well, before all that with Mack." She hung her head, and her mousy hair curtained her face.

"Oh. Of course. Is—is he out yet?" So Becky had been pregnant when Mack beat her up. Michelle's estimation of Mack Preston took another nosedive.

"His next parole hearing is in a couple of weeks. But he'll be out for good before the baby comes. No matter what." She sounded glad about it.

"Is he coming back here? Are you two still together?"

Becky tugged at the hem of her maternity top. "I don't really have much choice."

"Of course you do!" She hadn't meant to blurt it out like that. "Sorry. Not that it's any of my business, but . . . " She reached over to put her fingertips lightly on Becky's belly and was surprised at how firm it was. "Don't let this force you into something you don't want. You have to think about your babies."

"Could you support two babies on what you make at the *Beacon*?" Her voice held no malice, yet the implications of her question made Michelle wince.

"I—I don't know. I guess I've never thought about it."

"And I'll never find a job like yours. I was lucky to get out of high school with a diploma."

"Doesn't your husband have a job?" She backpedaled. "After he gets out, I mean?"

"We'll see. He's had trouble holding a job in the past."

"I'm sorry. I really don't mean to pry. I'm just worried about you."

Becky smiled. But it looked practiced . . . and sad. "I'm okay. We get by."

"Maybe we could get together for lunch sometime?"

Becky studied her, as if she thought it was a trick question. But apparently she decided Michelle wasn't just stringing her along. "I'd like that."

"I'll give you a call. Are you in the book?"

"Um, no. I don't have a phone . . . yet."

"Oh. Well, maybe we can just figure out a time right now. Are you free any days next week? Except Tuesday or Wednesday. Things are pretty crazy at the paper then."

"Take your pick."

Michelle wasn't sure what had prompted her to be so bold, but seeing the genuine smile her simple invitation had brought to the young mother's face, she was glad she hadn't talked herself out of it. "Okay. I only have an hour for lunch and my boss is pretty strict about that, but maybe we could meet at the café downtown?

A stricken look crossed Becky's face. "How about if I just fix us something here? It won't be anything fancy, but—"

Michelle suddenly realized that Becky must not be able to afford to go out to eat. She should have thought of that. "I have an idea. Since you're providing the house, I'll bring the food. And if you want to make something for dessert, that would be great."

Relief flooded Becky's features. "Sounds perfect."

"Is there anything special I need to bring for Eden?"

"Oh, I'll probably feed her first and put her down for a nap. Then she won't bother us."

Michelle was disappointed, but she didn't say so. "Okay. It's set, then. Shall we just plan on Monday?"

"That would be great. I'll see you then." Now that they'd settled on a time, Becky seemed more relaxed—buoyant, even. She climbed back into the car and closed her door. "I'm so glad you came by."

"Me too." And it was true.

She waved good-bye to Eden and was rewarded with another toothy smile.

A chilly gust made Michelle realize that she hadn't even noticed the wind and cold while she'd stood talking with Becky. Becky Preston wasn't the type of friend she ever would have steered toward before, but there was something in her that drew Michelle. And it would be fun to spend time with little Eden too. Maybe she could even offer to babysit once in a while after the new baby came.

But the image of herself in that house, with the possibility that Mack Preston might show up, stole away the warmth of the last few minutes. She'd have to tread carefully if Becky was serious about getting back with that monster.

CHAPTER EIGHTEEN

Michelle knocked on Becky's door and waited. The picnic basket full of food—and a little gift for Eden—was heavy in her left hand. She looked at the peeling paint and crooked shutters and counted to sixty before knocking again. The house seemed too still for having a toddler in residence. But she didn't want to ring the doorbell and wake the baby if she was napping.

Crisp fall leaves crunched under her feet as she went down the steps and around to the driveway where Becky had parked her car the other day when they'd talked. The door to the garage behind the house was closed, but judging by the tangle of tall, dried-up weeds poking through the gravel in front of the garage, it hadn't been used in a long time.

Michelle went back up on the front porch and knocked again. Was she mixed up on the date? No, she remembered them deciding on Monday. She couldn't call because Becky didn't have a phone, but she didn't want her to think she'd forgotten.

Feeling like a Peeping Tom, she went to the window overlooking the porch and peered in, praying she didn't get caught. The living room was strewn with toys and toddler paraphernalia, but there were no lights on and it didn't appear anyone was home.

Not knowing what else to do, she scratched out a note on a paper napkin from the picnic basket. *Hope I didn't get the time wrong. Call me at the* Beacon *if you can.*

She felt foolish, asking Becky to call her, since she didn't have a phone, but she didn't know what else to say. She decided to risk leaving the basket of food on the porch. It was cold enough out that nothing would spoil, and hopefully Becky would discover it before some dog roaming the neighborhood did. At least this way Becky would know she hadn't blown off their lunch date. And she could use retrieving the picnic basket as an excuse to stop by Becky's house again tomorrow.

She started to get back into her car then decided to walk around the block a couple of times. She could get some exercise in and maybe catch Becky before she had to go back to work.

She locked her purse in her car and set out around the block. She hadn't worn the best shoes for walking, and it was too cold for the light jacket she was wearing.

A twinge of worry niggled at the back of her mind. Something didn't seem right. More than likely something had come up and, not having a phone, Becky just didn't have any way to let her know. But still, it didn't seem like her new friend not to at least leave a note on the door.

When she got back to her car, she tried the door one more time. Again no answer. Resigned, she climbed into her car and drove back to the office. She was probably worrying needlessly, but she was going to ask Rob to help her find out whether Mack Preston had gotten out of jail yet. She knew Rob had access to the police reports each week, and if Becky's poor excuse for a husband hadn't been transferred out of the county jail, Rob would be able to find out his status. For Becky's sake, she hoped he was still locked away.

* * * * *

"Where's Michelle?" Rob tried to sound nonchalant as he stood at the tall layout desk and helped Joy place the finished ads on the week's page flats.

She looked askance at him. "How should I know? Am I my sister's keeper?"

"Well, excuse me. Sorry to trouble you." Could this woman's parents have chosen a more inappropriate name for her? He didn't know what he'd ever seen in Joy Swanson.

"Sorry. That wasn't very nice."

"You don't like her much, do you?"

"Michelle? I like her okay . . . "

"But . . . ?"

"But nothing. She's fine. Not saying we're going to become best buddies or anything, but I don't have anything against the girl."

"Then why are you so cool toward her?" Rob felt his defenses kick in. He really hadn't intended to launch this conversation, but he'd often wondered the reason, and now seemed as good a time as any to ask the advertising sales*woman*—emphasis on the woman, as she liked to say. Joy fancied herself a mover and shaker in the women's movement, which might explain why she wasn't a fan of the ultra-feminine college dropout and farmer's daughter, Michelle Penn. Or maybe it was because Michelle had landed the ice cream truck ad that Joy had never been able to nail down.

Joy glared at him. "Why do you care? Not that it's any of your business."

He stripped columns of waxed copy from last week's flats, tossed them into the barrel, and replaced them with the new ads. "Is the

Friends of the Library promo supposed to run again this week?" He knew when it was time to drop it with this woman. In a rare moment of insanity, he'd asked Joy out on a date shortly after he came back to work at the *Beacon*. In his defense, the woman had put on a sweet-and-pleasant front back then, and it hadn't hurt that she was good-looking.

It didn't take more than that first date before he saw her true colors. Unfortunately, he'd let her finagle a second date. He broke things off after that, and since then, she'd gone out of her way to win Grouch of the Year at the *Beacon* while also making it clear that she had no respect whatsoever for Robert Merrick III. He'd never tried to lord it over anyone that he was the son of the publisher, but in his position as managing editor, he *was* second-in-command.

After things went sour with him and Joy, his father had been adamant about the importance of keeping distance between himself and the other employees. But he wasn't about to let the thing with Joy ruin it for him with Michelle.

"The info is right here." Joy slid the ad schedule across the slanted desk to him. "Just like it is every week," she mumbled under her breath.

He chose to ignore that too, though if he'd had the authority to do so, he might have fired her sassy self on the spot. He turned to the bank behind him and started laying out the classified ads. It never failed that Myrtle let someone slip in an ad at the last minute on Tuesday morning, but he could at least get it started for Michelle. Where was she, anyway? She'd taken to walking over her lunch hour, but it wasn't like her to be late. Especially not early in the week.

It struck him that if it had been Joy or Myrtle or one of the typesetters, he could have cared less whether they were a few minutes late—if he even noticed they were absent. It wasn't fair for him to treat Michelle any differently, but didn't she know that the office was boring and stale without her?

It was 1:15 before he finally heard her come in the back way. He glanced up from the layout desk long enough to notice that her hair was pleasantly windblown and her cheeks were flushed.

She hurried into her cubicle, shedding her jacket as she went. She returned a minute later, rolling up her sleeves so she could work at the layout bank. "Sorry I'm late."

"I got the classifieds started for you."

"Oh. Thanks."

"Everything okay?" he asked, without looking up.

"Yes . . . At least, I think so."

He put down his craft knife and turned to lean one elbow on the sloped bank of the desk. "What's going on?"

"I was supposed to have lunch with a friend, and she never showed up."

He remembered her stowing food in the break room fridge this morning and had wondered what it was for. Not that *that* was any of his business either. But it had crossed his mind at the time that she might have a lunch-hour date, and he was relieved now to hear her say that *she* didn't show up. So it wasn't that kind of date. Good. "Did you call her?"

"She doesn't have a phone."

"Really? Who doesn't have a phone in this century?"

She looked disgusted with him. "People who aren't as rich as you, maybe?"

"Would you cut that out? Just because my dad is rich doesn't mean I am."

"That's not my point."

"Then what is your point?" Good grief, this was starting to sound like his conversation with Joy.

"Just that not everybody has all the advantages we take for granted."

"Okay. You're right. I'm sorry. So . . . your friend doesn't have a phone. And you never got hold of her?"

"No. And I'm worried. Would you—" She stopped short, as if weighing her words. "Would you be able to check some police records for me?"

Chapter Nineteen

"Police records?" Rob looked like an eager puppy waiting to hear where a bone was buried.

It reminded Michelle how much she lacked his journalistic instincts. "The friend I was having lunch with is Becky Preston."

Rob's brows went up, and she felt as if she were diving off a cliff into deep water.

"I'm worried about her, Rob."

"She's the one whose husband went to jail for beating her, right?"

She nodded. "She seemed really excited about our lunch. I don't think she would have just ditched me."

"And you want me to see if he's still in jail?"

She nodded. "I know he was supposed to get out before Becky has her baby, but I didn't think it was this soon."

"She wouldn't let him in the house, would she?"

She closed her eyes. "She's pregnant. She doesn't feel she has any choice."

"Oh, man . . . " He blew out a breath. "What kind of choice is that?"

She didn't have an answer for him. "Can you find out whether Mack Preston is out of jail yet?"

"I'll try. I don't usually go pick up the police report until Friday, but I can make an extra trip to check the records. Or the chief might talk to me—if I catch him in a good mood. Maybe you should go by her house again first, though, just in case your wires got crossed."

"That's a good idea. I know I've already eaten up my break time, but do you think I could leave a few minutes early today so I can stop by there?"

"Sure. I'll go with you. I can help you finish the classifieds so you're not behind in the morning."

"Thanks, Rob."

They worked silently for a few minutes before she sensed him watching her. She turned to face him, curious.

"Did you know her—Becky Preston—that day we went after the story?"

"No . . . well, not exactly. Why?"

"No reason. I just wondered how you got to be friends so quickly."

"She was in the class below me in high school. I didn't remember her, but she recognized me that day." She told him about running into Becky and Eden in the grocery store. "And then I saw her again one day when I was walking during my lunch hour. We struck up a conversation and"—she shrugged—"we just sort of ended up friends."

"Wow. That's pretty cool."

She shrugged. "What's cool about it?"

"Just that you befriended somebody under those circumstances."

She frowned. "You make it sound like I'm some kind of hero."

"Well, you are."

"Cut it out."

He didn't say anything else, and she had to admit she liked him thinking of her as a hero. But she wished she'd done something to actually earn the label. They finished up what they could of the classified pages then went out to Rob's car around four.

"You remember where it is, right?"

Rob nodded and headed east. He turned the knob on the radio, and Three Dog Night blared, "Mama Told Me Not to Come." She hoped it wasn't a sign.

He pulled into the Preston driveway a few minutes later. He started to open his door, but Michelle put a hand on his arm. "It might be better if you wait here."

"You're sure it's safe?"

"I won't go in if . . . he's there."

Rob looked reluctant, but he waited in the car while she ran up and knocked on the door. The basket of food she'd left for Becky was gone, and this time Michelle was certain she saw the curtains move in the window beside the door.

She opened the screen door and pounded louder. "Becky? It's Michelle. Is . . . everything okay?"

No answer. Maybe she'd seen Rob in the car and was afraid to open the door. Michelle tried the door and drew in a breath when it gave way. She started to close it, but then she saw Becky's little girl sitting crosslegged on the sofa, staring at her.

She pushed the door open and stepped inside. "Hi, Eden. Remember me? Is your mommy home?" Keeping one hand on the door in an effort to not appear as if she was trespassing, she waved at Eden.

The toddler popped a thumb into her mouth and peered out from under too-long bangs. Her eyes were as dark as her hair.

Michelle hollered again. "Becky? Are you here?"

The house smelled of stale cooking grease and sour milk. She dodged a menagerie of stuffed animals and toys littering the floor and went to the sofa. Holding out her hands to Eden, she smiled. "Do you remember me?"

The child kept her thumb firmly in her mouth but raised her left arm to Michelle.

She scooped Eden up and settled her on one hip. "Where's your mommy?"

The little girl pulled her thumb out of her mouth long enough to point at the back door and say, "Mama?"

Cautiously Michelle walked through the house, talking softly to Eden the whole time. She checked the backyard, but there was no sign of Becky. The kitchen was tidy, and except for a pile of clean laundry folded on the unmade double bed, the bedroom was in order too. Eden's playpen in the corner looked as if it served as a crib too, with a pile of blankets, discarded pajamas, and more stuffed animals.

Michelle hollered again for Becky before going back to the front door to motion Rob inside.

He turned off the ignition and trotted up the steps, stopping short when he saw the toddler in her arms. "Everything okay?"

"I don't think Becky's here. I didn't go upstairs, and I think there's a basement, but I hollered and nobody answered."

He frowned. "They left her alone here?"

She shrugged. "I don't know. Would you mind coming in to help me go through the house? I'm a little . . . scared of what I might find."

"Yeah, sure." He followed her into the house and panned the room. He cupped his hands around his mouth and shouted, "Anybody home?"

Eden jerked in Michelle's arms and burst into tears.

Cuddling the toddler close to her chest, she crooned, "Oh, honey, it's okay." She bounced Eden gently in her arms, trying to calm her, and sang a tuneless version of "Hush Little Baby" under her breath.

Rob eased over to them as if Eden were a frightened puppy. When she didn't cry, he patted the baby's back, laughing softly. "Sorry, little one. Didn't mean to scare you."

She snuggled closer to Michelle and peeked up at Rob, looking wary.

"I'm sorry," Rob said to Michelle. "I didn't even think about that scaring her. What's her name?"

"Eden." She patted her tiny back, loving the weight of the child in her arms. She gave Rob a reassuring smile. "It's okay. She's fine now."

"She's cute."

"Yeah, she is."

He looked around the room. "Do you think her mom is here? You want me to go through the house?"

She nodded. "We'll come with you."

"I hope we don't scare the mama to death like we did this little one." Rob pinched her tiny toes through dingy booties that sported a hole in one toe.

Michelle followed Rob up the L-shaped stairway, talking softly to Eden as they went. "Is Mommy upstairs? Huh? Where's Mommy?"

"Mama?" Eden sounded as puzzled as they were.

Rob stopped on the landing. "Man, it's freezing up here." He made his teeth chatter loudly.

Eden giggled over her thumb.

Rob chattered his teeth again. This time, Eden pulled her thumb out of her mouth and tried to imitate him. He cracked up, which made Michelle giggle.

A spark came to Eden's eyes and she leaned out of Michelle's arms, egging Rob on.

He obliged her, gnashing his teeth and crossing his eyes.

Eden reached for him, and Rob looked at Michelle as if seeking her permission.

"Sure . . . She likes you now." She transferred Eden into his strong arms, and the toddler bounced with joy, poking at Rob's mouth with pudgy fingers, trying to make him chatter again.

He indulged her then advanced to even sillier faces, which Eden did her best to mimic. Soon they were all laughing. They stood on the landing between the two flights while Rob made a charming fool of himself, getting Eden to giggle again and again. He quickly won the little girl over. The big girl too.

Michelle imagined the three of them—her and Rob and Eden—as a family. This was their house, and Eden was their daughter. In the space of a few seconds, she mentally redecorated the house into a cozy haven where they all lived and loved together, where there was another baby on the way and—

"Hey? Penn? Earth to Michelle . . . "

She was embarrassed to realize she'd spaced out. Rob waved his hand in front of her face, trying to get her attention.

"Where in the world did you go, Mish?"

"I—I was just thinking about where Becky might be," she lied.

"Well, let's look up here." He led the way up the next flight of stairs. It was like an icebox on the second floor, but not surprisingly, the two small bedrooms and tiny bath between them were empty. The upstairs rooms appeared to be used only for storage. And if Becky had been up here, she surely would have heard all the commotion they'd made with their giggling games.

They started back down the steps with Rob leading the way, Eden in his arms. He turned the corner to descend the next flight when a woman's scream pierced the air.

CHAPTER TWENTY

Becky Preston stood in the doorway, hands pressed to her throat, eyes wide.

"It's okay! It's okay," Rob said. He grabbed Michelle's arm and urged her down the stairs so Becky could see her. "I'm Michelle's friend. See." He put an arm around Michelle's shoulder, as if that would prove his statement. He noticed she didn't try to shrug him off.

"Hi, Becky." Michelle descended the last steps. "Everything's okay. We were just . . . worried about you."

Becky stood there frozen, obviously shaken and confused. She was noticeably pregnant, and her complexion was so pale it worried him.

"I'm so sorry," Michelle told her. "We really didn't break in. The door was open. We were worried about you. But Eden—she was sitting on the couch. Alone . . . "

Rob waited for the young mother to explain her absence. Instead, she burst into tears, just as Eden had when he'd frightened her with his yelling a few minutes ago.

"Becky?" Michelle hurried to her side. "What's wrong?"

Eden started fussing and struggled to free herself from his arms. He set the child gently on the floor, and she toddled over to her mother and wrapped her arms around Becky's knees. Rob couldn't help but think of the photograph he'd taken that hot August day, of Eden clutching her mother in the same way while the police dragged off her daddy.

Michelle reached over to stroke Eden's silky black hair, keeping her eyes on the baby's mother. "I'm so sorry if we scared you, Becky. I was worried when you didn't answer the door at lunchtime. I just"— she motioned toward Rob—"asked my friend from the *Beacon* to come with me to make sure everything was okay."

Rob gave her an anemic wave and shrank back onto the stairway.

Becky looked between them, trembling. "You won't tell anyone, will you?"

"Tell them what?"

"He needed me to bring him something, and Eden was napping. I thought . . . But it took longer than I thought it would and—" She put her face in her hands. "It was stupid. I never should have done it. I–I've never done anything like that before, but he said—"

"Who?" Michelle sounded as confused as Rob felt.

"Mack. He needed a few things, so I ran to the store. I was only gone for a few minutes. And she was napping . . . "

Surely Becky didn't mean she'd left the little girl here *alone*. "Eden was awake when we got here, sitting there." Michelle pointed to the sofa.

Becky shook her head. "No. She was in her crib . . . the playpen, I mean. She was in there when I left."

"How long were you gone? Because she was sitting on the sofa when we got here about . . . ?" She looked to Rob to fill in the blank.

He'd lost track of time but took a guess. "About twenty minutes ago, I'd say."

"That can't be. I wasn't gone that long . . . . And she was in her playpen when I left. Sleeping."

"How long ago?"

Becky looked sheepish. "I don't know. Maybe half an hour. Maybe not quite that long."

"Becky." Michelle's tone said *What on earth were you thinking?* But she only said, "Where were you?"

"Mack has a bad cold. They won't give him anything for it at the jail, and they won't let him go to the doctor. I—I ran to the drugstore for him."

"You really left the baby here alone?" Rob tried to temper his tone too late, and he heard the accusation in his own voice.

"She usually sleeps for at least two hours in the afternoon." Defensiveness crept into Becky's voice.

"But what if there'd been a fire or something?" He said it gently, but he could see in Becky's face that it stung.

"And apparently she does know how to climb out of the playpen," Rob said, unable to keep the indictment from his voice now.

Becky turned on him. "I'm not sure who you are, but you have no business telling me how to raise my daughter."

"It's okay, Becky." Michelle's voice was even. "He's my friend. From the paper."

"Yeah." She spoke in a monotone. "I remember him."

Michelle went still. "Where were you at lunchtime? Did you remember we were supposed to have lunch?"

Again, Becky hung her head. "Sorry, Michelle. I—something came up."

Rob didn't know what was going on, but there was something Becky wasn't telling them. A horrible thought nudged at him. Had Eden been here alone when Michelle came by for lunch earlier? Was Becky so irresponsible that she'd leave the baby alone for hours?

Michelle eased toward the front door. "I was worried about you."

"I'm fine. There's nothing to worry about. I'm sorry lunch didn't work out. And . . . thanks for the food. I'll get the basket back to you."

"It's okay." Michelle looked hurt. "Well . . . we probably should go. I'm sorry if we scared you."

"No big deal." Becky looked at the door as if doing so would hurry them out.

Rob tried to catch Michelle's eye. Surely she wasn't just going to leave. They needed to make certain this wouldn't happen again. Someone needed to talk to that woman and make sure she understood the severity of what she'd done. But Michelle opened the front door and unlatched the screen door.

Reluctantly, he followed her. "Nice to meet you," he told Becky as he passed by, even though Michelle hadn't officially made introductions. " 'Bye, Eden." He chattered his teeth again, but this time it didn't produce even a grin.

Outside, he and Michelle were silent as they walked to the car, even though Becky closed the door the minute they were off the porch.

But in the car, Rob had a fit. "We've got to report her. She left that baby alone for who knows how long."

"Do you think Eden climbed out of the crib on her own?"

He turned to study her. "Who else could have gotten her out?"

"No, that's not what I meant. I just mean—do you think Becky's telling the truth? That Eden was in bed, sleeping, when she left? Maybe she left her there awake. Watching TV or something."

"Was the TV on?"

"No. But Eden might have gotten hold of the remote. Babies figure that stuff out pretty quickly."

"I just can't believe she would leave her baby alone, wandering around the house, while she ran errands for that good-for-nothing husband of hers."

"Surely he doesn't wield that kind of power over her . . . ."

"It sounds like he does. Even from jail." Rob threw the Pinto in gear and gripped the steering wheel. "You said she planned to get back together with him?"

"Because of the baby . . . The one she's expecting, not just Eden." Michelle looked up at the house as he backed out of the driveway. "We should have asked her when Mack is getting out of jail."

"Do you want to stop by the police station and see what we can find out?"

"No. I think I'd rather just ask Becky. It feels a little underhanded, going to the police. And I think she might have talked to me if you hadn't been there."

Rob cocked his head, regarding her. "Can I ask you a question?"

"I guess."

He could tell he made her nervous when he got introspective like this. "Why did you take lunch to Becky Preston's?"

She squinted at him. "I don't understand what you're asking."

"She doesn't seem like the type you'd choose for a friend. I mean, she's nothing like your friends from college that I met. I'm just curious why you took an interest in her."

She looked at her hands in her lap, obviously debating how to answer. Finally she sighed and looked up at him. "I don't even know if I know the answer myself. Until I was eighteen, everything pretty much went the way I wanted it to. I grew up in a great family, parents who loved me, good friends at school. I had a great boyfriend, a bright future . . . But after graduation, things kind of—fell apart. For the first time, I realized that what I'd had wasn't guaranteed. That not everybody was blessed with the things I was blessed with." She worried the edge of her sleeve, looking as if she'd just bared her soul to a man she wasn't sure she could trust.

"That's true," he said, wanting to be worthy of her trust more than he'd ever wanted anything.

"When things fell apart, it kind of made me look at people differently. And it made me want to be on the giving end sometimes, instead of always being on the receiving end."

"Wow." He was deeply curious about what had happened to her.

Grinning up at him, she looked vulnerable—and beautiful. She gave a humorless laugh. "You thought I was going to say, 'Because it was the right thing to do.' Or 'Because I wanted to help someone less fortunate than me,' didn't you?"

"I honestly don't know what I thought you were going to say. That's what I like about you, Michelle Penn. You are never, ever boring."

"Aw, I bet you say that to all the girls." But her smile said she understood his compliment.

"No. I don't say that to all the girls." He pulled over and parked at the curb. He didn't want the distraction of driving while they had this conversation.

She seemed to understand his seriousness, her expression matching his.

His voice almost a whisper, he risked the question he'd been reserving. "Would I be out of line to ask what you meant about things . . . falling apart?"

She sighed. "I guess the easiest way to explain it is, I got dumped."

"Ah . . . That great boyfriend wasn't so great after all?"

"No, I think he was still pretty great." She struggled to swallow, and he could tell she despised the lump that clogged her throat. "He dumped me to go serve in Vietnam. Last I heard, he was in Phnom Penh."

Rob blew out a breath. "Whoa. So . . . are you waiting for him?" So much rested on her answer.

"No. I really mean it. He *dumped* me to go to Nam."

"But . . . surely he must have wanted you to wait for him?"

"I offered. He didn't want that. I think—" She bit her lip, but not before he saw it tremble. "I think Vietnam was the only thing Kevin could think of to let me know how serious he really was about not wanting to be with me."

"Ouch. I'm sorry, Mish. That had to hurt."

One tear slipped down her cheek, and everything in him wanted to sweep her into his arms and make everything right. But he couldn't do that. And even if he could've, he somehow knew that now wasn't the time.

It took every ounce of strength he had to stay on his side of the seat. Instead, he wrapped his hand around hers and squeezed. As if that feeble gesture could possibly say everything that was in his heart for her at this moment.

* * * * *

Michelle relished the feel of Rob's strong fingers gripping hers. His simple words of empathy were so different from the pity she'd felt from everyone when Kevin had first deployed and she had to explain why she wasn't waiting for him.

She stared through the windshield of Rob's car and the memories came flooding back. She knew there were still people in Bristol who probably thought that she'd cruelly dropped Kevin while he put his life in danger for his country. Her parents had long ago convinced her that it didn't pay to try to explain it to every person who wondered.

"It's between you and God what happened, Mish," her dad had told her one night when she could not seem to stop crying. "Let people think what they will. You know the truth, and God knows, and there's no reason to feel even worse over what happened just because people don't understand. Anyone who loves you will know that you couldn't have been more loyal to Kevin."

She still suspected that her parents—Dad for sure—were secretly relieved she wasn't getting married right out of high school. And after two years, she'd made peace with God about the whole mess. She hadn't seen the results yet—though Rob's presence in her life had certainly suggested some new possibilities. She trusted that God had something in mind to redeem everything that had happened to her.

She hadn't yet reached a place where she could trust that she'd *like* what God might have in mind for her life. But for now, she was willing to give Him the benefit of her doubts.

She squeezed Rob's hand again, grateful to have gotten this "secret" out of the way—and suddenly aware of an important truth. "You know, as hard as it was—the whole thing with Kevin—seeing what Becky's going through reminds me that it could have been so much worse."

Rob nodded. "That's always true, isn't it? We can always find someone worse off than we are."

"My mom always says she can choose her level of contentment by whether she looks out the south window, down to where the Martins' ranch is—one thousand acres and a beautiful, modern farmhouse—or whether she looks out the north window, to the trailer house, where one of Dad's hired men lives with his wife and three little kids—with one on the way."

* * * * *

Rob listened to Michelle and shook his head, feeling empty and wishing he could remember whether his mom had ever given him little tips for life the way Michelle's mother had. If only he could ask his dad. But Mom was pretty much an off-limits topic between them and had been for fourteen years now.

"Look north and Mom's happy," Michelle was saying. "But south, it's too easy to start dwelling on what she doesn't have instead of what she does."

"That's good advice. You're smart to take it."

"Yeah, well, I don't always. I try, but . . . " She shrugged.

"You do all right. And what you've done for Becky proves it."

"I haven't really done anything. Just tried to be friendly."

"That's more than most people would do. I wish there was some way we could help her," he said.

"Maybe there is."

He waited for her to explain, expecting it to cost him more than he was willing to give.

"Why don't we offer to babysit for Eden so she can have some time to herself? We could do it together." She looked up at him and smiled. "She likes you."

Her idea surprised him. But it felt like a gift, since it involved spending time with Michelle too. He wondered what his father would think of their plan. Didn't matter. At least it wouldn't if his own plans panned out. "That's a great idea. If we can talk Becky into actually taking us up on it. I don't think she was a big fan of me when we left there just now." He hooked a thumb over his shoulder toward Becky's neighborhood.

She grinned. "Good point. Maybe we should wait a day or two until she's had a little time to cool down."

"Okay. But I like the way you're thinking. Going together, I mean."

"You may like it, but I wonder what our boss will think."

"How could he be against such a mission of mercy?"

But even as he spoke the words, he knew exactly how his father would feel about it. And it made him all the more determined to set his plan in motion.

Chapter Twenty-One

"Please, Becky, let me in."

Michelle knocked again and tried the doorknob, remembering how it had given way last week when she and Rob had come to check on Becky. But it was locked tight this time. Still, she had a feeling Becky was home.

She waited a few more minutes and knocked again. This time she heard footsteps. And then the door opened.

"What do you want?"

"Becky, may I come in, please? I'd like to talk to you."

The door opened slowly and Michelle slipped in. "Are you okay?"

"I'm fine. Did you come to spy on me?"

Michelle felt as if she'd been slapped. "I was never here to spy on you. Is that truly what you think?"

"I don't know what to think. I come home and there's a stranger in my house holding my baby and accusing me of not being a good mother." Her voice cracked on the word, and she looked at the toy-littered floor.

"Rob wasn't accusing you, Becky. We were just worried, that's all. And we never would have come in if I hadn't seen Eden. When you didn't come, I was afraid something had happened—that you were sick or something. That's the only reason we were upstairs. We were looking for you."

Becky looked past Michelle as if she thought Rob might be hiding on the front porch. "Listen, I'm sorry I blew off our lunch. Like I said, Mack was sick and I had to get him some meds. They treat him like dirt at that jail."

Michelle bit her tongue to keep from mentioning that dirt was what he'd treated Becky like. "Do you know yet when he gets out?"

"There's another hearing next Tuesday. He's pretty sure he'll get out then—at least on parole."

"And he's coming back here?"

She nodded. "He's a good man. He's good to Eden, and he's actually happy about this baby." Becky put a hand on her belly.

It looked to Michelle as if she'd grown even rounder with child since the other day, but it was probably just the style of maternity top she had on.

Becky stuck out her chin, looking defiant. "I know you don't believe me, but Mack's changed. He—he was going through a bad patch last summer. But he's turned over a new leaf. He's trying to line up a job before he gets out. He already has some good leads."

"Well . . . that's good, I guess." She didn't know what else to say. She'd read too many articles in *Glamour* magazine and even *Seventeen* that made it sound like there was pretty much no hope for a guy who beat up a woman. But she also knew that people could change. She'd seen it in her own family. Not anyone who'd done what Mack Preston had, but Grandpa Penn had been an alcoholic—"a mean drunk," Grandma had called him. And he'd turned his life around. Or rather, God had—overnight. Grandpa had gone forward at a revival meeting when Michelle was a baby, and he'd never taken another drink after that. Her grandpa had died when she was only ten, but she'd heard Dad and her grandma tell the story many times. And they were eyewitnesses she trusted.

She wanted to ask Becky if Mack had found Jesus, but the girl was already on the defensive. It didn't seem like the right thing to do on the heels of the encounter she and Rob had had with Becky last week.

"What I was wondering . . . well, *Rob* and I were wondering . . . if we could babysit Eden some evening. So you can have some time to yourself. Or maybe go visit Mack? I don't know if they allow that in the evening—and unfortunately, that's the only time Rob and I could come, but—"

Becky eyed her with suspicion. "Are you two . . . an item?"

"Me and Rob?" Her laugh sounded forced, even to her. "No. We just . . . work together."

"Seems to me you get along really well for coworkers."

"Oh, we do. Get along, I mean. He's a great guy." She racked her brain to think of a way to change the subject. "He's excited about seeing Eden again. They really hit it off." She smiled, thinking about Rob's silly chattering-teeth game with Eden. For some reason, it had surprised her to see how he'd warmed up to the toddler. Because he was an only child, she hadn't expected him to be so good with kids.

"I don't know . . . . When were you thinking?"

Becky was acting reluctant, but Michelle got the feeling she really wanted to accept. "Is there a time that would help you out the most? Maybe whenever they have visitation at the jail? And if Rob can't do it that night, I'd be happy to come alone. It'd be nice to have something to look forward to—something more exciting than sitting home with a book. Really."

"Well, it *would* be nice to just have a night to myself. Maybe get groceries without having my little pack rat pulling things off the shelf and into my cart."

"Just name a night. Seriously."

"I don't get my check till next Friday, so it'd have to be after that."

"Oh, no—no. You don't have to pay us, Becky. I never meant that—"

"Oh . . . I just meant . . . " She seemed to be embarrassed. "I won't have a way to pay for groceries until I get my check."

"Sure . . . of course. That makes sense."

Eden's cries deflected the awkward moment.

"I'll go get her. Be right back . . . "

Michelle looked around the humble living room. As far as she knew, Becky didn't work. She must mean that her welfare check came on Friday. Michelle couldn't imagine how humiliating it must be to depend on the government to take care of her child. She found herself disliking Mack Preston more by the minute. What did Becky see in him besides the fact that he was Eden's father?

Eden burst into the room and raced for Michelle. Pleased beyond words, she scooped the featherweight into her arms and nuzzled her neck, giggling along with Eden. "Did you have a good nap?"

Eden's brow furrowed. "No nap!"

Michelle laughed. "No. It's time to wake up, isn't it?"

"Wake up," Eden parroted. "No nap!"

It was the most Michelle had heard her talk. Her cousin's three kids had all spoken in complete sentences by the time they were two. But then, Eden had been through a lot.

"Come here, silly girl." Becky held out her arms to her daughter. "Do you want some juice?"

Eden left Michelle's arms willingly for her mother's.

"Do you want something to drink? Hot tea, maybe?"

"Sure. That sounds good." She followed Becky to the kitchen.

Becky put a kettle on to boil and opened cupboard doors, revealing shelves that were as bare of food as the sink was full of dirty dishes. Michelle made a mental note to pick up a few groceries to bring over when she and Rob came.

Eden played in one corner with a stack of colorful plastic QuikTrip cups, and Michelle helped Becky wash mugs and spoons. Standing side by side at the sink she could feel Becky relax a little, and soon they were chatting like friends again.

Eden toddled over and lifted her arms to Michelle. Laughing, she lifted the toddler and shared an impromptu tea party while Becky finished the dishes.

When Eden grew tired of sipping tea, Michelle helped Becky dry dishes and straighten up the kitchen. When they were finished, Becky got out the baby book she was making for Eden. Each photograph glued to the page boasted an intricate pen-and-ink "frame" that Becky had drawn herself.

"Becky, this must have taken hours! You're an artist."

Becky shrugged. "Oh, not really."

But Michelle thought she saw a touch of pride in her response. "This is beautiful. An heirloom."

"You know what they say. Necessity is the mother of invention. Baby books were almost fifteen dollars. There was no way I could afford that, but I didn't want her to grow up without a baby book like I did." She looked embarrassed to have let that slip.

Michelle chose to ignore her comment and turned another beautifully designed page in the scrapbook. There was Mack Preston cuddling a newborn Eden in his arms. He looked like any proud father smiling down on his first child. Seeing him in this photo, Michelle got a glimpse of what Becky saw in him.

She stayed and chatted with Becky and Eden for almost an hour, and before she left, they'd settled on Saturday evening for her and Rob to babysit. "We can pick her up and bring her to my apartment so you can have the house to yourself, if you want."

"That'd be real nice, Michelle. I appreciate it. And Eden loves you. I know she'll be tickled."

Michelle shot up a prayer that Rob would be available that night and mentally ransacked her closet for something to wear that was cute but wouldn't look like she was trying too hard.

Eden actually cried when Michelle opened the door a few minutes later to head home. Her promises that she'd be back soon did nothing to assuage the little girl's tears, and by the time Michelle climbed into her car, the baby-shaped vacuum in her heart was big enough to drive a semitrailer through.

Chapter Twenty-Two

"Don't worry about a thing. We'll have her home by nine o'clock." Michelle stood in the doorway at the Prestons' house, bouncing Eden on one hip. The little girl was ready for the ride back to Michelle's apartment, bundled up in a pink coat with a ruff of pink fur around the hood and looking like an Eloise Wilkin illustration from one of Michelle's Little Golden Books. She had a collection of over fifty of the children's books in her hope chest.

But Kevin Ferris was the only one besides her parents who knew that. She pushed the thought aside. Kevin was the last person she wanted to think about tonight.

Rob planned to meet them at her apartment with a pizza in a few minutes. "Well, we'd better be going."

"You be good for Miss Michelle, okay?" Becky reached for Eden, suddenly reluctant to let her go. "Remember, you can call my neighbor if you need to get hold of me, okay?"

"I've got the number in my purse. We'll be fine. You just enjoy your evening. And don't you dare spend it cleaning house or doing laundry or something. You do something fun, just for you."

That smoothed the furrows from her brow. "Okay. I'll try. Thanks again, Michelle. I owe you one. And thanks for the groceries."

"No big deal. Have a great evening." She hurried down the steps and to her car before Becky could change her mind.

Rob's Pinto was parked in the driveway behind the house when she pulled in. He waved to them from the driver's seat. Good. He'd found her place okay. She checked her hair in the rearview mirror then went around to get Eden out of the car.

Rob met them at the door with a boxed pizza. The savory aroma wafted through the chilly night air, and her mouth watered.

"Pizza! Pizza!" Eden chanted, reaching for Rob.

"Oh, yeah, you just like me 'cause I made supper. Just like a woman." He pinched Eden's cheek and winked at Michelle.

"And you call that making supper? Just like a man."

"Touché."

His grin told her the evening was off to a good start.

She led the way up two flights of stairs to her apartment. She'd gone out to the farm this morning to rummage through the attic for some lamps and one of Grandma Penn's vases, which she'd filled with cut ivy that was still growing green on the side of the chimney. She'd talked Mom into letting her have—no, *borrow*—Grandma's everyday dishes too. They would use paper plates for pizza tonight, but the dishes looked nice arranged just so on the brick-and-board bookcases her brother had helped her put together when she first moved in.

She'd left the lamps on, and they gave the living room a cozy glow. The apartment smelled of lemon Pledge and Lysol, evidence she'd spent all afternoon cleaning. Beneath those clean scents, the smell of fresh-baked chocolate chip cookies wafted out. She almost hoped Rob didn't notice so she could surprise him later.

"Nice place," Rob said, when they were all inside. "Where do you want this?" He held up the box of fragrant pizza.

"I want it right here, actually." She patted her tummy.

"Pizza!" Eden chimed in.

Rob laughed. "Okay. Lead me to the dishes."

"Follow me." She led the way to the tiny kitchen at the back of the apartment. She got down paper plates for Rob, and he filled their plates and poured drinks while she got Eden out of her coat and settled her atop a stack of Sears & Roebuck catalogs on a kitchen chair.

"My grandma used to do that—and tie me in with a dish towel," Rob said, grinning.

"So did mine! And the dish towel is a good idea, actually." She scooted the chair close to the table and rummaged in a drawer for the largest cotton tea towel she could find. Folded on the bias, it made a perfect "seat belt" for Eden.

She cut a thin slice of the pizza into tiny bites and blew on them to make sure they were cool enough. She put them on a plate in front of Eden, who dug in immediately.

Michelle laughed. "Well, I guess we're not going to say a blessing."

Rob handed her an empty plate and a glass of pop, then plopped the pizza box on the end of the table farthest from Eden. "Dinner is served. And I'll say the blessing."

He sat down and bowed his head.

"Hey, Eden," she whispered. "Shhh. We're going to say grace."

"Heavenly Father," Rob began.

Michelle bowed her head then snuck a quick peek at Eden, who actually had her head bowed over her plate—even if she also had a death grip on the hunk of pizza in her tiny fist.

"God, we thank You for this food and for this chance to help Becky Preston out," Rob said.

"Mama!" Eden said.

Rob and Michelle exchanged a look. Did Eden recognize her mother's given name?

Rob chuckled and quickly closed the prayer. "Bless this food for our use, in Jesus' name. Amen."

"Amen!" Eden cheered and stuffed a bite of pizza into her mouth.

They ate in amiable silence, and as hard as she tried, Michelle could not help imagining what it would be like if they really were a family. It was as if she were getting a dress rehearsal of her dream. But God wasn't that cruel was He, that He would make her pretend at something she couldn't have?

Don't ruin a perfectly good evening with your fantasizing, Penn. She took her own advice and pushed aside the images that crowded in.

It was fun to see Rob like this, whether he was only a coworker or something more. He made goo-goo eyes at Eden and made her giggle like he had with the chattering teeth at Becky's house.

"Do you think she has a chance?" he asked, a winsome sadness in his blue eyes.

"What do you mean?"

"In life. Or will she just grow up like . . . you know?"

"Wow. I guess I hadn't thought that far ahead." They discussed Becky's situation, talking in code just in case Eden understood more than it appeared.

The little girl vied for Rob's attention, and he snuck a silly look in between his dialogue with Michelle. They were debating the earth-shatteringly important question of which Beatle was the most talented musician when a strange noise at the end of the table made them both look Eden's way—just in time for her to throw up all over the table and herself.

Michelle practically dove to pick Eden up, while Rob jumped out of his chair and backpedaled with a look of horror on his handsome face.

Michelle couldn't help but giggle, even as she tried to clean up the mess.

Eden whimpered a little, but she seemed more concerned that she was covered with liquid pizza than that her tummy hurt.

"Help me out here, will you?" She untied the tea towel to release Eden from the chair and carried her over to the sink. "Can you get the water nice and warm for me? But not too warm."

"I will if you promise she won't barf on me again."

Michelle cracked up. "She didn't barf on you."

"She almost did, the little vomit machine." He turned on the faucet while somehow managing to stay a safe distance from "the little vomit machine." He watched Michelle clean up Eden at the sink. "Do you think she has the flu?"

She frowned. "I don't know. It's probably just from snarfing down too much pizza in one sitting, but I think I'll call my mom as soon as we get her cleaned up. Just to be sure."

"Sounds like a good idea."

Ten minutes later, Eden was dressed in pajamas, smelling of shampoo and baby powder. Michelle went to the kitchen and dialed her parents' number. While she waited for them to pick up, she stretched the phone cord into the living room doorway. Rob sat on the floor in front of the sofa with Eden in his lap, turning the pages of a storybook they'd found in the diaper bag. Michelle wished she had her Little Golden Books here. She made a note to bring a few back to the apartment the next time she made a trip out to the farm.

"Hello?"

"Daddy, hi. It's Michelle."

He laughed. "You know, beings you're the only female on the face of the earth who calls me *Daddy*, you could probably dispense with the introductions from now on."

"Oh." She grinned. "I guess I never thought of that. Is Mom home?"

"She's upstairs. Is everything okay?"

"Everything's fine. But I'm babysitting, and I need to ask Mom something."

"Hang on . . . I'll get her."

She heard him lay down the phone and run up the stairs. A minute later, Mom came on the line. "Hi, honey. What's up? Who are you babysitting for?"

"Just a friend here in town." She didn't want to go into the whole explanation right now. "The baby is two and we fed her pizza for supper, but she threw it all up right after she ate."

"Who's we?"

"Huh?"

"You said *we* fed her pizza."

Oh, brother. She for sure didn't want to go into *that* whole explanation. "Oh. A friend's here with me. From work. Eden—that's the little girl—seems like she feels fine now, but do you think I need to be worried that she threw up?"

She could almost sense Mom kick into mothering mode. "Does she feel like she has a fever?"

"Hang on." She put the phone down and went to feel Eden's forehead with the palm of her hand. "No. Her forehead feels cool. She acts like she feels fine."

"The pizza probably just didn't agree with her," Mom said. "Pizza might be a little rich for a two-year-old's tummy. I'd just watch her and make sure she doesn't develop a fever. And be sure and let her parents know what happened so they can watch her over the next couple of days."

"Okay. Thanks, Mom. I knew you'd know what to do."

"Glad to help. Oh, and if she threw up her supper, she might be hungry again soon. But you might want to go easy this time. Maybe just a little applesauce and some saltines. I could bring something in to town if you want me to. What's the address where you're babysitting?"

"Oh no, you don't need to do that," she said, a little too quickly. *Please no.* The last thing she needed was her mother showing up at her door. "There are crackers in the cupboard, and I think there's some yogurt in the fridge." She made it sound like she was referring to someone else's kitchen.

"She should tolerate that okay. You might want to keep her quiet, though. No roughhousing. It's probably about time to put her to bed, isn't it? . . . So who's helping you babysit?"

Michelle glanced at Rob and took the phone back into the kitchen. "Just a friend from work. I really need to go now, Mom. Thanks again." She hung up before her mother could ask any more questions.

She went back into the living room and waited for Rob to finish the story—for the third time. "Are you hungry?"

"Are you kidding?"

She laughed. "I wasn't talking to you, silly. I was talking to Eden. Mom said she might be hungry again since she barfed up her supper."

Rob squeezed Eden and kissed her cheek. "Are you hungry, babe?"

Michelle's heart melted. This man was going to make such a good daddy someday. The thought sobered her. She'd had the very same thought watching Kevin coach Little League. And maybe Kevin would be a terrific father. Just not to *her* kids. She dare not put that monkey on Rob's back—even in her mind.

She knelt on the floor beside them and felt Eden's forehead again. Still cool to the touch. "Do you want something to eat, Eden?"

"Uh-uh." The little girl clamped her mouth shut and wagged her head. "Book?" She held the book up to Rob.

"Again? We've read this one three times already."

"Book! Book!" Eden bounced on his lap.

"How about I tell you a story instead?"

"Book!"

Rob took the book and slipped it under the sofa behind him. "Listen, Eden. Listen to this story. Once upon a time—"

She seemed to recognize the prelude to a new story and nestled herself deeper into his lap.

Michelle curled up in the easy chair beside them, smiling.

Rob spun a fantastical tale about a little girl named Eden and her pink puppy named Sweden. Michelle cracked up as his story became more ridiculous—and more rambunctious—as it went along. When Eden and Sweden suddenly learned to fly in the story, Rob swooped the real Eden into the air and landed her on the sofa behind him.

She giggled and dove over his shoulders, back into his lap. "Do again! Do again!"

He obliged, swooping her into Michelle's arms this time. Michelle thought about Mom's warning, but she didn't have the heart to ruin their fun. When a game of toss-the-baby ensued, she prayed Eden's stomach had settled and the game didn't turn into toss-the-cookies.

The next hour was pure delight, playing with Eden and seeing Rob Merrick in this new and amazing light. Finally Eden began to wind down, rubbing her eyes and twisting a hank of hair between her fingers.

"Are you sleepy, sweetie?"

In answer, Eden lifted her arms for Michelle to pick her up. She carried her to the rocker in the corner of the room. With the little girl snuggled in her lap, Michelle sang a Karen Carpenter medley at lullaby tempo. Within minutes, Eden was asleep.

Still humming softly, Michelle glanced up and saw Rob watching her. The look on his face made her heart turn a somersault.

Chapter Twenty-Three

"You're pretty good at that," Rob said, whispering so he wouldn't wake the baby.

Michelle quit singing, and her face flushed in the dim light of the lamp on the table beside the rocker. She'd seemed unaware of his eyes on her while she rocked Eden, but now she cringed and looked down, obviously self-conscious.

"No. Don't stop," he said. "It's working like magic." He motioned at the sleeping baby.

"Well," Michelle whispered, "I think she was tired enough that a freight train would have put her to sleep."

"She's a cutie. I'm glad we did this. It was a good idea."

"It was. Thanks for coming with me. Honestly, I don't know how Becky does it by herself."

He blew out a breath. "I was thinking the same thing. It's a full-time job. I hope she's having a good night."

"Yeah, me too. I bet the night flew by, though."

"I know it did for me." Only because he wished he had another four hours with this woman.

She glanced at the clock. "Don't speak too soon. We still have an hour and a half before we have to have her back."

"True. It will probably drag like crazy."

She eyed him as if she were trying to decide whether he was serious. But then that familiar spark came to her eyes. "Because I'm so boring, right?"

"Oh, yeah. I'm bored out of my gourd."

"Well, there's nothing that says you have to stay. I think I can get her down to the car without waking her up."

"No, I'll stay." No way was he going to let her talk him into leaving. He couldn't think of any place he'd rather be right now. If he told any of his college buddies that he'd spent a Saturday night helping a coworker babysit a two-year-old, they would have called him crazy. Even Doug Jensen would raise an eyebrow. And Doug understood firsthand the attraction the whole wife-and-kids thing held for him.

He could scarcely believe it himself. He couldn't explain it, but he felt content here. With Michelle, yes, but something about this little girl had reached in and taken hold of his heart too.

Michelle shifted in the chair. "Hey, would you mind spreading her blanket on the end of the sofa there?"

"Sure." He took the tattered quilt and unfolded it, making a little pallet in one corner of the sofa.

Michelle stood slowly, holding Eden close. The baby stirred, and Michelle bounced her gently, pacing the short length of the room until Eden stilled again. She brought her over to the sofa and laid her down, keeping a tender hand on her back until she settled back to sleep.

Michelle wrapped the corners of the quilt around Eden and tucked them underneath her.

"She looks like a little burrito," he whispered.

"She kind of smells like one too." She scrunched up her nose and pulled a face that made Rob laugh.

"Shh!" But she laughed too. "I'll change her diaper before we take her home, but I'm not going to wake her up now."

He nodded his agreement.

She propped sofa cushions strategically around Eden then straightened and moved toward the kitchen. "You want something to drink?"

"Do you have something hot? Tea, maybe?"

"Sure. Let me put the kettle on."

He followed her into the kitchen, and while she got down mugs and tea bags, he offered to fill the kettle with fresh water and put it on to boil.

When the tea was ready, they sat at the kitchen table—with a view into the living room in case Eden stirred—and talked.

He loved seeing this softer side of Michelle. Here, she seemed comfortable in her own skin, singing to the baby, making tea, and now sitting with her stockinged feet on the chair and her knees pulled up under her chin.

"You want your tea heated up?"

"Oh! I almost forgot!" She sprang out of the chair and went to a cupboard. "I made cookies."

He took the cookie jar she presented and peeked inside. "Oh, man," he said, "that's exactly what I was hungry for. How'd you know?"

She brought the kettle to the table, poured more water over their tea bags, and then curled back up on her chair, munching a cookie and looking as content as Rob felt.

He held up a cookie. "These aren't even burnt."

Without missing a beat, she took a bite of her cookie, gave his knee a jab with the toe of her thick socks, and smiled smugly. "That's because I didn't make them in a stupid microwave."

"Well, they're good. You could make these any time."

He couldn't quite interpret the look she gave him, but he thought it was something along the lines of, *And why, pray tell, would I have occasion to make you cookies again, Mr. Merrick III?*

"I'm glad we did this."

She grinned. "Yes, you said that already."

"Yeah, but I was talking about Eden before. Now I'm talking about you."

"Oh?"

"I don't care what the rules of engagement are at the *Beacon*, Mish. I like you, and I want to keep seeing you. And I don't want to have to make up some excuse every time, either."

She picked at a hangnail. "I don't know why you're telling me this. I'm not the one who made the rule."

"I know. Sorry. I—"

"I like you too, Rob, but I can't afford to lose my job. And I don't think your dad was joking when he called me into his office and said 'Leave my son alone, or else.'"

"No . . . I don't suppose he was."

"So that doesn't leave us too many options, does it?"

"What do you mean?"

"I just mean that as long as we're both working for the *Beacon*, we're going to have to keep things strictly professional."

"I think it's a little too late for that."

"No, it's not." She stared at him. "Why? You think he wouldn't call this professional?"

Before he could reason himself out of it, Rob slid off his chair, leaned across the table, and kissed her full on the lips. She gave a little gasp, but he noticed she kissed him back.

"I don't think he'd call *that* very professional."

"Um . . . no." Her eyes locked with his, and she reached up and brushed a strand of hair off his forehead. "Neither do I."

He kissed her again. In a totally unprofessional way.

Her arms came around his neck, and her fingers trolled through his hair. But after a minute, she pulled away, sucking in a breath. "Rob . . . we'd better get Eden home. It's almost nine." But she didn't let loose of him.

"I know. I know." He reached behind his head and grasped her hands. It was all he could do to extricate himself from her embrace. "We'd better get Rob home, is what we'd better do," he mumbled.

"What?" Her breath tickled his cheek and smelled of warm chocolate chip cookies.

"I'll go warm up my car. For Eden."

"I can just take her home."

"No. I'll go with you." He swallowed hard, not wanting to make a promise he couldn't keep. "I promise I'll bring you straight back home afterward. I won't even walk you to the door."

"Okay," she whispered. She leaned in to kiss him gently on the cheek, just below his left eye. "That's probably a good idea."

"Yes. Very good idea." He kissed her in the same spot on her own cheek. Her skin was smooth beneath his lips, like the petals of a rose. He placed a matching kiss below her other eye. "Very good."

Her giggle held all kinds of promise.

Chapter Twenty-Four

Rob rubbed sweaty palms on the knees of his suit pants and checked his watch for the tenth time in as many minutes.

He felt bad enough about being here in the offices of the *Wichita Eagle-Beacon*—the big *Beacon*—for a job interview. But worse, he'd told Myrtle—who would tell his dad—that he was out on a story. Now that he'd been out of the office for almost three hours, he'd better have a whale of a story to write when he got back. Or an explanation for where he'd been all morning.

He knew Michelle would be wondering too. And she was the last person he could tell. At least for now.

He glanced at the receptionist again. If he did manage to land a job, he wouldn't have to write that news story, because his father likely would show him the door—never mind that he had every intention of giving Dad the customary two weeks' notice. He realized that by doing so, he might be giving himself two weeks to find a new place to live too. But that was okay. Even with paying his father a little every month for "rent," he'd been able to sock away a decent amount in his savings account. Moving back home was only supposed to be temporary anyway. He'd work out the details. Somehow.

He cleared his throat and shifted in his seat, but the receptionist appeared to have forgotten he was here. Finally a door behind
her opened, and a man Rob recognized from his photo on the
op-ed page each week appeared.

"Mr. Merrick?"

Rob nodded.

"Come on back." Jim Clemson motioned him to his office.
"Merrick, huh? You any relation to Robert Merrick of the other
Beacon?" His voice held something close to disdain.

"Yes, sir. Robert Merrick is my father."

The lift of Clemson's bushy eyebrows told Rob he hadn't
expected that answer.

"What, the old man won't give you a job?" He gave a nervous
laugh, no doubt trying to extricate his foot from his mouth.

"Actually, I'm currently employed at the *Bristol Beacon*—
as managing editor."

"Looking to move up in the world, eh?"

Rob forced a laugh at a joke he didn't find humorous. Would
he have to answer to this turkey if he got the job? "I'd like the experience of working for a daily newspaper. I feel I could be an asset to
your editorial team."

The man shook his head. "We don't have any openings in editorial at the time. Can you type?"

He absently flexed his fingers. "Passably."

"We have an opening for a typesetter, and we need a couple of
pressmen."

"I really don't think I'd be interested in those positions. In the
interest of full disclosure, I don't think you'd *want* me in those
positions."

Clemson didn't seem to appreciate Rob's attempt at humor any more than Rob had appreciated his. "I can give you an application and let you know if something opens up. I assume you have a journalism degree?"

"I have a business degree, but I took quite a few journalism courses." Did *three* qualify as "quite a few" in anybody's book? He might be setting a personal record for lies told in a single day.

"I assume I could call your father as a reference?"

Rob froze. "I–I'd rather you not do that, sir. I can give you some names if you need references . . . ."

"Am I to take it that your father isn't aware you're looking to change jobs?"

He sighed. He'd reached his quota of lies. "That would be a fair assumption. As with any employer, I would need to give two weeks' notice before I could start work. I'll be twenty-five years old in February, sir. I don't need my father's permission to make a career decision." He might be cooking his own goose, but he didn't know how else to answer.

Clemson extended a hand across the desk, dismissing him.

Rob took the hint and rose to shake the man's hand. "Thank you for your time, sir."

"Give Dana your contact information before you leave." He shrugged. "I don't really expect there to be an opening any time soon, but you never know."

The editor ushered him out and closed the door behind him.

Rob left his résumé with the receptionist, but he knew a brush-off when he heard one. It was probably for the best. With his limited experience, he doubted anyone would pay him as generously as his father. And the payments on his Pinto weren't cheap. If he did find a job and had to get his own place, he might have to give up his new car.

He pushed the thoughts away. He was probably wasting his time on a pipe dream. Right now, his biggest problem was coming up with a story that would redeem his absence this afternoon.

* * * * *

Michelle was in the darkroom taking film from the canister when she heard a commotion in the office. Two male voices in an argument. Or was it three? Sometimes she couldn't tell Rob's voice from his father's when she was in here. But Rob had been out on a story all afternoon, and she didn't think he was back yet. She didn't recognize the other person in the shouting match, but it grew more heated by the second.

She was tempted to open the door and find out what was going on even if it meant ruining her film. But the photos she was developing were from the high school's Snowball Dance. She couldn't exactly restage the event, and she was counting on the photos to fill a half page. She quickly rolled the film into the canister and started its processing then went to the door and pressed her ear to the cool wood. Something pretty heavy was going on out there.

"I don't care what you say, you're gonna pay and you're gonna pay dearly!"

"You need to leave now." That was Mr. Merrick's voice, not Rob's. Maybe it was just the distortion through the door, but he almost sounded scared. She'd never heard that emotion in his voice— *ever*. "I'm not going to ask you again. If you don't leave, I'll need to call the police. I don't think you want them involved . . . ."

She had no idea why someone was threatening Mr. Merrick, but if Myrtle was hearing the same conversation Michelle was, the police had probably already been called.

She hoped they got here, pronto. From the sound of things outside the door, it had turned into fisticuffs.

"You leave me no choice, Mr. Preston."

Preston? Becky. Was Becky's husband out there? Was he out of jail? What was he so upset about?

Maybe it was about the story the *Beacon* had run back in August. They'd followed that story up with a report about Mack Preston's sentence. Maybe he thought—

A woman's scream curdled the air, and at the same instant, something hit the other side of the darkroom door so hard it knocked Michelle backward. She grabbed the workbench, struggling to regain her balance. Her heart felt as if it would beat right out of her chest.

She inhaled sharply, trying to catch her breath. A strange odor filled the air, and she wondered if she'd somehow spilled the chemicals when she stumbled. But it smelled more like burned toast. Or like when she'd burned the chocolate chip cookies in the break room microwave.

It sounded like the newsroom was in chaos, with people shouting and the sound of footsteps running past the darkroom door. The red light was on, so the employees had to know she was in here. She wished there was a lock on the door, but at the same time, she felt like she needed to get out of here.

Dismissing the film developing in the canister, she reached cautiously for the door. It flew open at the same moment.

Rob stood on the other side. When he saw her, his shoulders slumped. "Thank God."

"What is going on?"

He opened the door as wide as it would go and cast about the small room. "Are you okay?"

"I'm fine. What's going on?"

He inspected the door, and for the first time, she noticed a splintered circle of light coming through the wood.

"Did you get hit?"

"What are you talking about?"

He looked incredulous. "Didn't you see the bullet come through that door?"

"What bullet?"

He ignored her and flipped on the light then went to the back of the room, running a hand up and down the rear wall.

"What bullet?" she repeated.

He hooked a thumb behind him at the door. "The one that came zinging through this door two minutes ago."

She stared. "You're joking."

"You could have been killed, Mish." His tone said this was *not* a joking matter.

"Somebody fired a gun?"

"Yes. That idiot shot into this door. Didn't you hear the racket?"

"Of course I heard it. But I didn't know I was being shot at."

He moved to stand in front of her and ran his hands up and down her forearms. "You're sure you didn't get hit?"

"I think I'd know if I had a bullet in me, Rob." She shivered . . . more from his hands on her than from the thought that someone had tried to kill her. "I still don't understand what hap—"

"Everyone okay in here?" A shadow dimmed the light from the doorway and a police officer loomed in the doorway. Michelle had seen him around town before—Shepard, she thought his name was. He looked her up and down the way Rob had.

"Is he gone?" Rob asked.

"He's on his way to the station in a patrol car. I'm going to need statements from anyone who witnessed what happened."

Mr. Merrick appeared behind the officer. "I've got everyone corralled in the break room. You can question them whenever you're ready." He squinted, peering into the darkroom. "Rob, Michelle, you guys need to go on down to the break room."

Two more policemen arrived and escorted everyone out of the darkroom, presumably so they could locate the mysterious bullet.

Michelle started to follow Rob through the labyrinth of desks and machines to the break room, but she stopped short when she felt something wet and sticky on the sleeve covering her left arm. She brushed at the dark eggplant-colored fabric, and her hand came away red.

At her gasp, Rob turned to stare at her. "You're bleeding? Did you get hit?"

She took a deep breath. "I didn't think I did, but . . . I'm bleeding." She started to push her sleeve up and noticed it was torn. The fabric around the tear was scorched. She felt no pain, but it did seem like a lot of blood.

"We need to get you to the emergency room."

"I'm fine. It—it doesn't hurt." She rolled up her sleeve as far as it would go, but the wound was apparently higher up on her arm. "Just let me go in the restroom and check it out."

Officer Shepard must have overheard them, because he came over to her concern burning in his eyes. "You're hurt? Do we need to call an ambulance?"

"No, of course not. I'm fine. I must have just gotten grazed when the bullet came through the door." She didn't tell him she'd been standing with her ear pressed to the door when the bullet was fired.

An inch in any direction and she could have been seriously wounded. Or killed. The realization took her breath away.

She started for the break room again, but the policeman stopped her. "I think we'd all feel better if you went to the ER and had that checked out."

"Don't worry, the *Beacon*'s insurance will pay for it," Rob offered.

"I'm not worried about that." She was still covered under her parents' policy. Which reminded her. She needed to call Mom right away and let them know before they heard it from someone else—minus the detail that she was all right.

"I really think I'm fine," she protested.

Rob put a hand at the small of her back. "Please, Mish. Just go have it checked out. I'll drive you."

She dropped her head, feeling uncomfortable at being the center of attention. "I don't think it's really necessar—"

"Please?" He looked toward Mr. Merrick's office. "I know what Dad will say. He'll insist. Just let them check you out. It won't take long."

She blew out a sigh. "Okay . . . If it'll make you feel better. But don't we have to give the police our statements?"

"They know where to find us. We can talk to them after we make sure you're okay."

She shrugged, resigned. And not at all disappointed that Rob had volunteered to drive her to the hospital.

By the time they arrived at the ER parking lot, her arm was beginning to ache—as if someone had punched her with a sharp elbow. Rob was treating her like a complete invalid, and she decided to take full advantage of it.

He held her elbow then put an arm around her and ushered her through the door. Inside, he took charge. "We need to see a doctor."

The nurse behind the desk looked Michelle up and down. "What's the nature of your injury? Or illness?"

Rob stepped in front and leaned over the desk, lowering his voice. "This is Michelle Penn. A bullet grazed her arm, and we need to have it looked at."

"A bullet? Are you serious?"

Rob shot Michelle a look that made her stifle a grin. She knew exactly what he was thinking: *Would I joke about something like that?*

She liked sharing that knowing look with him, but it probably wasn't a good idea to be grinning like a Cheshire cat if she wanted them to take her seriously. She set her lips in a hard line and thrust her bloodied sleeve where the nurse could see it.

"Oh." The woman's eyebrows lifted. "Looks like you got zinged, all right. You're not feeling faint, are you?"

Michelle shook her head. "It just aches."

"Okay. Let me get some information from you, and then you can take a seat right over there"—she indicated the waiting room—"until we call you."

She answered the questions, but when they discovered she was still on her parents' insurance, the nurse insisted on calling Mom and Dad.

"All right, but let me talk to them. My mom will have a stroke if she gets a call from the ER."

The nurse handed the phone to Michelle, and she dialed, suddenly feeling a little queasy. When her mother answered, she lost it. Her hands trembled and she bit back a sob.

"Michelle? What's wrong?"

She tried twice to speak but knew she would fall completely apart if she said anything. Finally she thrust the phone into Rob's hand.

"Mrs. Penn? It's Rob Merrick from the *Beacon*. Michelle is fine, but we had a little excitement at the news office today, and I'm here in the emergency room with your daughter."

She heard her mother's shriek on the other end of the line. But Rob handled it with aplomb, speaking in a soothing tone, explaining what had happened, and asking her to meet them in the ER as soon as possible to fill out the insurance forms.

Another nurse came to usher Michelle back to an exam room just as Rob was hanging up.

"I'll be right here," he told her.

She started to follow the nurse then glanced over her shoulder, wishing Rob would come back with her. But she blushed when she realized they'd probably have to remove her blouse—or at least cut off her sleeve—to get to her wound.

Rob winked. "Break a leg, babe."

That made her smile even as the room spun and her legs turned to jelly beneath her.

Chapter Twenty-Five

Rob paced the waiting room, checking the industrial-issue clock over the reception desk yet again. Was the stupid thing even working? It seemed like it hadn't moved since the last time he'd looked at it.

Mrs. Penn had arrived about ten minutes after the nurse took Michelle back, and her father came rushing in a few minutes later—straight from the field, judging by his dirt-caked jeans and sweat-streaked forehead. Daniel Penn had told Rob to go on back to the office, but there was no way he could do that.

But now they'd been in the exam room with Michelle for at least a half hour, and no one had bothered to come out and tell him what was going on. He was starting to wonder whether Michelle's injuries were worse than they'd suspected. When they'd left the office, the police still hadn't located the bullet. Was it possible the slug was in Michelle's arm? But surely she couldn't have been so calm and pain-free if that were the case. Still, her arm had bled quite a bit.

Finally the door to the ER opened and Michelle emerged, flanked by her parents. Her left sleeve had been cut away and a thick bandage covered her upper arm, which was in a flimsy sling. Her face was pale, but she broke into a smile when she saw him.

Rob jumped up and met them halfway. He shrugged out of his jacket and held it out. Her father took it and wrapped it around Michelle's shoulders, taking care with her wounded arm.

Mrs. Penn beamed at him. "How thoughtful of you." He saw where Michelle got her straight, white teeth and high cheekbones.

"You didn't need to stay," Mr. Penn told him.

"I know, but . . . I was worried." He stole a glance at Michelle, but she avoided his eyes.

"Well, that's very nice of you." Mrs. Penn patted his arm, and a feeling of sadness and yearning shrouded him, as tangible as his coat draped over Michelle's shoulders.

Daniel Penn shook Rob's hand. "Will you please let your father know that we're taking Michelle home with us for a few days?"

"Of course. I'm sure—"

"No, Daddy. I'm fine." She looked at Rob and then at her father. "You and Mom can just take me back to my apartment. I'm perfectly fine."

"Are you sure, Michelle?" Her mother brushed a wayward curl off her face. "You look awfully shaky to me."

"I'm fine, Mom. I'd really rather go back to my place." She gave Rob a stern look. "Tell your dad I'll be back to work in the morning."

"I can take her home," Rob said, regretting the offer the instant the words were out.

The looks on her parents' faces confirmed his regret.

But Michelle smiled. "Thanks, Rob. That'd be great. I'm sure the police are still going to want to talk to us."

Mrs. Penn started to protest, but her husband put an arm around her and took her aside. Rob heard snatches of their hushed conversation to the effect that Michelle was a big girl now and if she said she was feeling fine, then they needed to trust her.

When they came back to speak to Michelle, Mrs. Penn's expression was stiff, but she hugged her daughter, being careful of the bandaged arm. "You call us if you need anything, you hear me?"

"I will, Mom, I promise. And honest, I feel just fine. It was just a little excitement, that's all."

Michelle's father gave Rob a hard look. "You're sure that guy's locked up?"

"Yes, sir. I saw them haul him off." *For the second time.* But of course he didn't say that.

"Okay. I'm going to hold you to that."

"Yes, sir."

Her dad hugged Michelle, being careful of her arm in the sling. "Take it easy, kiddo." Then he turned back to Rob. "Thanks, Robert. We appreciate you looking after her."

"No problem, sir." He went to open his car door for Michelle, aware that her parents were watching his every move. He'd prove to them that their daughter was in good hands with him. Even if he was breaking his own father's rules.

* * * * *

"You're sure you feel well enough to go back to the office? I'm sure you could give your statement later—or the police could even go to your place."

"I'm fine, Rob." She wished everybody would quit acting like she'd almost died. And she sure didn't want the police at her apartment. Her landlord would croak! "Let's go back to the office. I'd just as soon get it over with."

"Okay . . . if you're sure."

Michelle was the center of attention when she got back. Everyone gathered around, asking questions and recounting their own version of what had happened. It was the first time she'd heard the details of how the whole ruckus began, and it made her realize all over again how very lucky she'd been not to be more seriously injured. *No.* She corrected the thought. God had been watching over her, protecting her. "Thank You, Lord," she whispered.

Her thoughts—and her heart—went to Becky. "Oh, God, please be with Becky and Eden. They must be so scared and confused." She still didn't know exactly why Mack Preston had brought a gun into the *Beacon* office.

The police officers had already left the building, and Mr. Merrick broke up the powwow and sent everyone home for the day. "If you feel up to it," he told Michelle, "I'll call the police station and have them send over an officer to take official statements from you and Rob—and debrief you."

"Sure. I really am fine. The doctor said it was just a superficial wound." Even saying the words, it seemed unbelievable that she'd come *that* close to taking a bullet.

"Let's go back to the break room," Rob said.

"Yes," Mr. Merrick agreed. "Go get something to drink and rest until the police get here." He dug around in his pants pocket and handed Rob a few nickels. "Get her a pop, would you?"

"Sure." Rob put a hand at the small of her back and steered her to the break room.

He pulled out a chair for her and she sat down, grateful for the support. She was feeling a little light-headed in spite of assuring everyone how great she felt.

Rob fed the machine the nickels and brought her a cold Coke. "You look a little peaked."

"I think it's starting to catch up with me."

"You've been through a lot."

He reached across the table and put a hand over hers. "Just so you know, you scared me to death."

"Sorry." She tried to look contrite.

"Good grief, it's not your fault."

"I know." She took a sip from the can and set it down on the table. Her hand was cool from the can, and she placed her palm on her forehead. She was glad Rob was here. Something about his presence calmed her and made things seem normal.

Mr. Merrick popped into the room. "Officer Barclay is here. Rob, why don't you come talk to him first?"

Rob turned to her. "You sure you're okay?"

She nodded. "Go on . . . Break a leg."

His grin lifted her spirits more than anything else could have.

Left alone in the room, the events of the afternoon swirled in her head. Suddenly everything started to sink in. What had happened was serious. Someone could have been killed. She had come within inches of death. The details were sketchy, but from what some of the *Beacon* employees had said earlier, it sounded as if Becky Preston's husband blamed the newspaper for breaking up his marriage. He'd gone off the deep end and brought a gun to the office. But why had he shot into the darkroom? Did he know she was in there? Had he purposely targeted her?

The pop machine's motor kicked on, and Michelle's heart jumped into her throat. She assumed Mack Preston was in custody. Surely after what had happened, they wouldn't let him walk.

Maybe she should have gone home with Mom and Dad. Right now, the thought of going back to her empty apartment after the police dismissed her made her tremble. Was this how Becky had felt every night since Mack got out of jail?

Becky. She needed to talk to her. Would Becky and Eden have stayed at the house after what happened with Mack? Probably. They didn't have anywhere else to go, as far as she knew. She pushed back her chair and started for the door. Maybe the cops would give her more information about Becky's situation. But either way, she was determined to see her friend tonight and make sure she and Eden were okay.

She started down the hall toward Mr. Merrick's office, where they'd been conducting the interviews. She could see Rob standing near the door with one hand on the handle. Mr. Merrick and the cop were laughing about something, and Rob was smiling. Things must not be too serious.

She moved closer, wishing they'd hurry up. She felt an urgency about going to see Becky now. She cleared her throat loudly enough that all three of them turned to look at her.

"I'm sorry," she said, "but if it's going to be much longer, I wonder if I could wait until tomorrow to give my statement?"

"I'm finished," Rob said, looking at her with a question in his eyes. He came out into the hallway and lowered his voice. "Are you still doing okay? Do you want me to take you home?"

"I need to go see Becky. If she knows what happened, she must be terrified."

He nodded, sobering. "Why don't you go ahead and give your statement, and then we'll go together."

"Would you mind?"

"No. I'll go with you. The interview won't take long."

He shook the officer's hand and excused himself, telling Michelle, "I'm going to go work on a story until you're done."

"Okay. Thanks." She forced a smile and walked into Mr. Merrick's office.

Merrick stayed at his desk and observed while Officer Barclay asked her a series of questions about what she'd seen and heard while she was in the darkroom. She answered them as honestly as she could, alarmed at how fuzzy the whole incident was in her mind already.

"And you've never met Mack Preston."

"I've never met him, but—I was there when he was arrested at the end of August. I know his wife and daughter, though."

"Oh?" The cop's eyebrows went up.

"Mack went to jail after we did that story."

"They still get newspapers in jail, you know."

Michelle looked to Mr. Merrick, willing him to say something since she didn't have a clue how to respond.

Apparently her expression conveyed her angst, because her boss gave her a look that said, "Let me take it from here." He leaned forward. "Are you implying that the story we ran is what prompted Preston's . . . *visit* to the *Beacon* this afternoon?"

The officer shifted in his chair. "Well, the guy's not saying much since we took him in, but you said yourself, Mr. Merrick—and your employees concurred—that judging by his rant, he had a grudge against the newspaper. In particular, he wanted the photos that were taken the day of his arrest."

So that's why he'd shot through the darkroom. Had Becky told him about the photos? Michelle racked her brain to remember whether they'd credited the photo that ran with the story. They usually did put photo credits in the cutline, but she hadn't been aware of the paper's policies back then. She did remember telling her parents that she *hadn't* taken the photo, so maybe that meant there wasn't a credit line.

"Do—do you think Mack Preston thought Rob was in the dark-room?" She aimed the question at the policeman. If Mack somehow knew Rob had taken the picture, then his mission at the *Beacon* today might have been personal. Rob could have been killed!

She was certain she'd heard Rob's voice in the midst of the chaos, but she couldn't remember whether it was before or after the shot was fired. She hated that everything was such a blur. Of all the times she needed her memory to be sharp . . .

Officer Barclay took off his cap and scratched his head. "We're not sure about his motives, Miss Penn. But he's in custody now, and we don't believe anyone here at the *Beacon* is in danger. Until we've had time to review the evidence and the testimonies of witnesses, we really can't say more."

She nodded. "May I go home now?"

Mr. Merrick asked the officer's permission with a lift of his brows.

"Yes. We may have further questions as our investigation pro-gresses, but that's all for now. Thank you for your cooperation."

"Thank you." She pushed back her chair and rose to leave.

"Oh. One more thing, Miss Penn. You said that you're acquainted with Mack Preston's wife and daughter?"

"Yes." Something told her she shouldn't elaborate unless they forced her to.

"I strongly advise that you have no contact with Mrs. Preston."

"No contact? But why?"

"You may be called upon to testify if this case goes to trial."

CHAPTER TWENTY-SIX

The police officer's words left her speechless. First Rob and now Becky? This was America, last time she'd checked. And now she'd been forbidden to be friends with two people she cared deeply for. Three. She swallowed back tears at the thought of not being able to see Eden.

Officer Barclay's features softened. "There's no trial date at this point. We can't coerce you to have contact, or not, with any persons at this point, but you should be aware of the implications should you be called as a witness."

"I . . . understand. May I go now?"

"*I'm* finished." Officer Barclay looked for Mr. Merrick to concur.

"Yes, you may go. Thank you, Miss Penn."

Michelle left Mr. Merrick's office in a stupor and headed straight for Rob's cubicle.

He swiveled his desk chair to face her as soon as she stepped into his doorway. "Hey, how'd it go?" He studied her for a moment. "You don't look so hot."

"Did they say you couldn't talk to Becky or Eden?"

"What? No. Is that what they told you?"

She nodded, close to tears.

"But why? Preston is in custody." He moved a stack of old news releases off the extra chair in his cubicle and patted the seat. "Sit down. You look like you're going to faint."

She waved him off. "I'm fine." But she took the chair anyway.

"There's no way they're going to let Preston out on bail."

"It's not that. They said I might have to testify if it goes to trial." She eyed him. "Did you tell them Becky and I are friends?"

He shook his head. "I didn't say a word. *You* didn't tell them?"

"I guess I mentioned that we were acquainted." She told him about Officer Barclay's comment about Preston getting a newspaper in jail. "It sounds like Mack had a grudge against the paper. Did you hear him say that when he—went on his rampage?"

"He wanted the photos I took that day at his house."

"Why'd he wait till now?"

"Well, he hasn't been out of jail that long. I don't know . . . maybe Becky threatened to leave him. Did she say anything to you about it?"

"No. She rarely talks about Mack. She knows I've never thought she should stay with him."

"Hopefully she sees the wisdom of your opinion now."

"I have to go see her, Rob. This is going to kill her." She told him what the policeman had said about him not being able to coerce her.

"He may not be able to, but I bet my dad will try."

"What do you mean?"

"He's not going to like you talking to Becky, Mish. The woman's husband could have killed every person in this office today. This whole thing could have been tragic. God was looking after you today."

She hung her head. "I know." And she was grateful. But she *wasn't* killed today. And she wasn't going to let this dictate who her friends were. At least not where Becky was concerned. "This is not Becky's fault,

Rob. I'm sorry, but I don't care what anyone says. Mack has already stolen so much from her. I'm not going to let him steal her friends too. I'm going to find out if she's okay. See what kind of help she needs."

"I understand."

"It's bad enough your dad won't let us—" She stopped herself. One really had nothing to do with the other. And she didn't want to cause a rift between father and son. Besides, as far as she knew, Rob hadn't made an effort to challenge his father's stupid policy. If he didn't care enough to try to change things, then maybe she was fooling herself to think that he really cared about her.

"I'll go with you."

She looked up, surprised. "You don't have to. I don't want you to get into trouble."

"You know, I'm a big boy. I know you think I'm just my father's puppet, but that's not true. And you're right. Becky's suffered enough because of that turkey. She needs a friend now, more than she probably ever has."

"You don't have to go," she said again.

"I know I don't have to. But I want to. That little squirt Eden kind of wrapped me around her finger." He gave her a crooked grin that made her stomach do funny things. "Let's go."

"Okay. Let me get my stuff." She went to her cubicle and gathered her purse and the notes for a couple of stories she was working on.

"I'll drive," Rob said as he led the way through the office to the back door.

She climbed into the passenger seat of his Pinto, and he started the engine. They rode in silence for a few minutes. And the closer they got to Becky's house, the tighter the knot in her belly grew.

She looked over at Rob, who looked a little tense himself.

"I don't even know what to say to Becky," she told him.

He sighed. "I know. I'm sitting here trying to think how I'd want to be treated if I was in her shoes, and I can't even answer that question."

"I'd probably want to crawl into a hole and never come out."

"Yeah," he agreed. "And I know it's hard to face people at first, but once you get that over with, it's not so bad. Then you're glad to be around people . . . glad to have someone to talk to."

"You sound like you're talking about something personal."

He became intent on the road.

"I'm sorry," she said. "I didn't mean to pry."

He acted as if he hadn't heard her, but when they turned onto Donner Avenue, he pulled the Pinto over to the curb several blocks from the Prestons' home. He put the car in Park, turned off the engine, and angled himself in the seat beside her. "I was thinking about—when my mom died." His Adam's apple worked in his throat.

"How old were you . . . when she died?"

"I was nine. Nine and a half. It happened in the summer."

Michelle didn't dare breathe. "That must have been so hard. How—how did it happen?" She'd wondered so often about Rob's mother and why he never talked about her. Surely if he was almost ten when his mom died, he had plenty of memories of her. But as long as she could remember, Mrs. Merrick's death had always been talked about in hushed tones. And yet Michelle had never heard what could even be called rumors.

"She drowned."

Her hand went involuntarily to her mouth. "How awful. I'm so sorry, Rob."

He nodded and stared through the windshield, but it was obvious he wasn't seeing what Michelle saw beyond the glass.

He was silent for so long she grew uncomfortable. But he was the one who'd first opened the subject. She risked another question. "Do you mind me asking . . . how it happened?"

He closed his eyes, obviously in pain. Without looking at her, he grasped for her hand and when he found it, he squeezed so tightly it hurt.

He started to say something, but his eyes welled with tears and he looked away. "I'm sorry, Mish. I can't. I can't talk about it. Not yet."

Her heart swelled, feeling as if Rob's pain were her own. Almost fifteen years, and the anguish was as fresh for him as if someone had just given him the news of his mother's death. Was it her death that hurt so much, or did Rob's pain have more to do with his relationship with his mother?

After a minute, he glanced up, looked directly at her. But that far-away look still resided in his eyes, and she wasn't sure he was really seeing her.

"I'm sorry I asked, Rob. I won't ask again. Not until you're ready."

"I'm sorry," he said again. "I . . . just can't."

She raised their clasped hands to her lips and kissed the top of his hand then unwound their fingers and pressed the palm of his hand to her face. "It's okay. I understand."

But she didn't. Not really. How could someone carry such agonizing pain for so long? And how did he function the way he did, never giving a hint till now that there was so much pain, so much regret in his life? It made her wonder who else she looked at day after day, not recognizing the hurt they carried. *Oh, God, please open my eyes. Help me to see people with Your eyes. Help me to comfort Rob.*

Chapter Twenty-Seven

Rob let go of Michelle's hand. He reached for the keys, revving the Pinto to life. He ran a hand over his face, wondering how big a fool he'd made of himself. He hadn't meant to unload on her like that. Worse, he hadn't exactly "unloaded." No doubt he'd only left her with more questions than she'd begun with. He hated doing that to her. It wasn't fair. He would have hated it had the tables been turned and she'd been the one keeping everything inside. He would have been thinking the worst and dying to know the secrets she was hiding.

Well, his secrets were bad enough. But it would be worse if he tried to tell her and ended up blubbering like a baby, the way he had the few times in his life when he'd tried to talk about Mom.

The very thought of her felt like a stab wound. *Stop it, Merrick. Just stop thinking and start driving. This isn't about you. It's about Becky Preston. Talk about hurting . . .* It helped to get his mind on the reason they were in the car, the reason he'd found another excuse to be with Michelle. But even that involved a secret.

He hadn't told Michelle—or his dad—that he was looking for another job. He'd tried to convince himself that he would be looking even if it weren't for Michelle but he wasn't sure that was true. Things had been fine at the *Beacon*, working for his dad, before Michelle Penn came along.

He knew if he got the job in Wichita and was finally free to pursue her the way he wanted to, he'd have to share things about his life that were hard to talk about. But he didn't want Michelle to feel pressured by him. He didn't want her to think she was obligated to go steady with him if he did manage to land another job. It was just something he needed to do. For himself. And it made no sense to tell his father and get him all worked up over something that might not happen. It would probably be at least a week before he could even expect a reply. Still, as much as he wanted to land the job on his own merit, he'd hoped the Merrick name might carry some weight.

For the first time, it struck him that being a Merrick might be detrimental. It was beginning to appear that his father had exaggerated his importance in the newspaper world. They were only a small-town weekly, but Robert Merrick Sr. had served on several industry boards and the *Beacon* had won many awards—both state and national—over the years. But maybe that meant nothing—for Robert Merrick III anyway.

"You okay?" Michelle's voice broke through his pathetic, self-absorbed thoughts.

"I'm fine. And I promise we'll talk about—everything—some day soon. The question is, are *you* okay? Does your arm hurt? Why'd you take off the sling?"

She wiggled her arm and tried to hide a wince. "It hurts a little. It's probably going to be stiff. But I think I'll live." She grinned.

"That's not funny, Michelle. You're lucky to be 'living.' I don't think you realize how serious this whole thing was. If anybody should have taken that bullet, it's me."

"That's ridiculous, Rob. Mack is the only one to blame here. He's got major issues, and he needs help. That has nothing to do with us anymore, except when it comes to Becky."

"Okay." He wouldn't argue with her. "Speaking of Becky, let's go see how she's doing." He put the car in gear and drove on up Donner Avenue.

* * * * *

It was beginning to get dark, and the lights were on in the Preston house. Michelle led the way up the porch steps, trying to figure out why the place looked different. Then it struck her. Someone had raked the yard and swept all the leaves off the sidewalk in front of the house. The porch, too, looked freshly swept. Becky had mentioned that she was having trouble keeping up with the yard with Mack in jail, since that had always been his department. Had Mack raked leaves before he came and shot up the *Beacon* office?

"Do you think I should go back and wait in the car?" Rob tucked his hands into the front pockets of his bell-bottoms. "I think I make her a little nervous."

"No. Stay. I think you won her over the night we babysat." She winked. "Especially after she found out it was your idea."

"You told her that?" He gave her a look. "Okay. But . . . you do the talking."

"Gee, thanks." But she stepped in front of him and knocked on the door.

They could hear someone moving around inside. The porch light came on and the door opened a crack. Becky peeked out at them.

"Becky? It's me . . . Michelle. Rob's here too. Rob Merrick. Can we come in?"

"What do you want?"

Rob nudged her then aimed his words at Becky. "We're not trying to get a story."

Michelle hadn't considered that Becky might suspect that. "Oh! Becky, no . . . We're here as friends. This has nothing to do with the paper. We—we're just worried about you. Is everything okay?"

The door opened another crack, and Michelle took a tiny step backward, not wanting Becky to feel threatened. Even in the dim light from the porch lamp, she could see that Becky's eyes were swollen and red. Michelle looked closely, trying to see whether her face bore bruises, but it looked like the damage was only from weeping.

"Is there anything we can do to help? Can we just come in and talk?"

The door swung fully open and Becky stood aside while they came in, looking around the living room.

"Is Eden in bed?"

"Yes. I put her down early. She's pretty confused about everything that's happening."

Michelle reached for Becky, wrapping her in a hug and feeling the swell of Becky's pregnant belly between them. "I'm so sorry for everything you've had to go through."

"What was he thinking?" Becky sobbed. "He'll never get out now. At least not before Eden's all grown up. And this baby . . . "

Michelle just held her, not having a clue what to say. She knew Rob was probably thinking the same thing she was: it was for the best that Mack Preston had been locked away. It might have been Becky or Eden he hurt. Next time it likely would have been, given the anger Mack must have inside him to do what he'd done at the *Beacon* today.

Rob cleared his throat. "How about if I put on some water for tea?"

She could have kissed him.

"Okay," Becky said, shrinking from Michelle's embrace and slumping onto the sofa.

"I'll go help Rob." Michelle patted her knee. "I'll be right back with some tea, okay?"

Becky looked up at her and gave a pathetic try at a smile. "Thank you. For coming. I feel—so alone."

"You're not alone, Becky." But she knew even as she spoke the words that Becky *was* alone. Still, she tried to be positive. "We're here for now. We'll do everything we can to help. You okay if I go help Rob?"

She nodded. "Yes. Go. I'm fine."

Rob was opening cupboard doors one after another. "You don't know where she keeps the mugs, do you?"

"No, but I'll help you look." Their search turned up two mugs and a tin cup with a handle that would serve the purpose.

"Do you know if she takes sugar?"

"Yes, I think she does. Maybe two spoonfuls?" She remembered Becky stirring sugar into her cup when they'd had tea that day.

When the tea was brewed, Rob carried two mugs, and Michelle carried her own into the living room. Becky sat on the sofa with a sleeping Eden in her arms. Michelle hadn't heard her go upstairs and get the little girl.

"Man," Rob said. "She's grown just since I saw her the other night."

"Yeah, they do that," Becky said drily before taking a sip of the steaming tea.

Michelle decided to face the elephant in the room head-on. "Do you know why Mack brought a gun to the *Beacon* office?"

Becky closed her eyes and sighed. "We had a fight. Mack accused me of calling the *Beacon* with the story. He—he found out you two babysat for Eden that night, and he put two and two together and got five."

That explained a few things. "Do you think he was just trying to . . . scare us, or—?"

"I don't have a clue what he thought. He's— Jail changed him. And I don't mean in a good way. He was so full of anger. He hated everybody. Thought everybody had it in for him. I don't know how to handle him."

"Did he—hurt you again? Or Eden?" Rob asked gently. He reached over and smoothed a palm lightly over the little girl's head as she lay sleeping on Becky's lap.

Becky shook her head, and her forehead wrinkled. "No. That's what's weird. He hasn't laid a hand on me since he got out. But he's . . . paranoid. And seething with anger. You can almost feel it. And I guess . . . he finally blew today."

Becky shifted Eden on her lap, and Rob held out his arms. "Can I hold her?"

Becky handed off the sleeping child to him. "The police said nobody got hurt. They weren't just telling me that, were they?"

Rob and Michelle exchanged a look.

"Did he hurt somebody? Did he kill somebody? You have to tell me."

"Oh, no!" she and Rob said together.

"Nothing like that," Michelle said. "Didn't the police tell you?"

"Just that he'd fired the gun. And that's why they had to take him in."

"Yes. He fired a gun. Through the darkroom door," Rob said. "Michelle . . . was in there at the time."

Becky's eyes grew wide.

"I'm fine," Michelle said quickly, wishing Rob hadn't said anything yet understanding that Becky would need to know at some point. "The bullet just grazed my arm."

Becky put her head in her hands and rocked back and forth on the sofa. "I'm so sorry. It's my fault."

"What? Why?" Michelle went to sit beside Becky on the sofa.

"Those pictures . . . " Becky looked at Rob. "He wanted those pictures you took. He had asked about them, and I had told him Michelle was going to get them back from you, that he didn't have to worry about them. But when he asked about them today, I didn't have them yet. I just never had the guts to ask again."

"That was my fault," Michelle said. "I told you I'd ask Rob about them, and I never did. Don't blame yourself for that."

"I should have just told him I destroyed them."

"No, Becky. That wouldn't have been true." She didn't want to sound like the moral police, but she also didn't want Becky to think that lying about the photos would have been the right thing to do. Nor did she want Becky blaming herself, thinking she could have prevented what Mack did. "I should have asked Rob for the pictures like I told you I would."

"The photos are in my files at the office," he said. "I'll destroy them first thing on Monday morning. I've never given them to anyone. There was only that one we used in the paper. But I would never use them for anything . . . bad."

Michelle jumped in. "But I realize you didn't know Rob back then, Becky. And I can understand why you couldn't trust him. Why you wanted them back."

"Well, it wasn't worth someone getting hurt." Becky's voice cracked. "You could have been killed!"

"But I didn't get killed, and . . . it'll all work out." She knew it was a lame thing to say. It might *not* work out at all for Becky and Eden.

Mack would likely be in prison for a long time. And what would they do then? But she'd said it, and trying to take it back would only make matters worse.

Rob had distanced himself from the conversation and carried Eden to a dilapidated chair in the corner of the room. He sat there now, watching her sleep in his arms. Seeing him with the baby that way—the tenderness in his gaze as he looked down on the little girl—Michelle ached with a yearning she couldn't begin to express.

CHAPTER TWENTY-EIGHT

Mr. Merrick studied Michelle from across his desk. "How well do you know Becky Preston?"

She shrugged. "We've had lunch together a couple of times. I—I babysat for her little girl." Had Rob said something about them going over to Becky's on Friday night? She wondered if he'd told his father that he helped her babysit Eden. Of course that was before the whole mess with Mack Preston. Still . . .

She'd come in to work early this morning to make up the time they'd lost because of the shooting. She'd about jumped out of her skin when Mr. Merrick tapped on the wall of her cubicle, asking if she could please come to his office for a few minutes.

Now her boss looked at her hard. "You need to keep your distance from that woman. This thing could get messy, and the *Beacon* needs to stay unbiased. There can't be any conflict of interest here. Do you understand?"

She hesitated. "I understand, Mr. Merrick, but here's my problem. I'm about the only friend Becky Preston has in this town. And if she ever needed a friend, it's now. Would it—would it be best if I quit my job? Because I'm not sure I can just walk away from my friendship with Becky. She's going to need a babysitter so she can be at Mack's—at her *husband's*—hearings, and—" She stopped, shocked at what had just come out of her mouth.

There was no way she could afford to lose her job. She didn't know of another job in Bristol that would pay enough to keep her apartment, but she meant what she'd said about quitting if he was going to forbid her from seeing Becky. She doubted he could even do that, legally. But he had to know she wasn't going to take him to court over it if he did let her go.

Mr. Merrick looked at her sternly over the top of his reading glasses. "You're talking about something that isn't optional, Michelle."

She backtracked through their conversation in her mind, not wanting to make his edict more serious than it was—but needing to understand what he meant. "Are you saying that my . . . having a friendship with Becky Preston isn't an option? If I want to keep my job, I mean?"

"Well, now, don't put words in my mouth. I'm not making a threat, Miss Penn—"

"Oh, no. I—I wasn't saying you were." So she was back to being *Miss Penn* now?

He shifted in his desk chair. "I'm just letting you know that in the interest of what is best for the *Beacon* as we try to wade through the legal issues we're facing with the attack . . . Well, it would just complicate things if an employee was . . . *involved* with one of the opposing parties."

"But Becky Preston had nothing to do with her husband's actions. I can assure you, she feels awful about what he did."

"Be that as it may, you can understand why we can't appear to have a *friendship*, per se, with Mack Preston's family."

"Well, no. I'm not sure I do understand . . . " She prayed for the right words. "And I definitely don't see why *my* friendship with Becky would be construed as the *Beacon*'s friendship. I'm merely an employee. Why should my friendships have anything to do with your company? As long as it isn't harming the company, of course."

A muscle in his square jaw twitched. "And that's exactly my point. It *is* harming the company. Or maybe you don't view a man coming in, shooting up the office, and trying to kill you as harmful." Though his words were pure sarcasm, his voice held no hint of it.

"I didn't realize Mack was trying to kill *me*." She didn't believe Mack had targeted her, and she didn't think for a minute that Mr. Merrick thought that either. It was an out-of-control temper that had prompted Preston's actions. But her boss's sarcasm was contagious. "In fact," she said, "I think an argument could be made that Mack Preston came in here because of the photo that your son took and published."

She instantly regretted dragging Rob into the conversation. But if what Becky said was true, Mack had brought the gun to the *Beacon* because of Rob's decision to publish the photo taken that day Mack first went to jail for beating Becky.

Mr. Merrick rose and went to the door, opening it as he spoke. "I believe this conversation is over, Miss Penn. I'll not bring the subject up again, but I trust you will do what is in the best interest of both of us as long as you are in my employ."

Stunned, she stood and walked through the door he held open for her. She wanted to ask him what on earth he meant by that last remark, but she knew exactly what he meant. It was his way of threatening her without ever having to admit that he'd threatened her.

Well, two could play that game. If he was determined to believe that it was in the best interest of both of them for her to stay away from Becky, then she was determined to believe just the opposite. And if he ever dared to call her on it, she would feed him a line of his own psychological gibberish and tell him that yes, indeed, she had done only what was in the best interest of both of them.

She only hoped Rob didn't ask why his father had called her into his office. She would not tell him, because she had no intention of obeying Mr. Merrick's demands. And she didn't want to drag Rob into her rebellion.

* * * * *

Words strung themselves onto the page as Rob's Selectric tapped out the rhythm that seemed to come so hard these days. He'd finally hit his stride on the story he was working on. Michelle was waiting on him, needing his story to lay out the front page, and things were more tense than usual in the newsroom. But he had a full page and a half and was on a roll with the final paragraph when the phone on his desk jangled.

He bit back some choice words and pounded his desk, but quickly composed himself before picking up the receiver. "Rob Merrick III. How may I help you?"

"Robert, yes . . . This is Jim Clemson at the *Wichita Eagle*."

"Hello, Mr. Clemson." He lowered his voice, wondering if Clemson had identified himself to Myrtle when he called. He'd known it was risky to give the *Beacon*'s number as a contact, but they couldn't very well reach him at home on business hours, so he'd taken the risk. It wasn't inconceivable that the *Eagle* would be contacting him about a legitimate business matter, but knowing Myrtle's radar, she'd sniff out his betrayal quicker than a bloodhound on a wounded hare.

"I apologize for my timing. I know how crazy things are for a weekly on Wednesday morning, but we've been looking over your résumé, and we'd like you to come in for a second interview sometime next week. Is there a day early in the week that would work? Or, if not, we could wait until next Thursday, I suppose."

Rob bit his lip. Of all the lousy timing. And yet, he had a feeling it was a test. And he had no intention of failing. "Great to hear from you, sir." He ducked over his desk, hoping Clemson didn't pick up the muffling of his voice. "I'm available Monday or Tuesday any time. You just let me know when to be there." He'd have to jump through some hoops again to get away early in the week, but the fact they'd called him for an interview had his hopes high.

"Excuse me, Merrick"—Michelle appeared in his doorway— "are we gonna run that story this week or—" She clapped a hand over her mouth when she saw he was on the phone. Mouthing an apology, she slinked out of his cubicle.

"I'm sorry, Mr. Clemson. You were saying . . . ?"

They set up an appointment, and Rob thanked him and hung up. Composing himself, he ripped his story from the Selectric and walked the copy back to the typesetters.

"Okay, Penn, it's out of my hands." Coming alongside Michelle at the layout desk, he grabbed a metal pica pole and went to work arranging waxed strips of type on a page, trying to sound casual. "You can give typesetting all your grief now."

"Oh, yeah, try and shove the blame off on someone else."

"No shoving on anybody. Just the facts, ma'am."

"Fine." She ran a strip of printed galleys through the waxer and shoved them at him. "Could you please fit these on page three? They all need to run this week."

"Getting awfully bossy in your old age, aren't you?"

"Just the facts, sir," she deadpanned.

He whopped her arm with the pica pole.

She put on a good show like it hurt, but her laughter betrayed her.

Joy was checking ads on the finished pages a few feet away. She shot them the evil eye. He pretended not to notice, and he was pretty sure Michelle *didn't* notice. But he probably needed to mention to Michelle—sooner rather than later—that he and Joy had a history. An unimportant history for sure, but Michelle might not see it that way. Especially if she found out from someone else. Most especially if she found out from Joy.

That thought almost terrified him more than telling his father he might be interviewing for a position at the *Eagle*.

Joy finished and went back to her cubicle, and Rob grabbed the opportunity to ask Michelle about her meeting with his dad. "So . . . I saw you in the boss's office this morning. Everything okay?" It was always easier to ask hard questions while they worked side by side at the stand-up layout banks.

Still, it bothered him that she didn't meet his eyes when she answered. "Everything's fine. What are you, 007 or something?"

"So you're not going to tell me what that was all about?"

"Nope."

"Not even if I beat it out of you with this pica pole?" He wielded his weapon, trying for humor.

"Not even then."

"Woo . . . must be serious."

She sliced two paragraphs off a galley with her X-Acto knife before she looked up at him. "Just stop, okay? You don't need to always know my business." She said it in the same joking tone he'd used with her, but somehow he knew she wasn't kidding.

Okay, then. He didn't always need to know her business. But if he were a cat, he'd be dead from the curiosity right now.

CHAPTER TWENTY-NINE

By Friday afternoon, the *Beacon* office had cleared out except for Myrtle and Joy. Michelle opened the half-pound bag of wrapped candies she'd bought at the drugstore on her break and held it out to Myrtle as she came in.

The receptionist held up a hand, palm out. "Don't you tempt me, young lady! I appreciate the offer, but my figure can't handle such temptations the way yours can." She winked and lowered her voice. "And I'm saving some calories for all of the Christmas goodies that will start arriving in a few weeks."

Michelle laughed. "It's starting to feel like Christmas out there. I could swear I saw a snowflake."

"Don't even talk that way. I'm willing to wait for a white Christmas till December twenty-fifth."

"I know. I'm not ready for winter either. But I do love a white Christmas." She held up the sack of candy again. "Well, if you change your mind, you know where to find me."

She wasn't sure when things had changed, but sometime over the past few months she'd won Myrtle over. Unfortunately, she couldn't say the same for Joy Swanson. The advertising saleswoman had made it clear she had no use for Michelle, but Michelle had determined to be nice to Joy if it killed her. And it just might.

·

Seeing Joy in her cubicle on the other side of Rob's, she carried over the bag and held it out as she had for Myrtle. "Caramels and peppermints and gumdrops. Would you like some?"

Joy ignored her question and held up a copy of this week's paper. "Are you aware that the hardware store's ad was on the wrong page?"

"No . . . Where was it supposed to be?"

"It said right on the insert sheet that they wanted it across from the booster club ad on the sports page."

Why was Joy telling *her*? Rob always did layout for the sports page. And Joy always insisted on checking the ads before the pages went to the printer. In fact, Michelle was sure she'd seen Joy do just that on Wednesday. "Well, I didn't lay out that page, but I'll let Rob know. Do we need to run it again next week gratis?"

"It'll be too late next week. You know their specials come from the franchise. I can tell you, they are not very happy. They're probably going to want us to run next week's ad for free, and then *my* name is the one that will be mud. With Mr. Merrick *and* with Jesse at the hardware."

How in the world did the woman expect her to respond? "Well . . . Is there anything I can do to help?"

Joy's office chair squeaked as she swiveled forty-five degrees to face Michelle head-on. "As a matter of fact, there is something you can do. You can quit distracting Rob while he's trying to lay out the pages. None of this would have happened if you hadn't been over there flirting like a seventh-grade cheerleader."

"What? You mean—" The only responses she could think to come back with would likely get her fired and would most definitely require an apology later. She bit her tongue, trying to think of something to say that wouldn't accept responsibility for Joy's ridiculous accusation but that wouldn't sound patronizing either. Failing on both counts, she shrugged and, twisting the candy sack closed, walked back to her own desk.

She plopped into her chair, certain there must be smoke pouring out of her ears. The nerve! Had Miss Smarty-Pants given Rob the same lecture? Maybe that was why Rob had cut out early today. She'd heard him tell Myrtle he was leaving for the day and to take a message if anyone called.

But she couldn't very well ask him where he was going after giving him such a hard time for being a snoop about her meeting with his father. And since she'd taken lunch to Becky and Eden yesterday, now she felt like she had another secret to keep—not just from Mr. Merrick, but from Rob.

She was going home to the farm this weekend, and for once, she'd be glad to get out of town. Maybe she'd leave work early. Nobody else seemed to think they needed to be in the office today. She'd promised to babysit Eden tonight, but if she packed now, she could leave for her parents' directly from Becky's.

She typed up a short article from some notes she'd made after an interview, afraid she'd forget details by Monday. But when that was done, she tidied up her desk, and without so much as a fare-thee-well to Ms. Joy Swanson, she gathered her purse and her bag of candy and went out the back door. She would call Myrtle from home and tell her she was gone for the day and to please take a message if anyone called.

If Rob could do it, why couldn't she?

* * * * *

"We're pleased to have you on board at the *Eagle*, Mr. Merrick."

Jim Clemson pumped Rob's hand, smiling. Rob still had no idea why the lukewarm response he'd originally gotten from Clemson had changed to a job offer—especially after Rob had called and changed the interview to Friday—but he wasn't about to look a gift horse in the mouth.

"You're sure we can't talk you into starting any sooner?"

Rob shook his head. "I'm sorry, sir, but if it were the *Eagle* I was leaving, I would give you the courtesy of two weeks' notice. I can't do any less for my current employer—even if he is my father."

Clemson threw back his head and laughed. "*Especially* since he is your father. Wouldn't want to cut yourself out of an inheritance, now, would you?"

Rob didn't think it was quite as hilarious as Clemson did, but he laughed along with the man. No sense in starting out on the wrong foot with his soon-to-be boss.

Back in the parking lot, he pondered what he'd just committed to. Had his decision made an important point—that he needed to be free to make his own way in the world, including the choice of who he fell in love with? Or had he, as Jim Clemson jokingly implied, signed away his inheritance?

Before climbing into the Pinto, he shed his suit coat and loosened his tie—and rued the fact that he'd soon be wearing a striped silk noose to work every day. He'd have to do some clothes shopping. He wasn't color-blind, but he might as well be when it came to picking out shirts and ties that weren't the visual equivalent of fingernails on a chalkboard.

Maybe Michelle would come with him and help him choose his new wardrobe. Of course that meant he had to tell her *why* he needed a new wardrobe. But the thought of being able to drive to Wichita with Michelle in the passenger seat beside him—guilt-free—made it all worthwhile.

All he had to do now was figure out a way to tell his father he was leaving the *Beacon*.

He wasn't sure which prospect frightened him more.

* * * * *

Michelle put down her book and glanced at the clock in Becky's tiny dining room. Becky had said she expected to be home before nine, and it was already twenty after. Michelle had been happy for a chance to babysit Eden, but she was starting to worry. It wasn't like Becky to be late.

The weather had turned wintry. Thanksgiving was almost two weeks away, but Allen would be home for the weekend to help Dad move cattle to the north pasture and Mom wanted the house ready for Thanksgiving. It was a Penn family tradition to decorate the Christmas tree even before Thanksgiving, and Michelle had agreed to come and help.

She'd spent most of the evening peering through Becky's front windows, watching feathery flakes float down from a black sky. The streetlights illumined the swirls of white and gave the night a magical feel. The snow wasn't sticking yet, but she worried about getting home with the worn tires on her Oldsmobile.

Dad had been bugging her to replace the balding tires, but money was still too tight to make a purchase like that, especially when she only put a few miles on her car each week. Dad would buy them for her in a heartbeat if she only mentioned that she needed them, but she was determined to make it on her own. She just needed time to save up a little.

She wished Becky at least had a telephone so she could let her parents know not to worry about her. But Mom knew where she was, and she knew about Becky's phone situation, so hopefully she wouldn't worry too much.

She got up and went to check on Eden again. The nursery was heavy with the mingled scent of baby powder and sleep. Michelle turned on the tiny lamp on the dresser and went to peer into the crib.

There was something so vulnerable and precious about a sleeping baby.

She stroked Eden's cheek, almost wishing the baby would wake up so she could hold her again one more time before she left for the farm.

When she got to heaven, surely one of the first things she would ask the Lord was why He gave her such a passionate love for children, such a yearning to be a wife and mother, only to plop her into the life of a single career woman. It wasn't fair.

The sound of the front door opening made her start. She quickly wiped away tears she'd shed unaware and prayed that Becky wouldn't notice.

Chapter Thirty

"Where on earth have you been? I was worried sick." Beth Penn wrapped her terry-cloth robe tighter around her and gave Michelle a hug and pulled her into the warmth of the farmhouse kitchen.

"It's not even ten yet, Mom. Becky was a little late in getting home. You didn't want me to leave a two-year-old home alone, did you?" She cringed inwardly, remembering that Becky had done just that not so long ago.

"Of course not," her mother said. "But I wish that girl would get a telephone. What if the baby gets sick and she needs to call an ambulance?"

"It costs fifty dollars just to get the phone hooked up. Never mind how much the monthly bills are. She's barely squeaking by as it is."

Mom shrugged. "Well, I guess your grandmother managed to raise my mother without a telephone, but it would worry me to no end if you didn't have a way to get in touch with the outside world."

"If *you* didn't have a way to get in touch with me and Allen, you mean."

"You two *are* my outside world."

Michelle rolled her eyes. "Oh, joy."

Her mother gave her *that look*, but there was a twinkle in her eye.

"Speaking of Allen . . . " Michelle pointed to the door behind her. "I didn't see his car. Is he home yet?"

"He's out with Mike and Gary. Said he'd be late. And he wouldn't give your dad or me any details, but he broke up with that Piper woman. Forgive me, but I could not be happier."

"Mom! I hope you didn't tell Allen that."

Her mother looked askance at her. "I'm not completely heartless."

"Did Dad go to bed already?"

"Yes. He was up at six hauling cattle. He didn't get home for supper until almost seven. He said to tell you 'hi' and he'll see you at breakfast."

"He thinks I'm getting up for breakfast?"

Her mother sniffed. "Of course you're getting up for breakfast. But I might be able to talk Dad into staying in bed till eight."

"Oh, please. That would be lovely. Nine would be even lovelier."

"I'll see what I can do. If this snow keeps up, you might get your wish. Now let's get that tree decorated."

"You still want to do it tonight?" She shrugged out of her coat and hung it on the rack in the hallway.

"Sure. I'm wide awake now," Mom said. "Come and see the tree."

Michelle had smelled the rich pine the minute she entered the house, but walking into the living room, the scent overpowered her and brought with it a parade of happy memories. Dad had outdone himself this year. He'd always cut a tree from their pasture, and every year she and Allen begged for a bigger one. In its stand, this tree almost touched the nine-foot ceiling of the old house. She jumped up and down and clapped, feeling like a little girl again.

Mom laughed and lugged a box of indoor lights from the sofa to the floor beside the tree. "You game?"

"Sure. We'll surprise Allen when he gets home."

For the next hour and a half she and Mom talked and laughed while they got out ornaments and decorations, each one bringing back a precious memory. She'd been extremely blessed to grow up in this house with the parents she'd been given. She had taken her happy childhood for granted until she got out into the world and saw how other people lived. She made a silent promise that she would never take lightly the gifts she'd been blessed with. And she'd do better at showing her appreciation too.

They were putting the finishing touches on the tree when they heard the back door open and Allen whistling as he clomped up the back steps.

She and Mom hurriedly put away the empty boxes and straightened the skirt around the Christmas tree. Michelle flipped off the living room lights for effect as her brother came into the room.

"Hey! Looks good."

"Good? That's all you got? Come on, baby brother . . . it looks great, and you know it."

He shrugged and gave her the crooked grin that had always been able to infuriate and charm her in the same minute.

He came over and proceeded to give her what Dad had always called a Dutch rub, holding her head in a viselike lock with his elbow and rubbing her scalp with his fist till it burned.

She squealed and punched him with the point of her own elbow. They scuffled playfully until Mom intervened.

"Cut it out, you two. Allen, you're going to hurt her arm."

Allen backed off, looking genuinely alarmed. "I forgot. You okay?"

"I'm fine." She shot Mom a look. "I told you, it barely grazed me."

"In that case—" Allen slugged her.

"Ouch!"

Mom gasped. "Allen James Penn! You're going to wake up your father. Not to mention, you're going to knock over the Christmas tree before we even get one gift under it."

"Hey, wait a minute." Michelle put her hands on her hips. "What happened to all the angst about my arm?"

"You said you were fine." Allen punched her again and ducked out of her reach. "I'm heading to bed." He went to the fridge, poured a glass of milk, and raised his glass to the twinkling tree. "Nice work, ladies."

Michelle turned to her mother, beaming. Her heart was so full right now—and so happy to be part of this family. She'd never really thought about the phrase before, but was this what they meant by the "Christmas spirit"?

After her brother was out of earshot, she turned to her mom. "He seems like he's doing really well, don't you think?"

"I think it did him good to go out with his friends. He was a little down when he first got home. He put on a good front, but he almost cried when he told us about the breakup."

"He did? Oh . . . Poor Allen."

Mom shook her head. "No, it's for the best."

"Don't you want him to be happy, Mom?"

Her mother looked at her as though she'd never considered the question before. "I do want him to be happy. I want both of my children to be happy," she said pointedly. "But not just happy for the sake of happy, but happy because they are at the center of God's will."

"But how do you know?" She'd rarely had these heart-to-hearts with her mother when she lived at home, but after she went to college, something changed between them. She knew it was mostly her own attitude that had changed. But she had a newfound respect for Mom. Especially after seeing what Becky went through as a young mom.

Mom studied her. "How do you know God's will? Oh, honey, that's the question of the ages. I don't have an answer. I don't think anyone really does. Except that I think if you're asking Him to show you His will, He'll do it. Through the Bible, through good counsel . . . If you ask for wisdom, God isn't going to give you a counterfeit."

Michelle remembered a story from Sunday school about a boy asking his father for bread and Jesus saying that the father would not give his much-loved son a snake if he asked for bread. Or something like that. She was ashamed to admit she hadn't read her Bible much lately. In fact, she'd probably cracked it open twice in the whole time she'd lived in her own apartment. And she only went to church enough to keep her parents satisfied. Maybe those things needed to change. And not just for her parents' sake.

Could she be happy if the center of God's will for her life didn't include a husband and children? She didn't see how. But maybe for the first time in her life, she was willing to admit that all her dog-paddling and orchestrating were not getting her any closer to where she wanted to be. Maybe she could finally, truly trust that God would work it all out.

And there was Rob. If he wasn't part of God's plan—and she had no clue whether he was or not—well, he certainly was a pleasant diversion.

She fell asleep pondering the idea that maybe God had spoken something of His will to her this very night. It was a start.

* * * * *

Rob leafed through the phone book until he came to the *P*s. There it was. *Penn.* He picked up the phone and dialed, feeling as nervous as he had the first time he'd asked Julie Holcomb to the Snowball Dance his freshman year of high school.

"Hello?" He recognized Michelle's mother's voice.

"Mrs. Penn? This is Rob Merrick. We met at the emergency room that night of the . . . "

"Of course. Hello, Rob."

"I wondered if I might speak to Michelle."

"Of course. She's right here. We just finished breakfast."

"I hope I'm not interrupting."

"Not at all."

He heard muffled voices, and then she was on the line. "Hi, Rob."

"Did you get the tree up?"

"We did. Stayed up past midnight last night. It turned out really pretty."

Her tone was friendly, but he could tell she was preoccupied. Whether because of something going on at home or because she was curious about why he was calling, he couldn't tell. "I'm sorry to bother you at home, but I was wondering if I could talk to you about something."

"Yeah. Sure."

"Oh . . . sorry. Not over the phone. I meant in person. Tomorrow, I was hoping? Will you be home by then? Back in town, I mean?"

"What time?" Her curiosity was clear now.

"I was thinking lunch, but whenever it works for you. I'm free all day."

"Oh. Well, I'm going to church with my family and we usually go out to eat after, but—"

"He's welcome to come with us." Rob heard her mother interrupt in the background and then Michelle shushing her.

"How about if we make it tomorrow evening?" he said. "We could go for ice cream or something."

A long silence, and the background voices faded, as if she'd stretched the phone cord into another room. "Is this business or pleasure, Rob?"

He thought for a minute. "I guess you'd say a little of both."

"You really have me curious. You can't give me a clue?"

"Sorry. I'd rather wait. It's not a huge deal. Well, I guess it sort of is."

"Okay . . . " He heard people talking in the background again.

"I'd better let you go. I know you're trying to spend time with your family. How about if I just call you after supper tomorrow? Sound okay?"

"Sure. I'll wait to hear from you."

He hung up, wishing he'd just gone ahead and told her. His news was going to hit her completely by surprise—or maybe he was flattering himself to think she would even care.

And he still had to figure out how to tell Dad he was leaving the *Beacon*.

Life was about to get interesting.

Chapter Thirty-One

The choir's song ended and Michelle shifted in the pew, trying to ignore her brother, who was scribbling something on his bulletin. He slid the folded program close to her on the pew between them.

She read his cryptic quip. *Row 2, 3 from L, hat looks like Purdy—postmortem.*

She snorted, masking her laughter with a hard cough. Purdy was the orphaned raccoon they'd raised, and Mrs. Highlam's hat did indeed look like a dead raccoon.

Her shoulders shook, and she dared not look at Allen because she knew he was cracking up too and just raring to egg her on. She felt Mom glaring at them and knew without even looking that her mother was remembering the countless times she'd had to separate Allen and Michelle in the pew for just such antics. Laughter bubbled up into her throat, threatening to escape.

If she looked at Allen or Mom or Mrs. Highlam—*especially* Mrs. Highlam—she would lose it altogether. She had no choice but to pretend to pray. But she made the mistake of "praying" with her eyes open. Glancing over at Allen's lap, she saw that he was rendering a portrait of a very dead raccoon—complete with *X*s for eyes—atop a lady's hat.

She had no choice but to rise, dip her head, slip past her brother and three other parishioners, and hightail it down the aisle and out into the foyer. She ignored the usher standing at the end of the hall and ducked into the women's restroom. Thankfully it was empty. But now that she was alone, the whole episode didn't seem nearly as funny.

She checked her hair in the mirror, composed herself, and opened the door. She went to the foyer and stood in the doorway to the sanctuary, waiting for a time in the service when she wouldn't be noticed slipping in. Unfortunately, the pastor had already begun his sermon. She stood there for a few minutes, trying to get up the courage to go in.

She felt a gentle hand on her shoulder. "Michelle?"

She turned at the sound of her name spoken by a voice she felt she'd known forever—but hadn't heard for more than two years now. "Kevin."

"I thought I saw you slip out," he whispered, nodding toward the sanctuary and folding the garrison cap he held. "I probably started a dozen rumors by following you . . . ."

His hair was crew-cut, military-style, and he wore an army-green dress uniform. It was odd—and a little intimidating—to see him that way. And yet his smile hadn't changed a bit in all those months. Her instinct was to hug him, but she restrained herself. "When did you get home? Are you back—for good?"

He shook his head. "Home on leave. I go back the day after Christmas."

"How—how are you?" She could hardly believe she was talking to him. Had anyone in town known he'd be home?

"I'm doing good. Drove down from Kansas City last night."

"Oh, that's right. Your parents are there now, aren't they?"

"Yeah. They followed the grandkids. I've got three little nieces there and one on the way."

"That's great." Why had Kevin come back to Bristol? His two sisters had moved to the Kansas City area when they got married, and his parents followed suit once grandchildren came along. "Well . . . tell them all hi for me."

"I will." His expression turned serious. "I wanted to talk to you, Michelle. Could you get away for lunch, maybe?"

"Lunch?" First Rob and now Kevin. And she had no clue what either of them wanted to tell her. Though she could come closer to guessing at Kevin's intentions by the look in his eyes. A look she hadn't seen since he was . . . a mere boy. Had they really been only fifteen when they started dating? "Kevin, I—"

"Just give me a chance, Michelle. Please. Let me explain myself."

She cast about, looking for . . . what? An escape? But he was only here for a few weeks. And he was going back to a horror she could imagine only from the dim black-and-white images that flickered on the television.

What if he'd changed his mind about her? What if he wanted her back?

The thought made her a little panicky. All those months when she'd prayed so desperately for a letter from him saying that he couldn't live without her, that he'd been wrong, that he wanted her back, wanted her to wait for him . . .

To her shame, she'd even fantasized that he would be wounded and shipped home—with injuries just severe enough to keep him from going back to Nam, of course.

And now he was back. She couldn't deny that he still had an effect on her, still stirred her blood the way he always had.

But then there was Rob.

Oh, Lord, why is this happening? She stopped herself. She was jumping to conclusions. She didn't even know what Kevin wanted. For all she knew, he might be wanting to ask her for her chocolate chip cookie recipe.

It struck her that he'd said "give me a chance to explain." Maybe he merely wanted to apologize. He didn't really owe her an apology, though for a long time she'd thought he did.

She could hear Pastor Davis in the sanctuary. It sounded like he was winding up his sermon. In just a few minutes, people would spill into the foyer and she and Kevin would both be fair game for friends who hadn't seen them in a while. Who would be surprised to see them together. "I guess we could go somewhere for lunch," she said. "I'll need to let my parents know."

He grinned, suddenly looking boyish again. "That'd be great." His eyes cut to the crowded sanctuary. "I don't really feel like seeing a lot of people. Could I just meet you somewhere and then we can drive to Wichita or Hutch for lunch?"

She captured the corner of her lip with her teeth. "I have . . . plans for tonight, so I really can't go too far. Would you mind eating at Milt's?"

He arched a brow. "They're open on Sundays now?"

She laughed. "Almost everything is. But you still can't buy a beer in Bristol."

"Not that you ever have a hankering for beer, though, right?" He gave her a *just-checking* look.

"Root beer, maybe. And *that* you can buy here."

"Whew!" He made a show of wiping his brow.

She laughed, relieved they'd found a more comfortable place with each other. "Can you save us a booth at Milt's?" She winked. "If you hurry, you can beat the Presbyterians."

"I'm on it!" He gave a sharp salute and turned on his heel. "See you there," he called over his shoulder.

She watched him unfold his garrison cap and place it on his head before ducking through the door.

How different this day was turning out from what she had planned or expected.

Kind of like her entire life as an adult.

CHAPTER THIRTY-TWO

There were still a few parking spaces on Main Street when her parents pulled up to Milt's to drop off Michelle. She opened the door and looked back, to see that Mom's forehead wore deep furrows.

"Are you sure you want to do this, honey?" she asked Michelle for the second time.

"Mom, we're just going to talk. He's going back the day after Christmas."

"I just don't think it's good to go backward."

"Beth . . . " Dad reached across the bench seat and patted Mom's knee.

"It's just that she was past all that, and now he's stirred things up again."

She'd thought she was past all that too—until she saw Kevin. So handsome in his uniform and seeming like he'd grown up a lot over there. No longer a boy, but a man.

"It'll be okay." Dad said it in a way they all knew was code for Mom to drop the subject. Dad stretched his arm across the back of the seat and turned to look at Michelle. "You call us if you need us to come and pick you up, Mish, you hear?"

"It's okay, Daddy. Kevin's going to drop me off at home when we're done . . . at my apartment, I mean."

"What about your clothes? Your makeup?" Mom was grasping at straws.

"There's nothing I really need. I can get my stuff next time I'm home." She gave Allen a quick hug. "Be good up there, college boy. Don't do anything I wouldn't do."

He pushed her away. "Good grief. I'll be home in a few days for Thanksgiving. You act like I'm the one going off to war."

"Allen!" Mom and Dad both said at once.

He grinned at Michelle and slugged her hard on the bicep. "You want me to come in with you and give that loser a piece of my mind?"

"Don't you dare." She slugged him back. "See ya, bud."

She climbed out of the car, took a deep breath, and steeled herself for another encounter with Kevin Ferris.

* * * * *

Rob ordered another Coke and folded the paper from the drinking straw accordion-style. He and Dad ate meals out so often during the week that they usually barbecued at home on Sundays after church. But his father had gotten home late from a meeting with his accountant last night and hadn't had time to clean the grill, so they were letting Milt do the cooking today.

Under ordinary circumstances, it would have been the perfect time to tell his father about the position he'd accepted with the *Wichita Eagle*—if there was such a thing as a perfect time to deliver that kind of news. But he wanted to tell Michelle first. That was important to him, since she was the reason he'd sought work outside the *Beacon* in the first place. He didn't want her hearing it from someone else, and he wanted to use the announcement as an excuse to "declare his intentions" to her.

That had been Doug Jensen's idea. "It worked with Denise," his buddy said when Rob had told him about the job the other night after they shot hoops at the high school gym. "A woman wants to know what your intentions are toward her. You tell her you're pursuing her, she'll make the game interesting, while making sure you do eventually catch her. But you keep her guessing about your intentions, she may lose interest and find a guy who's truly in the hunt."

Rob didn't know why Doug suddenly fancied himself an expert on women just because he'd managed to catch one himself. But this time his friend's logic made sense. Now if only he could find the words to convey his intentions. Doug hadn't gotten that far before he had to go home to the wife who'd made him such an expert on love.

"This steak isn't half bad," Dad said over a mouthful of top sirloin.

"Neither is the brisket. Do you want some of my fries?"

His father shook his head, distracted, watching something over Rob's shoulder. "Isn't that Michelle?"

"Where?"

"Right over there . . . In that booth." He pointed past Rob.

Rob turned to see Michelle sitting with her back to them in a booth on the other side of the dining room. She sat across from a good-looking soldier. She was laughing and leaning across the table. He couldn't see Michelle's face, but there was no mistaking the intent on the soldier's face.

Rob broke out in a cold sweat. What happened to "I'm going to church with my family"? Soldier Boy had to be the guy who'd dumped her to go to Nam. If he was still in uniform, that meant he wasn't out for good. Must be home on leave for the holidays. But why had she made up some story about eating dinner with her family after church? She could have just told him she had a date.

No. Scratch that. She shouldn't be on a date! He and Michelle had a thing going. He hadn't imagined that. The only obstacle between them was his dad, and he'd taken care of that. Okay, to be fair, Michelle didn't know that yet. But couldn't the woman have a *little* patience? According to her, she'd been willing to wait for Soldier Boy for however long it took. She couldn't give Rob Merrick two weeks?

He would've worried about what he'd say if she spotted him, but the way they were giving each other googly eyes, he had nothing to worry about. She wouldn't have noticed if a UFO had landed in the middle of Milt's.

He'd told her he'd call her this evening about getting together. He wondered if she'd tell him where she'd had lunch. And who with. Not that she owed him anything. She didn't. Not really.

But he was disappointed. Deeply disappointed. She'd lied to him, and she was sitting twenty feet from him, flirting with another guy. Two huge strikes. Maybe he just wouldn't call her. Or maybe he'd call her just to test her. If she said nothing about her lunch date, that was it. Three strikes and she was out.

Somebody had put a quarter in the jukebox in the front of the restaurant, and Rob found no comfort in the fact that the machine was belting out Bobby Sherman's "Easy Come, Easy Go."

*　*　*　*　*

Though she was laughing on the outside, another knot twisted its way into Michelle's stomach. She still couldn't believe he was here, sitting across the table from her. Kevin Ferris. Why couldn't she be having a lousy time with him? Why couldn't it feel awkward and uncomfortable, being together again? Then, at least, she would be sure that it was time to move on, time to seek another direction for her life.

But that was exactly the problem. She thought she *had* moved on. Now, being with Kevin, she wasn't sure about anything. Was this God's way of guiding her? Of giving back to her what she thought she'd lost?

Still, they'd only talked about old times, laughed at funny memories, skirting around the things they really needed to talk about.

Their laughter died down, and Kevin's expression turned serious. He reached across the table and took her hand. "I'm sorry, Michelle. I don't know what was wrong with me. I just . . . I looked at the future and it scared me. I didn't want to just settle and then regret it."

"Just settle, huh? Wow. Thanks."

"Oh, man . . . " He smacked his forehead comically. "That didn't come out right. I didn't mean you. What I meant was, I didn't want to just settle down in Bristol, USA, without knowing what else was out there. If I chose—if I *choose* this place to live out my life, I want it to be because I've seen what else is out there and I know that this is what I want. Not just what I ended up with." He captured her gaze and squeezed her hand. "Am I making any sense at all?"

She nodded, her throat too tight to speak. "Kevin . . . " She worked to compose herself. "I do understand. It just . . . when it happened, it felt very personal."

"I understand that. Now. And I'm sorry. I wish I could have expressed, back then, how much it wasn't about you. And that should have told me something in itself. I was too self-centered and immature to have anything to offer you. I'm sorry."

"And I was the same," she said. "We were both too young to know what we wanted. Who we wanted."

"I'd like to think I've grown up a little bit over these past two years. Maybe by the time I get out . . . if I come home—"

"Please don't talk that way."

He shrugged. "I'm sorry. That probably sounds like I'm trying to make you take pity on me. That's not my intention at all. It's just the way we learn to think over there. I don't even give it a thought anymore. It's just . . . reality."

She gave a little shudder. "Is it awful?"

That shrug again. It made him look vulnerable and boyish. "I've seen things no man should ever have to see. And I'm not sure I even know what I'm fighting for."

Her heart broke for him. *War was hell.* How often had her dad said that? "Are you afraid—to go back?"

"I'm not afraid to die, if that's what you mean. I know where I'm going . . . if anything happens. I settled things with Him"—he cut his eyes to the ceiling—"long before I got on that plane."

"I'm so glad. So glad, Kevin." Relief flooded her. In all the prayers she'd said for him those many months after he broke things off, her most fervent was that Kevin was right with God. That he hadn't lost the faith he'd professed when they were teenagers. They hadn't talked a lot about spiritual things back then. Probably hadn't taken their faith seriously enough, either of them. But they'd been in youth group together and she'd always hoped Kevin truly believed the things they'd been taught about God, about faith in Christ.

Their waitress came and cleared away their dishes. "Can I get y'all some more Cokes, or maybe coffee and dessert?"

Kevin looked to her. "Will you split a piece of pie with me?"

"No, thanks, but I'll take some coffee while you eat your pie."

"We'll take an apple pie with vanilla ice cream and two coffees." He winked at the waitress. "And bring us two forks, please. I happen to remember that this woman can eat me under the table when it comes to apple pie."

Michelle kicked him under the table, but the humor brought a much-needed diversion. And veered the conversation away from a direction she feared it'd been headed.

Chapter Thirty-Three

"The driveway's right here . . . on the right." Michelle pointed at the windshield. "You need to drive back behind the house. I live in the apartment upstairs."

Kevin turned the rental car onto the narrow driveway, creeping around to the back of the house.

"This is good right here. Thanks." She put a hand on the door handle. *Oh, how to say good-bye?* There was no way to not make this awkward.

Kevin put the car in Park. He raked his cap off and set it on his knee. "It's so good to see you. I sometimes thought I might have lost you forever. Mish . . . if that was true, I would have lost the best thing that ever happened to me."

What was he saying? "Kevin—"

He held up a hand. "Hear me out. Please. I know it's not fair to ask you to wait for me"—he gave a sheepish grin—"especially when you already offered and I turned you down." He pivoted in his seat to put his arm up over the backrest. "I've never stopped thinking about you, Michelle. I've never stopped caring for you. You were a huge part of my life—a good part of my life—and I'd like to try again. To see if maybe—"

"Oh, Kevin. I'm so sorry. I—" She swallowed the lump that crowded her throat.

His jaw dropped, and realization sparked in his eyes. "There's someone else, isn't there? I should have known you wouldn't still be available." He shook his head. "I took you for granted. I'm sorry."

Oh, Kevin. It's too late. "No . . . I'm sorry," she whispered. "You will always have a tender place in my heart. And I'm grateful for what we had together. But I'm also grateful you made the decision you did. I'm not sure I would have ever discovered who I am, what I truly want out of life."

He folded and refolded his cap between his fingers before he looked down at her with a crooked grin. "Funny, there was a time I got the impression pretty strong that it was *me* you wanted out of life."

She sighed. "It was. It was, Kevin. At least that's what I thought I wanted. I'm . . . grateful for what we had. I'll always cherish the memories of that first love. But when you left, I—I had to move on. I don't know if I can go back again." It would be cruel to tell him now that back then, she'd been more in love with *love* than she'd been in love with him. But it struck her now that maybe it was the truth.

Was that the case with Rob Merrick? Was she so desperate to be in love that she'd fall for any man who showed an interest in her?

"I need to go, Kevin. Thank you for lunch. I'm glad I got to see you. I really am. I pray God keeps you safe. I–I've prayed for you a lot."

She opened the door and the interior light came on, making harsh shadows across his face. He reached out his hand and she held it, but loosely, terrified he might try to draw her into an embrace.

But he didn't. He squeezed her hand then let go. "Thank you for that. I need all the prayers I can get."

She started to get out but he called her name, louder than he needed to.

She turned back to look at him. His eyes held more sadness than she could bear.

"Don't write me off, Michelle. Keep an open mind, okay? I can't make any promises. I know you understand that. But just—keep me in mind, would you? Remember what we had together. And maybe write to me once in a while?"

She nodded slowly, wanting to lay some parameters, wanting to tell him she couldn't make any promises either. But like before, it would seem like such a cruelty to leave him that way. To send him back to Nam that way. And the truth was, she *would* keep him in mind. He'd been too important a part of her life not to. She would never forget what they'd had. Never forget that he'd been her first love.

And so she nodded and smiled softly and went into the house with a heart that was heavy—and more confused than ever.

* * * * *

Rob paced the back deck, hoping his dad wouldn't see him and come out to ask what was wrong. But he was too antsy to stay caged in upstairs another minute.

He looked at his watch and sighed. Michelle was probably expecting his call about now. He was tempted to call her and play dumb about seeing her and that soldier at Milt's this afternoon. Would she tell him about it, or would she string him along the way she apparently had been doing for a while now?

No. That wasn't fair. He was jumping to conclusions. Maybe that guy was her brother and he was in ROTC or something. But Rob knew better. The uniform was real. And nobody looked at their sister the way that guy had looked at Michelle.

He felt sick to his stomach. And now he had to call her and tell her he'd quit his job for her sake. Maybe it wasn't too late to turn down the job at the *Eagle*. He hadn't told Dad yet. He could call Jim Clemson and say that something had come up, and he was going to have to decline the offer.

But if he did that, he'd be stuck in the *Beacon* office, sitting in a cubicle beside Michelle every day. Smelling her heady perfume and knowing she was off-limits. He wasn't sure he could survive that.

Well, nothing was going to change because he paced a hole in the deck. He might as well go make the call and get it over with. *Lord, let me be kind, and don't let me say something I'll regret.*

He went inside and heard his father talking on the phone in the den down the hall. He went to listen at the door of the den for a minute. It sounded like Dad was deep in conversation with someone about newspaper-industry stuff. *Great.* Judging by how those conversations usually went, it might be another hour before he could get to the phone.

Times like this, he couldn't wait to get his own place. He'd toyed with the idea of getting an apartment in Wichita. His salary was more than enough to rent a decent apartment, especially if he wasn't spending money on gas commuting from Bristol. Of course if he was with Michelle he'd be driving back to Bristol—

Stop it, Merrick. He rubbed his face and went back out to the kitchen. He wasn't going to be with Michelle. Might as well brace himself for the truth.

And might as well get it over with. He scribbled a note to his dad and went out to the Pinto. There wouldn't be anybody at the office on a Sunday night. He'd call her from there.

* * * * *

Main Street was a ghost town, and the alley behind the *Beacon* office was empty. Rob unlocked the office and relocked the door behind him. The path to his cubicle was lit by dim overhead lights that were always left on at night so the police could see into the building. He plopped into his chair, steeling himself to make the call. He dialed Michelle's number and waited, his mouth all cotton.

"Hello?"

"Hi . . . it's me."

"Hey, Rob. How's it going?"

He hesitated, trying without success to read her demeanor over the phone lines. "Are you still wanting to get together?"

Nervous laughter. "I thought you were the one who needed to talk to me."

"I just meant . . . does it still work for you?" He hadn't meant to be so short with her, but under the circumstances he wasn't sure he cared.

"Yes, any time is fine."

"I'm at the *Beacon*. Do you want to come here? Or I could come to your place . . . ."

"I'll come down there. Are you ready now?"

"Any time. I'll leave the back door open."

"Okay, I'll come right now."

He unlocked the door then went to the break room to put some decaf on to brew. When he brought two steaming mugs out to his desk, she was just coming in the back entrance. Bundled in a heavy jacket, a scarf wound loosely around her long, slender neck, she looked beautiful. Her cheeks were flushed from the cold, and unruly ringlets framed her face. She sure wasn't making this easy.

He went to meet her and held her coffee while she took off her coat and scarf and hung them on a hook in the back entry.

"Hi." He handed over one of the steaming mugs.

"Hi." She studied him. "You really have me curious, you know."

"Yeah . . . Let's go sit in the reception room."

She nodded and followed him through the labyrinth of desks to the front of the building. They took opposite ends of the wide couch. She curled one leg up under her and sipped at her coffee, eyeing him over the rim of the mug.

He took a deep breath. "I'm just going to be blunt here. Are you back with your boyfriend—Kevin?"

Her eyes widened. "Where did you get that?"

"I saw you with him today. At Milt's."

"You were there?" She scooted deeper into her corner of the couch. "What, were you spying on me?"

"No. I was there with my father. Having lunch. Are you back with him?"

She shook her head, though not convincingly. "I didn't even know he was home until he showed up at church this morning. We went out to lunch, that's all."

"I'm sorry, but it looked like you were pretty cozy."

She opened her mouth and started to say something, but then she heaved a sigh and dropped her head.

"What's going on, Michelle?"

When she looked up again, he was surprised to see tears in her eyes. "I don't know. I'm feeling a little . . . confused right now."

"About . . . ?"

"Kevin and I were together for three years, Rob. He was my first love. It's hard to just—"

"I thought he dumped you."

"I guess he's reconsidering."

"So he wants you back? Is he out of the service?"

"No. He has at least two more years to go."

"But he wants you to wait for him?"

"Something like that."

"And did you tell him you would?"

"No. No . . . " She shook her head emphatically.

And it gave him a little hope. Maybe cruel hope, but still, his spirits rose a notch. But then, his spirits did that just being in her presence. "So . . . what's the deal?"

"What do you mean?"

"Michelle, I don't want to play games." He scooted forward on the couch until his knees touched the low coffee table. "I think you know what I mean," he said, without looking at her.

"Rob, I'm so confused right now. I don't *know* what 'the deal' is. With Kevin. With you. With anybody."

He looked over at her. "I'm not interested in pursuing a woman who's already spoken for, so I'd appreciate it if you'd just tell me if it's over between you and me."

"I don't want it to be. I don't." Her voice cracked. "But . . . "

"But . . . ?"

She shook her head and seemed to struggle for words. "I wasn't aware there was exactly anything *between* you and me."

He chose to ignore that and went for the more important question. "Do you love him?"

She closed her eyes and rested her head on the back of the couch. "I think a part of me will always love him a little bit. Don't you have a special place in your heart for your first love?"

He nodded. "Yes. I do." He didn't tell her that *she* was his first love.

"Then you understand."

"Maybe. But I'm not the kind of guy who likes chasing someone who's playing hard-to-get. I'm not going to chase you if I know there's no hope of catching you."

"I'm not asking you to chase me. I–I'm asking you to be patient. Can you give me a little time to sort things out?"

"Define 'a little,' please."

"I don't know."

"Michelle"—he angled himself toward her on the couch—"what is it you want? What do you really want out of life?"

"Out of life?"

"Yes. If money was no object, what would you do with your life? Do you want to go back to college? Be a journalist? Join the army?"

"Hey!" She frowned at him like a stern schoolteacher.

"Kidding. Just seeing if you were listening."

"Of course I'm listening. But you know what? The last time I told a guy what I really, really wanted—in my deepest heart of hearts—he dumped me and, well, joined the army. So you can understand why I'm a little hesitant to just spout off about my dreams." She shifted and curled both legs underneath her. She was close enough he could smell her baby-powder scent.

"He dumped you because of your dream? What on earth would make—" Suddenly it hit him. "Is it singing? Is that what you want to do with your life?"

Her expression revealed nothing.

"You have a gorgeous voice, Mish. As good as Karen Carpenter. Better, even. You could totally make it in the music—"

"No, it's not that." She shook her head and gave a nervous laugh. "Good grief. Being a singer is the *last* thing I ever dreamed of."

"What is it, then? Hey . . . " He waited until she met his gaze.

"I promise you I would never make fun of your dream. No matter what it is. You surely know me well enough to know I'm a liberated kind of guy. I can handle a woman with aspirations to greatness."

"Oh, yeah?" She rolled her eyes. "Can you handle a woman who wants nothing more than to stay home and have babies? Lots of babies?"

He looked askance at her. "Are you serious? That's it? That's what you want."

She nodded then dipped her head, looking ashamed.

"Is that why he dumped you?"

She shrugged.

"He's a fool." He reached to tip her chin with one finger, forcing her to look at him. "I think that's the most amazing aspiration you could possibly have. And now you're probably thinking I'm a male chauvinist pig to say that."

She ignored that. "Really? You think that's amazing?"

"Well, hang on a minute . . . " He held up a hand like a stop sign. "How *many* babies?"

That earned sweet laughter.

Before he could weigh the consequences, he closed the gap between them on the couch. "Michelle, I think *you're* amazing." He took her face in his hands and kissed her.

Her arms came up around his neck and she kissed him back, stroking his hair.

He came to his senses and gently pushed her away. He unfolded himself from the sofa and went to stand on the other side of the coffee table. Michelle straightened and looked up at him. He thought he saw longing written in her expression, but how could he know it was for him? He couldn't. For all he knew, she'd kissed Kevin the same way only hours ago.

She had to decide. And he had to know for sure that if she chose him, she was choosing for the right reasons. Not on the rebound. But first, he had to tell her what he'd called her here to tell her. He stuffed his hands into his front pockets, trying to think how to say it.

"What's wrong, Rob?"

"I'm leaving the *Beacon*."

"What?"

"I've taken a job with the *Wichita Eagle* . . . as a reporter."

"But . . . why?"

"A lot of reasons. And some of them don't matter anymore, I guess." He dropped his head, gathering his thoughts.

"But . . . when do you start?"

"I'm giving Dad my two weeks' notice tomorrow."

"Why, Rob? I don't understand."

"Honesty is the best policy." His father's words echoed in his head, ingrained in him almost from birth. "The truth is, I wanted to be free to be with you, Michelle. But I can see that's not an option right now."

"You did that for me? Rob . . . "

"Yes. And no offense, but it was a stupid thing to do."

She looked at him the way she did when she was trying to figure out whether he was teasing. He wasn't, and he watched her expression change as she realized it. "I'm sorry. I'm sorry if I made you think I was—"

"No." He shook his head. "It's not your fault. I jumped the gun. Or maybe there never was a gun."

"No, Rob. You didn't misinterpret my—*interest* in you. Not at all. It's just that, well, Kevin showing up . . . ? I thought I was over him. I think I *am*. But—"

"I know. You have to be sure. I understand that. I do. It's just lousy timing."

"I'm sorry, Rob. I don't know what else to say."

"I'm sorry too. About the kiss." He pointed to the scene of the crime.

She gave a little smile. "I'm not."

Anger swelled his throat, and he glared at her. "How can you say that in one breath and that you're not sure you're over Kevin in the other? I don't get that, Michelle."

"I'm sorry," she said again. "I shouldn't have said that."

"Listen . . . I need to tell you something, and then that's all I'm going to say on the topic."

She eyed him with curiosity.

"You take some time to think about what you want. And when you decide what that is, come talk to me. I won't wait forever, Michelle, but I'll tell you this much—I know what I want. I've known for a long time. And I've been willing to do what it takes to go after it. But I'm not going to chase a dream that can never be mine."

He paced the short length of the reception area. "I think it's good I won't be around here. Yes . . . it's good." He was thinking out loud and trying to rationalize, he knew. Trying to save face, even.

Michelle rose, looking distressed. "I need to get my things." She headed toward the back entry.

He was afraid she'd leave without saying good-bye, yet something wouldn't let him follow her.

But she returned a minute later with her coat and scarf. She slowly wound the scarf around her neck. "Rob, I'm so sorry. I can't say that enough."

Well, she had that much right.

She slipped her coat on and buttoned it from the bottom. "Can we still be friends?"

"As long we keep our distance." Again he pointed to the couch, where they'd kissed. Where even now, he wanted to go back and feel the warmth of her in his arms again.

Instead, he watched her walk away and wondered if he'd lost the dearest friend he had ever known.

Chapter Thirty-Four

The highway was pitch-dark beneath a white fingernail moon. It might scare her parents to death for her to show up on their doorstep at this hour, but Michelle had to go home. She wasn't sure she could even talk to Mom and Dad about everything that had happened with Rob—and with Kevin. But she couldn't sit alone in her apartment for one more minute.

At least she could sleep in her childhood bedroom tonight. Maybe she would find some comfort in that.

She pulled into the driveway a few minutes later to find the house dark and no one home. Like always, the back door was unlocked, so she went in through the garage, flipping on lights as she went.

She wandered through the farmhouse she'd grown up in, feeling strangely as if she'd gone back in time. There were such precious memories here. This was the place where she'd become the woman she was now. Mom had lovingly decorated the house over the years when the harvest was good or cattle prices were up—and walking through the house now, Michelle saw it with different eyes. No longer a place she couldn't wait to launch from, the house now felt like a shelter she could always come back to.

But tonight it felt empty too. Where were Mom and Dad? It wasn't like them to be gone this late on a Sunday night. Or any night, now that she and Allen had left home. She hoped everything was okay.

In the kitchen, she raided the fridge and found a parfait glass of Whip'n Chill. Her favorite—and she hadn't tasted it in forever. She grabbed a spoon from the dish drainer and took the dessert to the dining room table, where she could watch the driveway.

She sat there in the dark and enjoyed the fluffy dessert. When Mom and Dad hadn't shown up by 11:45, she was alarmed. Five minutes later, as she was trying to decide whether to contact the police, she heard a car on the gravel driveway. She went to watch out the dining room window.

It was them. Relief coursed through her. Instead of pulling into the detached garage, they parked behind her car on the drive. The kitchen door opened, and her mother called for her.

"Michelle?" Mom's voice came closer. She flipped on the dining room light and gave a little start when she saw Michelle. "What are you doing home? Is everything okay?"

"Yeah." She shrugged. "I just didn't feel like being alone."

Her mother studied her with that suspicious look that was so familiar from her high-school years. "Did everything go okay . . . with Kevin?"

Another shrug. "I guess."

Her dad peeked around the corner just then. "Mish! What are you—" His gaze landed on the empty parfait glass on the table. "Hey! You didn't eat that last Whip'n Chill, did you?"

She ignored the question. "Where have you guys been, anyway?"

"Your dad took me out to dinner and a movie."

"Yes," her father said, winking at Mom. "When the mice are away, don't think the cats just pine away in the empty nest."

Her parents had always been openly affectionate with each other, but there seemed to be a fresh spark between them. It embarrassed

Michelle, even as it made her heart swell, and reminded her of the longing she carried inside.

"The question is," Dad was saying, "what is this little mouse doing home? It's Sunday night. Don't you have to work tomorrow?"

She affected a pout. "Can't a girl come home for a visit without getting the third degree?"

She couldn't see Mom's face but could tell by her demeanor that she was giving Dad the tread-lightly signal.

Dad yawned and stretched. "Well, you girls can stay up as late as you like, but this old cat has to get up early. I think I'll hit the hay." He caught on a lot quicker than he had when she was in high school. Either that or he and Mom had perfected their silent communication skills.

She went to give him a hug.

After he disappeared up the stairs, Mom looked at Michelle again—a piercing gaze that said, *Are you really okay?* "So you talked to Kevin. After all this time . . . " Her parents had always liked Kevin, but Mom sounded almost wistful. "How was he? How's he holding up?"

"Okay, I guess."

"How was it, seeing him again?"

"Kind of weird. He . . . sort of apologized."

"For breaking up?" Mom sounded surprised.

Michelle nodded. "He wants me to 'keep him in mind.'"

Mom wrinkled her nose. "What does that mean?"

"I'm not sure. He said he can't make any promises."

"Well, he can't, Michelle. Not where he is."

"I know that, Mom. But now I feel . . . like I *should* wait for him."

Her mother pulled out a chair and sat down across from her. "I remember a time not so very long ago when that was all you wanted . . . to wait for that man."

She blew out a sigh. "I know. I'm just . . . Oh, Mom, I'm just so confused. I don't know what I want."

"What's going on, honey? Is there something you're not telling me?"

She looked at her mother, willing her to provide some answers. "Do you think it's possible to be in love with two people at the same time?"

"Is there someone else?"

Michelle sighed again. "I just came from the *Beacon* office . . . talking to Rob. Mom—" She cast her eyes down, afraid to say the words aloud. "I think I might love him."

"You were just there tonight?"

She nodded.

"Was there anyone else at the office?"

"No. Why?"

"I don't think that was very wise, Michelle." She had on her stern face.

"Are you serious? Mom, Rob wouldn't hurt a flea."

"That's not what I'm talking about. It's just not a good idea to be there alone . . . together. It—well, you know."

Did her mother really think they were going to—do something like *that*—right there in the newspaper office? Good grief. "Mom, nothing happened. Nothing was going to happen."

"That's not the point. People talk. And once a rumor gets started, you can never convince some people that it isn't true."

"It's not my fault if people want to talk about something that never happened."

"Well, you don't need to give them any fuel for the fire."

Michelle rolled her eyes and waved a hand as if she could brush the subject aside. "I'm tired. I'm going to bed."

Her mother cringed and closed her eyes, but she didn't try to stop her.

Twenty minutes later, tucked into bed in her old room, she heard a soft knock at the door. "Come in."

Her mother slipped in, closing the door behind her. "I'm sorry." Mom flipped on the bedside lamp and sat down on the side of the bed. She patted Michelle's hand. "I forget sometimes that you're not my little girl anymore."

Michelle smiled, but her face melted into a frown and she felt tears hot behind her eyelids. "What should I do, Mom? I don't know how to feel about either one of them. I think I love them both. How can that be? I thought I was over Kevin, but seeing him . . . I missed him. But then, when I was with Rob tonight . . . Oh, Mom, he's so wonderful. He's amazing. What do I do?" The words came out in a moan.

"Michelle, you know what to do. You know the answer. If I tell you, you'll just roll your eyes and accuse me of preaching at you. But your dad and I have taught you since you could barely walk what to do when you're scared, when you're confused, when you have a problem, when you don't know the answer, when you're hurting. You *know* what to do." She reached up and turned off the lamp. "Oh, sweet daughter of mine"—she planted a kiss on the crown of Michelle's head—"I love you more than life itself, and I'm going to leave you alone now. Everything will turn out fine. Just maybe not by tomorrow." She gave a serene smile and closed the door behind her, leaving a slash of golden light from the hallway across the worn carpet.

Michelle looked at the back of the door, her heart full of love for her mother, for this home full of love that she'd grown up in. All the tension drained from her body, and she closed her eyes and sought the One who held every answer she needed. The One who had been waiting for her all along.

Chapter Thirty-Five

It was well after ten when Rob crept into the house. His father usually went to bed early on Sunday nights, but there was a light on in the den, so Rob started up the stairs without raiding the kitchen for his customary bedtime snack. He wasn't hungry anyway.

And he sure didn't feel like talking.

He took the steps two at a time to avoid the creaky stair tread, but before he reached the first landing, Dad called his name from the hallway.

Rob turned around, one hand still on the bannister. "Hey, Dad. You still up?"

"Where have you been?"

"Didn't you see my note?" He nodded in the direction of the kitchen.

"It didn't say where you'd been."

"I just—went in to the office for a while. Caught up on some work." That much was true. He'd stayed for an hour after Michelle left, just trying to sort things out.

"I just got off the phone with Harv Slabaugh."

Not good. Slabaugh was a bigwig at the *Eagle*. Rob stood still, no doubt looking like a possum caught in the headlights.

"Harv called to apologize for stealing my son away from the *Beacon*. You want to tell me what's going on, son?"

"Dad—" What could he say? He hadn't thought to tell Personnel at the *Eagle* not to mention it to his father yet. He shouldn't have needed to. Whatever happened to discretion and privacy? "I was going to tell you."

"*When* were you going to tell me? Do you know how foolish I felt, hearing that news from Harv?" In the harsh light from the hallway lamp, his father looked a decade older than his fifty-eight years.

"I was waiting—" He'd started to say he was waiting until he told Michelle, but there was no way he was going to tell his father that now. Not only would it make him look like a bigger fool than he was, but it might get Michelle into trouble too. "I don't start for two-and-a-half weeks. That should give you time to find someone else, and I'll be sure to—"

"That's not the issue . . . not the issue at all, Robert." His dad walked slowly to the bottom of the stairs and looked up at him, his shoulders hunched as if they carried a heavy burden. "Are you that unhappy at work?"

"No, that's not—"

"Why didn't you say something? Are they paying you more? Because if you ask me, you're getting a pretty good deal right here." His jaw clenched. He looked more angry than hurt now.

"Dad . . . " Rob came halfway down the flight of stairs and sat heavily on a step, resting his forearms on his thighs. "I don't want you to think I don't appreciate everything you've done for me. It's not that at all. It's just that . . . I need to do some things on my own. Not always be in your shadow. I don't even know if I have any talent in this business."

"You have talent, son. You just need some experience to develop it. That's what I thought I was offering you."

"I know. And I do truly appreciate it."

"You're leaving us shorthanded. You know that."

"That's why I made sure they knew I'd need two weeks before I start."

"This doesn't have anything to do with Michelle Penn, does it?"

He knew his silence said far more than he wanted his father to know. "I don't agree with your policy on that. But it's more than that—my reasons for leaving, I mean."

"If I lifted the ban on fraternization, would that change your mind?"

"I don't know if that's even an issue anymore, Dad." He knew he should tell his father the whole truth—that Michelle had been almost his sole reason for wanting to leave the *Beacon*. He could see in the slump of Dad's shoulders and in the dullness of his eyes that his decision cut deeply. But he wasn't ready to share about Michelle yet. He was hurting too. And confused and embarrassed that he'd made such a huge decision for a woman whose heart he wasn't even sure he'd captured.

That was something he simply couldn't admit to his dad. Not when he could barely admit it to himself.

* * * * *

Michelle slid a pencil behind her ear then twisted a tendril of hair around it. Her concentration was shot, and she still had two stories to finish before five o'clock. But all she could think about was the man in the cubicle beside hers.

Rob had kept to himself all day, his nose to his Selectric, whenever she caught a glimpse over the partition. But from the silence of his keyboard, he wasn't having any better luck getting the words to flow than she was.

To make matters worse, things were taut between Robert Sr. and Robert III. If it hadn't been drilled into her to "avoid clichés like the plague," she would have said the tension was so thick, you could cut it with a knife. She hadn't heard father and son so much as speak to each other all morning, but Robert Sr. was making up for it by growling at anyone else who crossed his path.

No announcement of Rob's impending departure had been made yet, so Michelle had to sit on that news and let the other employees wonder what on earth was going on in their formerly mild-mannered newspaper office.

"Michelle?" Joy poked her head in to Michelle's cubicle. "Do you have the ad copy for Milt's?"

"Milt's, the restaurant?"

"Who else would I mean?"

She counted to ten. Joy Swanson had had it in for her since the day she'd first walked through the doors, but the woman had ramped up her animosity lately. "I don't know, but I never got any copy for Milt's, so that's why I asked."

"What do you mean, you never got any copy? I put it right there on your desk."

"I'm sorry, but I never saw it. When did you put it here?"

"I don't remember. Last week some time."

Michelle made a show of searching through the papers on her desk, even though she knew exactly what was there and when it had been put there. She was quite certain there had never been an ad for Milt's. She finally shrugged. "I'm sorry. I don't remember ever seeing it. Is there someplace I can help you look?"

"Yes. On your desk. Because that's where I put it."

She spun her chair around to face Joy. "I've already looked on my desk, Joy. And it's not here. Would you like me to call Milt's and see if I can get another copy from him?"

"I guess you'd better. I just hope he still has it."

"Um, excuse me . . . " Rob popped over the partition, waving a sheet of paper. "Is this what you ladies are looking for?"

Joy ripped the paper from his hand and inspected it. "How did you get that?"

"It was on my desk."

"Why didn't you say something?" Joy was indignant.

He glared at her. "Unlike some people, I was working and not eavesdropping on your conversation."

Ordinarily Michelle would have come back with some quip like, "How did you know what we were looking for if you weren't eavesdropping?" But since Rob had all but ignored her since he'd arrived at the office this morning, she decided silence was golden.

"Here—" Michelle took the ad from Joy. "I'll get it typed up."

"I need it by ten at the latest." Joy stomped off to her cubicle.

Michelle sat down and started typing out the ad. She didn't know why they didn't have the typesetters take care of ad copy as well as news. She and Rob had all they could do to keep up with, writing the news stories and filler. But that was how it had been since she started here. She couldn't imagine how they'd keep up after Rob was gone, especially if they didn't replace him right away. And even then, they'd have to train someone. She wondered who would be sitting in Rob's cubicle two weeks from now. Whoever it was, she already resented them.

She heard a rustling overhead and looked up to see a sheet of paper fluttering over the partition. She reached up and took the paper from Rob's hand. It was written in his familiar all-caps hand:

THAT WAS BIG OF YOU TO OFFER TO TYPE THE AD. LET
THE RECORD SHOW: SHE OWES YOU AN APOLOGY.

She smiled and scribbled a note underneath his:

Thanks for the vote of confidence, you eavesdropper, you.

She added a smiley face and folded the note into a paper airplane. She stood and lofted it over the divider.

Except, she put a little too much muscle behind her throw, and the airplane sailed right over Rob's cubicle and took a nosedive into Joy's airspace.

She gasped and scrambled to Joy's cubicle. Fortunately, Joy was over at the banks laying out ad pages. With a furtive glance in that direction, Michelle darted into the space and retrieved the paper missile from beneath Joy's chair. With the airplane firmly in hand, she peeked out of the adwoman's cubicle and, seeing that the coast was clear, she made a dash for her desk.

Rob stood in his doorway, his shoulders shaking with silent laughter.

She glared at him and stuffed the airplane into his hands. "Here."

Back in her own cubicle, she heard him unfolding the missive next door. Then his quiet chuckle.

They laughed together from opposite sides of the divider. Still smiling to herself, she silently thanked Joy Swanson for what was assuredly an accidental mending of the rift between Rob and her.

She went back to her story. There was a lot to do, since next week's paper would come out a day early because of the Thanksgiving holiday. She'd so looked forward to the holidays with Rob, and now she couldn't let herself think too long about what this place would be like without him. What her life would be like without him.

Maybe the *Wichita Eagle* had an opening for her too. But she dismissed the thought the instant it came. Being near Rob was exactly her problem. Following him to Wichita wouldn't solve anything.

Chapter Thirty-Six

"Pass the spuds, would you, sis?" Allen reached across the table and took the proffered bowl of mashed potatoes from Michelle. She wasn't sure what had gotten into her brother, but he was actually using his manners today.

Eden leaned across the high-chair tray, her eyes sparkling. "Me spuds."

Becky shushed her, looking embarrassed. "You have turkey and dressing to eat first, sweetie."

Eden pouted, and Becky concentrated on her own plate.

Michelle could tell that Becky felt awkward with her family. And seeing the farmhouse through Becky's eyes, Michelle caught a glimpse of how she must feel "intruding" on their family holiday.

Mom had the house looking—and smelling—wonderful, with taper candles aglow and the traditional crepe-paper turkey centerpiece gracing the table. The good dishes and silver were placed just so atop a freshly ironed russet-colored linen tablecloth, and fancy printed napkins from Bristol Drugs were folded at each place. But Michelle couldn't enjoy any of it for comparing her parents' house to Becky's.

Michelle could tell Mom was trying hard to put Becky at ease. But that was just it—she was trying *too* hard. Yet if Michelle said anything, it would only make things worse.

Dad cleared his throat loudly. "So, Becky, Michelle tells us you live over on Donner?"

"Yes, sir."

"That's a nice little area of town." Mom's voice held a false note of cheer.

Michelle had to fight not to roll her eyes. She knew her mother's intent was pure, but now she was just patronizing Becky.

"Hey, Eden. Watch this." Allen came to the rescue, picking up a handful of black olives from the relish tray and tossing one high into the air. He caught it in his mouth then did the same with two more in quick succession.

Eden giggled and reached across the high-chair tray toward the relish plate. "I do it."

Allen cringed and gave an apologetic shrug in Becky's direction.

To Michelle's surprise, Becky giggled too. "I never could figure out how to do that."

"It's all about keeping your eye on the 'ball.'" He demonstrated with another olive and was rewarded with more giggles.

"Allen, you're going to get the child in trouble." But Mom's warning lacked its usual bite and was accompanied by a smile.

Allen gave Michelle a conspiratorial glance before scooting the relish tray within Eden's reach. Michelle laughed under her breath, and Becky tossed a shy smile in Allen's direction before placing two black olives on Eden's plate. "Maybe you can try it later," she whispered. "Outside. And *after* you eat your turkey."

Eden took a tiny bite of turkey, but the minute Becky looked away, she gave a gleeful smile and lobbed the olive over her head. Allen caught it before it hit the floor and just as quickly tossed it back into the air and caught it in his mouth.

The entire table erupted in cheers and laughter, and Eden did an encore with the olive remaining on her plate. Only this time, she merely pretended to toss the shiny orb, instead bringing her chubby fist to her mouth and nabbing the olive like a snapping turtle would a fly.

Registering the taste of the black olive, her face scrunched up and she stuck out her tongue and made spitting sounds.

Dad howled and slapped his knee. "I don't blame you, Eden. I don't like those nasty things either."

Allen looked appropriately chagrined. "Sorry about that, squirt. I didn't know you weren't crazy about black olives."

"She's never had them before." Becky looked embarrassed again.

Michelle tried to deflect her discomfort. "This big lug"—she punched Allen's arm—"used to get me in trouble at the supper table almost every night. He'd make me taste something gross and then—"

"Hey!" Mom frowned. "I never made anything gross."

"Oh, there *was* that one time . . . " Dad took up the story, with Allen contributing details, Mom trying to defend her reputation, and everyone laughing.

Becky relaxed and seemed to enjoy the rest of the day. But later, when Michelle drove her and Eden home, Becky's melancholy silence puzzled her. "Everything okay?"

"You guys are so happy . . . your family." Her voice held awe— or maybe it was skepticism.

"Yeah, I guess we are."

"It's like you really like each other."

She shrugged. "I guess we do."

"Don't ever take that for granted. You don't know how lucky you are."

The sadness in Becky's eyes put a lump in Michelle's throat, and she thought about her friend's words long after she'd driven away from the little house on Donner Avenue. She'd always taken her happy family for granted. Her happy childhood. Now, her heart broke for Becky. And for Eden too. The sweet little girl would probably never have the kind of memories Michelle had of her own childhood.

Until she'd met Becky, Michelle hadn't appreciated nearly enough all that she'd been privileged to grow up with. But now, on this day set aside for giving thanks, she closed her eyes and sent up a silent prayer— and promised herself she would be more grateful for what she did have and gripe less about the things she was still waiting and hoping for.

And speaking of things she was waiting and hoping for, she wondered how Rob had spent his Thanksgiving. Had he and his dad fixed a turkey and all the trimmings? Somehow she doubted that. And the thought left a deep hollow inside of her.

* * * * *

Two weeks past Thanksgiving, the city crews had finally hung the Christmas decorations along Main Street. Michelle wasn't sure why they were so late, but at last, Bristol was dressed in its Christmas finery. In spite of the unsettled feeling she'd carried ever since Rob left the *Beacon*, Michelle reveled in the holiday mood that pervaded the little town.

Walking down the frost-dusted Main Street at dusk, watching multicolored lights twinkle from shop windows and eaves, she felt the doldrums of the drab autumn weather lift. Work had finally settled into a routine, and if not for missing Rob, she was actually enjoying her days at the *Beacon*.

She'd grown to enjoy the writing assignments—well, except for covering the school board meetings. School *bored* meetings, Rob had always labeled them in his sluglines. She sighed. The *Beacon* office was not the same without him.

Rob had agreed to come in after-hours to work until they could find a replacement, so she'd seen him a couple of times as she was leaving the parking lot. He always waved and smiled, and once they'd talked for twenty minutes from their respective car windows, which only made her realize how much she missed him.

Mr. Merrick was crabbier than ever—crabbier than Joy, even— which was saying a lot. Michelle wasn't sure how she would survive at the Beacon once they hired a replacement and Rob was really gone for good.

Although she felt guilty about it, she'd purposely missed a deadline with a story today so she'd be "forced" to stay after-hours and be there when Rob arrived. She was nervous about how he might behave toward her, but what did she have to lose?

The clock inched toward five. Rob usually came in shortly after that. Michelle went to the restroom to freshen her makeup and tame her hair.

When she came out, Rob was at the coatrack in the back, stripping a red tie from around his collar. Wearing a still-crisp white shirt and dress pants, he was a treat for weary eyes. "Well, hey, stranger," she said, feeling as nervous as she had the day she'd realized he was Mr. Whoop-dee-do.

He whirled around, seeming surprised to see her. "Hi there." A grin bloomed on his face. "What are you doing here so late?"

"Oh . . . " She cut her eyes to the dusty wood planks beneath her feet, feeling the weight of guilt about her deception. "I need to finish a story. Christmas feature."

"Listen . . . I feel bad about that."

"What?"

Now it was his turn to study the floor. "I feel responsible for the extra hours people are putting in. And I'm afraid Dad's not working too hard to find my replacement."

As if anyone could ever replace him. "Right before Christmas is probably a pretty hard time to find someone."

"Maybe. But I still feel bad." He clapped his hands together. "But you don't need to hear all my woes. I'm keeping you from your work."

"Oh, no, it's okay. I needed a break. In fact, would you have time to look at a couple of paragraphs I'm having trouble with?"

"Sure." He led the way to her cubicle.

She showed him two random paragraphs that she'd struggled with earlier but pretty much already decided how to fix. Could he see right through her pathetic ruse? If he did, he didn't let on, patiently giving his opinion in a way that made her laugh—and miss him all the more.

He straightened and glanced past her toward the front window. "You want to get out of here for a little while?"

"Where'd you have in mind?"

He shrugged. "Just go for a walk or something . . . Get some fresh air. Where's your coat?"

"I'll get it." She was glad she'd bundled up before she came. She hurried to the back room and donned her gloves and scarf, sneaking a peek at her reflection in the small TV that sat silent on the counter. She tried to tame the curls that frizzed around her forehead but quickly admitted defeat and went out to meet Rob at the front door.

He was peering through the plate glass into the night sky. "Did you know it's snowing?"

"Really?" She'd dared to hope for a white Christmas, but not this early. Sure enough, snow was falling in thick, wet flakes—what Mom called snowdrops. "You still want to walk?"

"Sure." He grinned as if she'd issued a challenge and held open the door. "After you."

She ducked into the air-lock entry and headed out onto the street. "Careful, it's slippery," she called over her shoulder.

He caught up with her and grabbed her hand, tucking it into the crook of his elbow. She savored the warmth of him. The Christmas lights on Main Street wore halos of red, green, blue, and gold. Despite every tenth one needing to be replaced, the effect was magical. They strolled arm in arm along the uneven sidewalk, their breaths mingling in the crisp night air.

They'd walked two blocks when the tinny strains of Christmas carols floated from the courthouse at the center of town. "Silent Night" died away, and Elvis crooned a new rendition of "Silver Bells" that did Bing Crosby proud. As they got closer, the music grew louder and Michelle sang along, bungling most of the lyrics but too happy to care.

Beside her, Rob chuckled.

"What's so funny?"

"I was thinking how opposite from this song everything is."

"What do you mean?"

"No city. No busy sidewalks. No children laughing. No people passing. No strings of stoplights. Not a silver bell in sight."

"You Scrooge! What about the strings of streetlights? And those red-and-green lights are blinking. See?" She pointed up at the court-house tower. "And can't you hear the snow crunch?" She stomped her boot in snow that was mostly a mushy puddle.

He smirked. "That sounded more like a *slosh* to me."

"Okay, but there is a feeling of Christmas in the air."

He laughed and tugged at her hand, twirling her to face him. "Fine. I'll give you that."

He let go of her hand and stroked a mittened finger gently over her eye. "You had a snowflake caught in your eyelash."

"Ha!" She gloated. "That's just me—dressed in holiday style." She swallowed a giggle, tickled at her own joke.

Across the street a car door slammed, and a father helped two dark-haired little girls from the backseat. Their musical laughter wafted on the night air as they pointed up at the courthouse lights.

"Children laughing!" Michelle declared.

The father took the sisters by the hand and started across the street.

"And people passing!" she crowed.

Rob tweaked her nose between two mittened fingers. "Ooh, aren't you clever?"

"I really am." Laughter bubbled up from her throat.

It was apparently contagious, because Rob laughed out loud. "Come on." He grabbed her hand and pulled her along.

"Where are we going?"

He didn't answer but did slow to match her gait. They walked briskly, hand in hand, with snowflakes swirling around them, the sky a black canopy overhead, as if they were caught inside a magical snow globe.

Elvis's velvet voice receded behind them as they approached the bridge over the creek at the edge of town. The snow was falling heavily now, piling up on the guardrail, speckling their coats and scarves, and netting their hair with icy crystals. They were going to be soaked by the time they finally got back to the office and thawed out. But Michelle couldn't have cared less.

Rob stopped in the middle of the bridge and turned to look over the rail. The creek was barely a trickle and mostly covered up with snow now. But under the glow of the last streetlight in town, it had an ethereal beauty.

"Listen," he said, cupping a hand to one ear.

She did likewise. The gentle trickle echoed in the hushed cavern the snow had created. It was its own kind of music. "Beautiful," she breathed. "All of it."

"*You* are what's beautiful," he said, then looked away, as if he hadn't intended for that to come out.

Before she could think how to respond, he looked back and took a step toward her. He took her face in his hands and kissed her. Briefly, tenderly . . . an almost innocent gesture.

Still, Michelle felt something far stronger simmering beneath the surface. She didn't dare kiss him back. But when he pulled away, she brought her fingers to her lips, as if she could seal in the warmth of his lips.

"We'd better get back," Rob said, sliding his hand down the arm of her coat and catching her fingers up in his again. "That is probably a road to nowhere."

For a split second she thought about playing dumb, but she knew exactly what he meant and instead went for broke. "Don't be so sure, Rob Merrick. Don't be so sure."

It wasn't until her head hit the pillow just after midnight that she realized she hadn't given Kevin Ferris one thought the entire day.

* * * * *

"Becky, you look fantastic!" Michelle could hardly believe the transformation in her friend. It was Saturday, and she'd been babysitting Eden most of the day to give Becky a break. And Becky had come home with her hair styled and frosted and wearing makeup in the hip, barely-there tones all the women's magazines were advertising. "What's the occasion?"

Becky looked embarrassed. "Does there have to be an occasion? *You* wear makeup every day, and your hair always looks nice." She put a hand on her growing middle. "Besides, it helps me not to think about how fat I'm getting."

"Stop it!" She felt bad for putting Becky on the spot. "You look great! Like a million bucks, as my dad would say. And you are not fat. That's all baby. Beautiful baby." She reached to touch Becky's belly, pushing away the twinge of jealousy that came. The baby wasn't due until mid-January, but Becky looked as if she could pop any day.

"I just don't want to be one of those moms who lets herself go, you know?" Becky looked sheepish.

"Yeah. I've thought about that too. If I ever get to be a mom, I mean . . . "

Becky looked taken aback. "Of *course* you'll get to be a mom."

Michelle ignored her, sorry she'd brought up the subject. "I don't know how you do it. Every time I babysit for Eden, I'm wiped out after only a few hours."

"It's hard sometimes. Not having anybody to give me a break—" Becky stopped and shook her head. "That didn't come out right. Here you are doing exactly that. I appreciate you letting me have some time away today. I didn't mean to sound ungrateful."

"I know what you meant. And you deserve it. Besides, you know I love watching Eden."

As if on cue, Eden toddled in from the dining room, where she'd been stacking building blocks. She started for her mother then stopped short and burst into tears. "Mama?"

Michelle laughed. "She doesn't recognize you!"

Becky knelt and held out her arms. "Come here, baby. It's me. Do you like Mama's hair?"

Eden must have been convinced by the sound of her mother's voice, for she reached up and touched the platinum streaks in Becky's brown hair. "Pretty?"

"You like it, huh? Well, we'll see what your daddy says."

Mack had pleaded guilty and had been sentenced to eighteen months in the pen at Leavenworth. It was almost six hours round-trip, and Becky's car wasn't dependable enough to make the trip. Michelle couldn't imagine how they would maintain any kind of relationship for that long. And while Michelle knew it was hard for Becky to be a single parent with a husband in prison, she also was glad Becky had some time to decide what she wanted to do when Mack got out. She hoped he didn't get out too soon—and that he would get help for his problems while he was serving time. Mostly, she hoped Becky would do whatever it took to keep herself and Eden safe.

"Mama pretty." Eden plucked at Becky's hair again and jabbered something Michelle couldn't understand.

But Michelle noticed that Eden had started talking more now that the issues with Mack were settled. Becky seemed more at peace. Maybe it had more to do with the fact that she was working full-time now, waitressing at Milt's while Eden stayed with a woman who babysat for five other toddlers.

Becky had cried on Michelle's shoulder when she realized she'd have to put Eden in day care, but she really had no choice now that Mack wasn't contributing a salary. It wasn't easy, but at least Becky and Eden were safe now, and that was worth a lot.

"I'd probably better get going," Michelle said. "I promised my folks I'd come for dinner tonight."

Becky laughed. "You make it sound like a chore. I'd be turning cartwheels if someone was cooking for me."

"Oh. I didn't mean it to come out that way. Really, I didn't." Becky had been good for her, helping her to not take her blessings for granted. It gave her an idea of another way she could help Becky. Michelle had enjoyed cooking in her apartment, but it was hard to cook for only one person. It would be an easy matter to make double and bring meals to Becky once in a while.

Driving to Mom and Dad's later, she remembered Becky's gentle chiding and thanked God again for the loving parents and the happy family she'd grown up in. She'd taken them for granted far too long.

But even in her "thanksgiving" mode, she felt a desperate sense of—she couldn't even put her finger on it. It wasn't that she was depressed or angry or even bored. She didn't mind her work—enjoyed it even, most days—but if someone told her she would still be here even one year from now, she would despair.

Something about her life right now felt like she was "on hold." She wanted to feel passionate about something again. And she did feel passion when she thought of Becky and Eden and her own family—Mom and Dad and Allen. But that was exactly the point. It was the idea of family that made her heart beat faster, that made her feel *purpose* surge through her veins. She wanted that for herself. And more and more when she thought of family, she thought of Rob.

So I'm back to this again, Lord. I can't seem to help it. I want a husband, and I want babies. Is that wrong of me, God? Is it too much to ask?

She got no answer, but she was learning to wait. She'd made her request. And now she would be patient and trust that the answer would come when God's time was right.

Chapter Thirty-Seven

Traffic on Kellogg was the worst he'd ever seen it, and for the hundredth time, Rob wondered why he'd ever wanted to work in Wichita. And to make matters worse, he hated his new job. With a passion.

Maybe it wasn't fair to make that judgment after only a few weeks on the job, but he found himself living for the weekends and feeling grateful he'd at least had the sense to get a Monday-through-Friday schedule. Since the *Eagle* was a daily paper, he was fortunate not to be on the weekend staff.

At least not yet. After working for Clemson for a few weeks, Rob was starting to suspect that the man actually had a vendetta against Dad and was summarily taking it out on Robert III.

The bottom line was: unless something changed in the near future, he'd made a huge mistake. To top it off, he was coming back to Bristol every night and putting in three or four hours at the *Beacon* as well. What was really sad was that those overtime hours were the highlight of each day.

Of course that was because if he hustled, he could usually get to the *Beacon* before Michelle left for the day. Most of the time he got there only in time to wave at her as she left the parking lot. Still, it was better than not seeing her at all.

The weeks had gone by in a blur of trying to learn the new job while keeping Dad happy at the *Beacon*. Since their walk that snowy night, he'd only really seen Michelle twice for any length of quality time. Once when he'd run into her in the library and they'd sat and talked till old Mrs. Beakman kicked them out at closing, and another time when they happened to be at the Bristol Grocery at the same time. All those encounters had done was remind him what a fool he was for leaving the *Beacon*. And as much as he'd wanted to, he hadn't been able to finagle another kiss on either occasion. Oh, but the memory of that night on the bridge kept him hoping.

He glanced at the clock on the dashboard: almost five already. He ordinarily got off work at four, but they'd had a stupid news meeting this afternoon, and since it was Thursday, Michelle would likely have gone home early. His hopes for another encounter with her were pretty much shot.

But when he pulled in behind the *Beacon* office, he was pleased to see her car was still there. Immediately guilt replaced his pleasure, since it was probably his fault that she was having to work late on a Thursday.

Dad had been quick to express appreciation for the extra hours Rob put in, but he feared those hours kept his father from hiring a full-time replacement—that, and Dad's hope that Rob would change his mind and come back to the *Beacon* full-time. Unfortunately, the time he put in here wasn't enough to keep the other employees from having to take up the slack, and he'd gotten a less-than-friendly reception the first couple of days he showed up back at the office.

He went in through the back door. The office was quiet. He heard Myrtle on the phone in Reception, and he'd seen Joy's car in the parking lot, so she was here somewhere. And of course Dad was always here until late. But Rob would have Michelle mostly to himself. His spirits lifted exponentially.

He found her in her cubicle looking beautiful as ever. She wore her hair loose today, spilling over her back and shoulders like a cape. She was hunched over the Selectric, deep in concentration.

He stood and watched her for a minute before he spoke. "You're working late again?"

She jumped at the sound of his voice, but when she saw it was him, she rewarded him with a smile. "I'm just finishing up. Stupid school board meeting."

He knew she was thinking of the way he used to tag them "school *bored* meetings." They cracked up at the same moment.

"Well, I guess I'd better get busy." He sighed, knowing she would think he was exhausted from his day at the *Eagle*, but in truth, it was a sigh of disappointment that she would soon be leaving.

But she winced and said, "Hey, I have a huge favor to ask."

"Shoot."

"Would you mind helping me with some film? In the darkroom. I'm trying to purposely overexpose some film and I'm not sure about the settings."

"Now?"

She shrugged. "Whenever you have time. I've got stuff to work on until you're ready."

"I'm ready now. What speed film are you using?"

"I don't know. Whatever was in the drawer." She jumped up, scooped the camera off her desk, and led the way to the darkroom.

He followed her in and shut the door behind them. Michelle set to work fixing the chemical baths, moving about the small space with the familiarity of someone who'd done this many times.

"Look at you," he said. "I remember when you first started. You didn't know a canister from a banister."

She laughed. "Sad but true."

"You're an old hand at this now. I'm impressed."

She smiled up at him, her eyes sparkling in the yellow light from the single bulb overhead. "I learned from the best."

"Well, I don't know about that. I kind of miss the photography, though."

"Oh? You don't ever take pictures for the Wichita paper?"

"No, the *Eagle* has full-time photographers. That's all they do. Any time I go out on a story—which isn't very often, unfortunately . . . But anyway, if I'm doing a story that needs pictures, I take a photog with me."

"Must be nice." She picked up the camera. "Okay, I'm ready. Would you hit the light for me?"

They chatted about their respective jobs while she prepared the film. He talked her through the developing, relishing being enclosed in this familiar room with her. She was in a playful mood, and he was loving every minute.

He knew it'd been hard for her to come back into this room that first time after the shooting. But judging by the way she was flirting with him—there was no other word for it—he was pretty sure the shooting wasn't what she had on her mind now.

When the photos started to come to life, he moved closer, intent on giving her a happier memory of the darkroom. He had a feeling she was expecting it. Maybe even anticipating it. He didn't want to disappoint her.

She sloshed the photo paper in the bath with the photo tongs. "Do you think it's been long enough?" She looked over her shoulder at him.

"I think it's been too long," he said, purposely misinterpreting her question. "Way too long." He took the tongs from her hand and placed them on the counter. Then, taking her by the shoulders, he turned her to face him. He placed a featherweight kiss on her forehead, testing.

She leaned into it, her breath quickening. Needing no more encouragement, he kissed the tip of her nose, working his way to her waiting lips.

"Rob . . . " She came up for air, and even in the dark he could see the longing in her eyes. "I've missed you so much."

"Not as much as I've missed you. It's murder without you filling my days."

"I know what you mean," she whispered against his cheek.

A quick rap at the door made them both gasp.

"Just a sec!" Rob shouted. Too late.

The door swung open and the light flickered on.

At the same moment, Michelle dove to save the film and Rob dove to turn out the light.

"What the—" His father stood there blinking. "What are you two doing in here?"

Rob evaded the question. "Didn't you see the red light?"

"I saw something that looked a little like a red light *district*—"

Michelle gave a little gasp that turned into a giggle.

His dad gave him a pointed look. "No, son, the red light was not on." He glanced over Rob's shoulder to Michelle. "Apparently you were too distracted to turn it on."

Rob felt Michelle go still behind him. He reached behind him for her hand and squeezed it reassuringly. For some odd reason, Dad didn't seem all that upset.

His father looked toward the ceiling as if trying to think how to handle this. Finally he sighed and put a hand on the doorknob. "I hope that film wasn't important. You two salvage what you can and meet me in my office in ten minutes."

Or maybe he was so furious, they were only seeing the calm before the storm.

* * * * *

Mr. Merrick was waiting behind his desk when Michelle reached his office. Rob had sent her on ahead while he finished cleaning up the darkroom, which she thought was pretty cowardly of him. It was his dad after all. And his idea to go and kiss her like that.

Well, that wasn't exactly true. She'd definitely had the idea long before Rob's lips ever touched hers. But he was the one who'd acted on it first.

It struck her that in only five months of employment, she'd sat in this office waiting for Mr. Merrick to chew her out more times than any individual ought to and still remain employed. But tonight may have been the last straw.

Rob came in and she glanced up at him, but he only threw her a little smile. One she couldn't quite interpret.

"Close the door, Robert," Mr. Merrick said.

Uh-oh. That was never a good sign.

Rob reached around and gave the door a nudge without getting up from his chair.

Mr. Merrick looked back and forth between them. "Are you two trying to send me into early retirement?"

"Sorry, Dad. It was my fault. Don't blame Michelle. It won't happen again." Rob glanced at her and winked. "Not in the darkroom, anyway."

Even Mr. Merrick couldn't keep a straight face at that. But after a minute he sobered. "All right. This is getting ridiculous. You two are obviously crazy for each other. Your antics are going to get you both into trouble."

Michelle held her breath.

"So here's what I suggest." Mr. Merrick looked hard at Rob and shook a finger at him. "You need to go get a ring and propose to this girl. And *you*"—he turned to Michelle—"need to put him out of his misery and say yes."

Her jaw dropped. She snuck a glance at Rob. Surely she'd heard wrong. But, no, Rob looked as bewildered as she felt.

"As you both know," Mr. Merrick went on, "we have a strict no-fraternizing rule at the *Beacon*. But we have no rules against nepotism. You two get married and you can do all your kissing at home and come in to the office ready to work and, if at all possible, ready to keep your hands to yourselves during work hours."

Was he serious? This was not how she wanted her marriage-proposal story to go. *Good grief!*

Rob rose from his chair, still looking shell-shocked. "We—we will take that under advisement, sir." He spoke slowly and deliberately, as if he couldn't believe what he'd just heard, either. "May Michelle and I have a minute, please?"

"Tell you what . . . " Mr. Merrick opened the top drawer of his desk and withdrew several bills from the tray. He placed the stack of cash in Rob's hand. "Take the woman to dinner and talk it over. On me."

Chapter Thirty-Eight

"What on earth is wrong with your dad? Is he *serious*?" Michelle sat across from Rob in a corner booth at Milt's, suddenly feeling self-conscious and vulnerable with him.

"I think he was dead serious."

"But . . . we've only known each other for five months," she said, still shocked they were even discussing this.

"So what, Mish?" He swept a hank of hair out of his eyes. "Is . . . what he proposed out of the question for you? We've worked together almost every day since we met. I think we know each other pretty well by now."

"No, Rob. We don't."

"As well as anybody *can* know someone before they marry them and live with them for a while? Do you think your parents knew each other as well as they do now when they first got married?"

"Well, no . . . of course not, but—"

"That's what marriage is about. I think God's brought us together so we *can* get to know each other better. We have our whole lives ahead of us. To learn to know each other." An ornery gleam came to his eye. "I want to get to know the wonder of you, Michelle."

His reference to the Elvis Presley song prompted an anemic smile. Then she realized—"The Wonder of You" was playing on the jukebox. She rolled her eyes. "Don't you dare break into song on me, buddy."

He held up a hand. "Don't worry. I'll leave the singing to you. Believe me, the world will be a better place for that. In fact, I can't believe you're not singing along."

She waved him off. "I don't sing when I'm stressed."

"Ha! You sing *all* the time."

"I do not."

"Fine. Have it your way. But seriously, Mish, are you listening to what I'm saying? We may not know every single thing there is to know about each other, but it's not like we have any deep, dark secrets from each other."

"You don't have *any* secrets?"

"Well, maybe one." He looked sheepish.

"What's that?"

"I was going to say something, I swear I was." He held up a hand. "It's about Joy."

"Joy Swanson?" Now he had her worried.

"It was nothing, I swear, but we—"

"You sure are doing a lot of 'swearing' for something that was 'nothing.'"

"We dated for a while," he blurted.

"You and Joy? Dated?"

"Guilty as charged."

Well, that explained a *lot*. "Did you—love her?" She was almost afraid to hear his answer.

But the look of horror he shot her said everything. And made her laugh. "So I have nothing to worry about?"

"Less than nothing."

"Who broke up with who?"

"Whom."

"You're seriously going to correct my grammar? *Now*?"

"I broke up with her."

It had never crossed Michelle's mind that Joy's resentment toward her might have something to do with Rob, but she remembered an expression Dad had used once: "*Hell hath no fury like a woman scorned.*" "Okay. Well, maybe I can give her a little slack, then."

He looked relieved that she wasn't upset. Or maybe he was just glad for a change of subject. But she wasn't going to let him off so easy. "Since we're divulging secrets . . . You're not the only one who has them."

He stared at her. "*You* do?"

"Yes. I do." She ran a finger around the rim of her coffee cup. "Rob, you know the shape of my lips and the way my stupid curly hair feels between your fingers . . . . You know what it feels like to hold me in your arms—"

"Cut it out, woman. You're making me want to go develop some photos."

She glared at him. "Could you be serious for two seconds? You know some things about me, Rob, but I'm not sure you really know me."

He frowned. "What secrets are you keeping from me?"

She shrugged. "Maybe not deep, dark secrets. But still . . . things we need to talk about. Things you don't know about me. And other things I still don't know about you."

"Like?"

"Like your mother."

He flinched as if she'd struck him. But he recovered quickly, sighing with resignation. "Okay. Fine. Tell me what you want to know."

"What happened to her? I mean, I know she died when you were nine—nine-and-a-half," she corrected, remembering he'd done the same the first time she'd asked about his mother. "I know she . . . drowned, and that it's hard for you to talk about. Understandably. And I'm so sorry. But . . . you never talk about her at all, Rob. About when she was alive. You surely remember her . . . ."

A light of incredible tenderness came to his eyes. "I remember her. She was—" He seemed to be collecting his thoughts with great care. "She loved me. No, she delighted in me."

"Oh, Rob. That's a beautiful way to put it."

"Like your mom delights in you."

She tilted her head, questioning.

"It was obvious that day at the hospital. Both your parents take pure delight in you."

"Really? You saw that—that day?"

He nodded. "Your folks were worried about you, yes. But anyone could see, spending two minutes with them, how proud they are of you and how much they enjoy being around you."

"Wow. I—I know I've taken them for granted."

"Don't ever do that. You're blessed, Mish. Very blessed." He looked pensive, as if collecting his thoughts. Finally he blew out a breath. "So you want to know about my mom?"

She nodded, afraid to speak, lest he change his mind.

A faraway look came to his eyes, and she had to strain to hear him. "We were on our boat. Dad had a boat back then." He shook his head. "I don't know why, because Mom was terrified of the water. Anyway, we'd taken it to one of the lakes down by Branson. I don't even remember the name of the lake now. I guess that's good. I don't want to know how to get back to that place."

"Oh, Rob . . . " The café was empty except for a middle-aged couple on the other side of the room. Michelle got up and came around to slide into the booth beside him. She leaned against his shoulder and slipped her hand in his.

He looked down at her, his eyes gleaming with unshed tears. "I say I don't want to know, and yet I won't set foot in the lower half of Missouri for fear I'll accidentally come upon that site. Her gravesite."

"Her gravesite? I don't understand."

"They never found her body. They dragged the lake for two days."

"Oh, Rob. How awful." She knew her voice reflected the horror she felt. But she couldn't hide it. And maybe she shouldn't try. What had happened *was* horrific.

"I pretty much hated my dad for a while after that."

"Because of the boat?"

"Yes. Because he had to have that"—he clenched his jaw, and she knew he was tempering his words out of respect for her—"that boat. And because he made her try to swim." His voice was hard, making her suspect the hatred he'd spoken of in past tense wasn't buried all that deep beneath the surface. "Mom had asthma. She was deathly afraid of water. But Dad taught her to swim. And she learned too, but—" He bowed his head. "They think she had an asthma attack while she was swimming and—she drowned."

She reached for his hand and he let her take it, squeezing back. "When I see other people with their moms, even now, I feel this"—he brought their entwined hands to his chest, clenching his fingers around hers in a fist—"this *weight* . . . this heavy weight . . . that I never really knew what it was like to grow up with a mom. And I never will."

"I'm so sorry, Rob," she whispered. "I can't even imagine what that must have been like."

"I've survived. Dad and I have survived. God's gotten me through, and I expect He'll continue to do that. But you're right—it's something I should have told you. Because it has a lot—maybe everything—to do with why I am the way I am."

She squeezed his hand again and looked up at him. "I happen to really like the way you am." She grinned.

"I like the way you am too." He dropped a kiss on the top of her head, and she thought she'd never loved him more.

In that moment, Michelle decided she'd write a letter to Kevin before another day passed. She'd thank him for their memories, but then she'd tell him her heart belonged to someone else.

Chapter Thirty-Nine

Rob exhaled and felt the tension seep out of him. Why hadn't he talked about his mom before with Michelle—or with someone? How could thirty minutes have made such a difference? But it had—getting the story out there where he could view it through the eyes of someone more objective, where he could see it through the filter of time—and with a man's perspective instead of that of the bewildered and angry nine-year-old boy he'd been when Mom died.

"Thank you," she whispered, putting a gentle hand on his back.

"For what?"

"For trusting me with all that."

He nodded. "That's what I like about you. I can trust you."

"No." She shook her head slowly. "See, that's exactly what I was talking about. You think you can trust me. That just proves you don't know me."

"Okay, so it's your turn. What's your big secret?" He tried to make it come out sounding lighthearted, but a frisson of alarm had gone through him at her words.

She closed her eyes. After a long minute she looked up at him. "This is hard."

He twined his fingers through hers. "It's okay. You can tell me anything."

"You know that day in the library?"

"Yes?" They'd run into each other in the public library shortly after he started working at the *Eagle*. But he had no idea where she was going with this.

"And the grocery store that night?"

"Yeah. Fun night." He smiled, remembering. He'd clowned around, juggling fruits and veggies. And making her laugh. One of his favorite things to do.

"Listen to me, Rob. You're not hearing me. Today, did you notice that I 'just happened' to still be at work when you got there?"

"Yes . . . ?"

"Rob, I–I've manipulated everything. Running into you. Being where I knew you'd be. Making excuses to stay at work late . . . I've practically been stalking you!"

"*That's* your big secret?" He angled his body on the narrow bench seat of the booth so he could look her in the eyes.

She nodded, looking like he'd just caught her shoplifting.

"Are you serious? This is what's been eating at you?" It came out louder than he'd intended.

She shushed him. "How could we ever say *God* brought us together when I've practically orchestrated the whole thing?"

"Wait a minute . . . " His life since he'd met Michelle flashed before him. He eyed her with suspicion. "You didn't take the job at the *Beacon* because of me? That whole *whoop-dee-do* and—"

"No!" She looked horrified. "No, I promise you. I had no clue who you were back then. You don't think that's how I'd try to make a good first impression on a guy, do you? No . . . It was after you started at the *Eagle*. I was afraid I'd never see you again. And then there'd be no chance for us to ever—be together."

"Michelle." Was she really so naive? "Mish, that's what men and women *do* when they like each other. Since the beginning of time, men have invented ways to be wherever the woman they love is. And you've proven that women obviously do the same." He winked. "You don't really think I needed help developing all those pictures, do you?"

"Rob!" She gave a little gasp. "Robert Merrick the third!"

He laughed. "Well, good grief, how do you think Adam and Eve ever got together? You think ol' Adam just *happened* to be out picking apples one day?"

She laughed, egging him on.

"And Samson and Delilah? Mary and Joseph?"

She slugged him. "Cut it out. I think God might have had a little bit to do with that last one."

He turned serious. "And you don't think He had anything to do with this one?" He motioned between them. "Even if you did feel the need to help Him along a bit?"

"I'm starting to think He just might have something to do with it."

Rob pushed their coffee cups to the edge of the table and fished in his pocket for his wallet. He left several dollar bills on the table along with his loose change. "You ready to go? We can continue this discussion in the car."

"Sure." She slid out of the booth and followed him out to the car.

He started the Pinto's engine, but he didn't put it in gear. Instead, he turned to her and put the palm of his hand along her smooth cheek. "I want to tell you something, Michelle. And just so you know, my dad has absolutely nothing to do with this."

Her gorgeous eyes held a spark of curiosity and a glint of anticipation.

He took a deep breath and exhaled a cloud of steam into the cold car. "I'm starting to be pretty sure that this—you and me—is God's doing. And I'm starting to be pretty stinkin' happy about it."

Her smile lit her face and he bent to kiss her, feeling more sure about his future than he had in—well, *forever.*

The kiss was just getting good when she pushed away from him. "Rob . . . wait. There's one other thing. Not a secret really, because we talked about it a long time ago. But as long as we're getting things out in the open, I just want to be sure you remember."

"What's that? And is it really so important that you needed to interrupt a perfectly good kiss for it?"

She put a hand flat on his chest, holding him off. But she was still smiling.

"Okay. What is it?"

"I want twelve kids. And I want to stay home with them."

He gave a low whistle. "Twelve, huh?"

"Well, the number might be negotiable. But I want a bunch of them."

"Four?" he said, bargaining.

"Nine."

"Six. And no more."

"Deal."

They shook on it, laughing. "God providing," he answered, shooting up a prayer that God would be reasonable when the time came.

"Hey, no fair," she pouted.

He captured her face in his hands, cradling it there. "Michelle, I want you to be able to have your dream. Whatever that is. I want to make your dreams come true. You could even pursue your singing if you wanted to."

She stilled.

"What's wrong?"

"I don't want that. I've never wanted that."

"But you have so much talent—"

"I'll tell you what I want, but . . . you'll think I'm stupid."

"Never. Tell me."

"I've never thought God gave me a good singing voice for any other reason than to sing lullabies to my babies. I guess I just don't have an ambitious bone in my body."

"I think wanting to raise twelve kids is pretty ambitious."

"Six," she corrected him.

"Oh. Right. Six. And I don't think that's stupid at all. I think it's beautiful."

She cocked her head. "Are you being sarcastic?"

"No!"

She looked skeptical. "I can never tell with you."

"I'm not being sarcastic, Mish. Or facetious or ironic or anything except dead serious. I love the thought of you following in your mother's footsteps. In *my* mom's footsteps. I think it's a beautiful thing for a woman to aspire to be a good wife and mother. I know a man's not supposed to say that in polite company anymore, which, by the way, I think is a crying shame."

She grinned up at him. "Oh? So you don't consider me polite company?"

"Definitely not." He leaned and kissed her.

She responded and deepened the kiss.

He pulled away. *Needing* to, but not wanting to. "That was definitely not polite."

She laughed. "No, it wasn't, and you'd better take me home now."

He put the car in gear, knowing she wasn't kidding about that. And it applied double for him. The woman was a serious temptation, and he couldn't wait until they were married so he could give in to her charms.

CHAPTER FORTY

Michelle carried the pizza box up the porch steps and rang the doorbell.

She heard Eden's happy squeals inside and then Becky's footsteps.

The door opened, and Becky swung it wide to accommodate her girth. She was only two-and-a-half weeks from her due date now and at the waddling stage.

But she took one look at Michelle's offering and whooped. "Oh! Bless you. How did you know I was dreading trying to figure out what to make for supper?"

"Probably because I was dreading it too. And then I drove by the Pizza Hut and it smelled too good to ignore. But who wants to eat pizza alone?" She tried to look sheepish. "Can I come in?"

"Oh! Of course. Don't mind me. My brain is fried." She opened the door wider and turned behind her. "Hey, Eden, look who's here!"

The toddler looked up from the middle of the plush-animal menagerie on the living room floor. When she spotted Michelle, she gave a squeal of delight and scrambled to her with outstretched arms.

"Here." Becky reached for the pizza box. "Let me rescue our dinner before it's too late."

Michelle passed off the box in the nick of time then swooped Eden up in her arms and nuzzled her neck. The little-girl giggles warmed her heart. "Why don't we pick up your toys so we can go eat some pizza, okay?" She turned to Becky, who was distributing plastic picnic plates around the table in the dining room. "I should have asked first . . . . Can Eden have pizza? I remember it not sitting very well with her once when Rob and I fed it to her."

"As long as we scrape off any of the spicy stuff . . . She probably shouldn't have pepperoni. Speaking of Rob, how's he doing?"

"Okay, I guess. I hardly ever see him."

"Well, that's not good."

"I don't know. Maybe it is."

"What do you mean?"

"It's just so—complicated—between us."

"What's complicated? You said his dad wants you to get married. So get married."

"I don't want us to get married because his dad *told* us to." She tucked Eden into her high chair and chose a small slice of pizza for her.

"Does he want to marry you?"

Michelle nodded, curbing a smile. "I'm pretty sure he does."

"Do you want to marry him?" Becky cut Eden's pizza into small bites.

"Definitely. I mean . . . as much as I could possibly know that. How do you know if someone will be a good daddy or not? How do you know if someone will change after you're married?" She felt bad asking the questions, because obviously Becky had proven how important the answers were.

But Becky didn't seem offended. "You *don't* know, Michelle. But you get some pretty good clues pretty quick. And just so you know, I got those clues with Mack . . . and I ignored them."

"Really?" Michelle found a slender thread of hope in her friend's words.

"Mack . . . " Becky hung her head. "He shoved me around plenty before we said 'I do,' and he showed his selfish side plenty often. I should have seen it, but you know, that's how my dad was with my mom—before she kicked him out. I wish I could say I didn't know better, but deep in my heart, I knew. I just made the mistake of thinking that being with a guy like Mack would be better than not having a guy at all. I wasn't sure I'd have another chance, not being pretty. And, well, I wasn't popular like you—"

"Becky! Who told you you weren't pretty?"

"Mama pretty!" Eden parroted.

Becky laughed and kissed her daughter's cheek, but then she turned serious. "I have a mirror, sweet friend. I don't need anyone to tell me."

"Well, you need to return that mirror to wherever you bought it, because it lies! You are a beautiful woman. And not just on the outside."

Becky looked away, as if she'd never heard that concept. It broke Michelle's heart. Who had been so cruel to this attractive woman that she could look into a mirror and not see the truth? Then and there, Michelle made a promise to herself that she would do everything in her power to encourage Becky and help her to realize what a beautiful woman she was, what gifts she had to give. If only she could have become friends with Becky before she took up with someone like Mack.

Becky looked up, wearing a shy grin. "Enough about how stunningly gorgeous I am. Back to the subject at hand. Rob Merrick. Look at how he is with Eden, Michelle."

"Rob?" Eden perked up at his name. "I see Rob?" she asked over a mouthful of pizza.

"Not today, sweetie. Some other time." She turned back to Michelle. "How can you doubt for one minute that Rob would make a great daddy?"

"I know. I can't."

Becky cocked her head. "Has he ever laid a hand on you?"

"Only in a good way." Michelle grinned and felt her cheeks heat. "And I mean that too. He's been a perfect gentleman." Remembering the darkroom kisses, she wasn't so sure her mother would have called his behavior *gentlemanly*, exactly. But although Rob had made no secret about the fact that he was looking forward to the privileges of marriage, and though they were both tempted in that way every time they were within two inches of each other, he had treated her with respect in every way.

"You're a lucky woman, Michelle. You have everything going for you. Look at how you grew up. Your parents are amazing. I still can't believe what they've done for me."

Michelle nodded, agreeing. A week ago, Mom and Dad had bought a top-of-the-line telephone for Becky, arranged to have it hooked up, and paid a year's worth of phone bills.

"You don't bring all the baggage Mack and I did into marriage," Becky said. "You grew up with a living example of what marriage is *supposed* to look like. Believe me, that puts you at an advantage right off the bat. And neither one of you has a selfish bone in your body, so—"

"Well, I don't know about that." Michelle shook her head. "I've been known to want my own way from time to time."

"That's just human nature. But I've seen you. Don't fool yourself, Michelle Penn. When the chips are down, you do what's right. Rob too. You guys will be just fine." Tears welled in her eyes and she turned away.

"Becky? What's wrong?" Michelle felt awful. It had to be hard for Becky to watch her happiness with Rob and then face the reality of her own situation. "I'm sorry. Here I am going on and on . . . . I'm being totally thoughtless."

But Becky waved her off. "No, it's not that. Not at all. I just feel bad that watching me and Mack has made you leery of marriage. I'm so afraid it'll be that way for Eden too."

Michelle jumped up and put her arms around Becky. "What Eden is going to see is a woman who did everything she could to make a good life for her daughter. It's not your fault, what Mack did to your family. Don't ever think that. You're one of the bravest women I know."

Becky wiped her tears and offered a forced smile. "Thanks, Michelle. I don't know what I would do without you."

"And I don't know what I'd do without you. So that's settled, okay?"

"Okay." Her smile turned genuine.

"Now what do you say we eat this pizza before it gets cold?"

Becky's smile morphed into a grimace, and she wrapped her arms around her middle. "I'm not feeling so hot all of a sudden. I think I'll pass on the pizza for now."

Michelle studied her. "Is everything okay with the baby?"

Becky stumbled to the sofa and eased into one corner, wincing. "Ooh! If I didn't know better, I'd think that was a contraction."

"Was it? Could you be in labor?"

"I doubt it. Eden was almost a week late. And they say it's usually the same with— Oww!" She rubbed her belly through the fabric of her maternity blouse.

"Okay, now you're scaring me." Michelle found it difficult to catch her breath. "Stay here. I'm calling my mom." She went for the phone in the kitchen.

"Michelle—"

The urgency in Becky's voice made her turn.

"I think . . . you'd better call the hospital instead. My water just broke."

CHAPTER FORTY-ONE

Rob checked the clock again just to be sure it was working. But the steady, quiet tick told him it was. And it was after ten. Where *was* Dad? It wasn't like him to stay at work this late. Especially not on a Sunday night. And so close to Christmas.

He went to the phone in the kitchen and dialed Dad's extension at the *Beacon*. No answer.

He waited another twenty minutes and called again with the same result. It was probably nothing, but he had an odd feeling about this. He grabbed his car keys off the kitchen counter and headed for the garage.

Entering the back door of the *Beacon* office, Rob called for his father. No answer.

He flipped on lights as he walked through the newsroom to Dad's office. A small lamp burned dimly on the edge of his desk, but Rob thought Dad left that one on all the time.

He unlocked the door, feeling a little guilty, even though Dad had given him a key to his office years ago. Nothing seemed amiss inside, so he relocked the room and started for the break room.

He turned on the hall light and almost tripped over his father's prone body.

"Dad!" He knelt beside him, grabbing his wrist to feel for a pulse. Relief surged through him the instant he detected a beat. It was thready, but it was there.

He patted his father's cheeks gently, trying to rouse him. When he got no response, he shrugged out of his jacket and wadded it into a pillow beneath Dad's head. That done, he ran to the nearest phone and dialed the hospital's emergency number.

It seemed like forever before the ambulance came, but when the technicians administered oxygen and Dad finally stirred a little, Rob felt better. He rode in the ambulance, holding tightly to his father's hand until they made him let loose.

Rob couldn't remember a time in his life—ever—when his father had not been in complete control. To see him so vulnerable and weak now shook him to his core. He sent up a stream of prayers that consisted of a few words repeated over and over. *Please don't take my dad. Help him, God. Please.*

Once in the ER, the techs made Rob stay in the waiting room while they worked on Dad, first on a gurney in the hallway and then on a bed in one of the exam rooms.

With his head in his hands, Rob begged God to spare his father's life. He didn't know how God felt about bargains, but in the same breath he promised that if God would answer his desperate prayer, he would do everything in his power to mend his relationship with his dad. He'd spent too many years resenting a man who'd surely done the best he could to be both father and mother in the midst of his own grief.

"I'm sorry, God. Forgive me," he whispered, not caring if anyone heard. It was time to put the past behind and—if God saw fit to grant them more time together—to learn a better way to be a son to his father.

When the doctor finally came out to talk to him, his words were more encouraging than the grim look he wore on his face. "It doesn't look as though there's been permanent damage to the heart, but we'll run more tests tomorrow before we can say for certain. We'll get him settled in a room shortly. You can probably see him there in a half hour or so. You can expect him to be here for at least four or five days, depending on what the tests reveal tomorrow."

Consumed with guilt, Rob thanked the doctor and headed for the lobby, where the nurse had said he could find a pay phone. This never would have happened if he hadn't quit the *Beacon*, piling on Dad not just physical stress, but emotional too. He would never forgive himself if anything happened to his father.

Rob spotted the pay phone just inside the entrance to the lobby. He hated to wake Michelle so late, but he knew she would want to know.

Who are you kidding, Merrick? Yes, Michelle *would* want to know about his father, but Rob was calling because he needed her. He needed her arms around him, her gentle touch, her sweet smile. He needed her with him, pure and simple.

He dialed her apartment and relief seeped into his taut muscles even at the sound of the phone ringing on her end. It rang three times. Four. But then, on the fifth ring, he heard her voice calling his name. *That's weird.* It almost sounded like she was in the room with him.

He held out the receiver and looked at it, trying to figure out what was going on.

"Rob?"

He turned to see her standing in the middle of the lobby, holding a sleepy-looking Eden in her arms.

He wasn't sure he'd ever been so glad to see two people in his life.

* * * * *

"What are you doing here?" Rob's forehead furrowed, and his eyes were dull. The PA system urgently paged a doctor with an unpronounceable name.

For one horrible moment, Michelle thought Rob's appearance might mean that something had happened with Becky. But how would he have known she was here?

"Becky's in labor," she said, unable to curb the smile that had been stretching her mouth ever since she'd said good-bye to Becky at the labor room door. "But . . . what are you doing here?"

"It's Dad. They think he's had a heart attack."

"Oh, Rob!" She rushed to embrace him, and he wrapped strong arms around her, sandwiching Eden between them.

They waited together in the waiting room, Rob updating Michelle on what the doctors had said about his father. "They're doing some tests tomorrow, and he'll probably need at least a stent put in, but they think he's going to be okay. But it'll be a while before he can come back to work. I've already decided. I'm calling the *Eagle* tomorrow and giving my notice."

Michelle nodded and tried to curb the joy that news filled her with.

They invented games to entertain Eden and found the games to be an equally good distraction for the two of them.

When Eden finally grew drowsy, they took turns holding and rocking her until she slept.

Chapter Forty-Two

Rob and Michelle arranged a sofa and a couple of chairs to carve out their own private little corner in the empty waiting room. They took turns entertaining Eden and catching catnaps.

With the help of medication, Mr. Merrick was sleeping well. Every half hour or so, Michelle went to ask the nurse for an update from the labor room.

"She's progressing just like she should be, honey. But these things sometimes take hours, days even. You may as well go on home. We can call you when she gets closer."

There was no way Michelle was going to leave. And besides, the company she was keeping was altogether pleasant.

Midnight came and went with still no baby. Eden awoke with a second wind, but she finally wound down again an hour later and drowsed on her little blanket that Michelle had spread on the sofa.

She and Rob had been talking quietly off and on about nothing in particular, but after a few minutes of silence, she felt Rob's eyes intent on her. She looked up at him and smiled. "What?"

"Just look at us, Mish. We're playing house here." He nodded toward Eden, who'd finally fallen asleep with her head on Rob's lap. "We're both wishing she was ours—or at least that we had one like her—and we're both wishing we had a claim on each other."

She stared at him, dumbfounded.

His eyes challenged her. "Am I wrong?"

"No," she stuttered. "But—I didn't think men thought that way."

"Oh, you'd be surprised how men think."

She giggled. "I like it. My stupid brother would never play house with me."

He pulled a face. "Well, don't think I'm going to start dressing up Barbie dolls or anything."

She laughed but stopped when she saw him watching her with an enigmatic smile. "What?"

"We both have a lot of growing up to do, but is there anything that says we can't do that *together*?

She looked skeptical. "Do you think that's wise?"

He tried to convince her. "We've already made strides. We both know where our weaknesses are and what we need to work on. We're both asking God to help us become what He wants us to be."

"But how do we know what that is, Rob?"

He thought for a moment. "I think we know by the gifts He's given us. One of those gifts is you, Mish. I don't even want to think about a future without you."

"Then don't."

He cocked his head. "Do you mean that . . . the way I think you mean it?"

She made sure Eden was safe on the sofa on the other side of Rob, then she scooted close to him, reaching up to caress his stubbled cheek. "I mean it with all my heart, Rob Merrick. I don't know what took me so long to see the light."

"Michelle . . . how is it you're always turning worst days of my life into best days?"

"I could have sworn it was the other way around."

"Never." He gave her an impish grin. "Well, maybe sometimes."

"But not anymore. I promise."

The smile he gave her in return filled her with joy.

"Hey," he said, eyeing the clock over the nurse's station. "Almost two a.m. Do you know what day it is?"

She shook her head, frowning.

"December twenty-fourth. Christmas Eve."

"That's right. It is! Becky was hoping for a tax deduction. She got a Christmas present too." She reached behind her to pull the blanket up around Eden's shoulders. "We'll have to see if we can find something in the gift shop to celebrate."

"I wonder if they have diamond rings there." Rob sounded dead serious.

"You'd better not be—" She stopped short, seeing a doctor in green scrubs ambling down the corridor smiling. She rose and started to gather Eden in her arms, but Rob nudged her out of the way.

"I'll bring her. You go find out the news."

"Okay, but—" She grinned. "About that diamond?"

"Yes, ma'am?" The eyes that had been dull just a few hours earlier now sparked with life.

She poked his chest with one finger. "I'll hold you to that, buddy." She turned on her heel and hurried to meet the doctor. But at the nurse's station, she turned back to see if he was behind her.

He was. With Eden in his arms, his shoulder cradling her head, and his cheek nestled against the toddler's jet-black hair. It was about the sweetest sight she could imagine—outside of the day when it would be their own precious child he carried in his arms.

EPILOGUE

"Look, Eden. Look what Rob got for you!" Michelle shook the fluffy white bunny and rubbed its red suede nose on Eden's button nose. The little girl giggled and made a face.

Eden's cheesy grin prompted an identical one on Rob's face. It was good to see the stress lines ease from his handsome face.

"Do you want to go see your baby brother?"

Eden hugged the stuffed bunny and brightened. "Baby!"

"That's right," Rob said. "You got a new little brother, didn't you?"

"Not all that little," Michelle said. "He was nine pounds four ounces."

Rob's eyes grew wide. "That's a full-grown football player right there."

"Oh, you!" She administered a playful slug. "Enough about football."

While Eden took her bunny to the child-sized table in the corner of the waiting room, Rob winked and dug into the pocket of his jeans. "I got something for you too."

"You did?" She frowned. "I hope it's not chocolate."

"Even better." He opened his hand and presented what looked, at first glance, like a wad of foil. Grinning, Rob dropped to one knee.

Michelle inspected the misshapen lump he held out to her. It did look a little like the diamond ring he'd promised her last night. On closer inspection, she saw that the band was fashioned from a shiny foil gum wrapper. And it held a sparkly, rather impressively sized "diamond" that looked suspiciously like a hunk of the rock candy they'd bought in the gift shop earlier. She laughed and let him slip the concoction onto her finger.

"It's beautiful," she said, looking down at him and making her voice supremely genuine. "I'll treasure it all my life." She couldn't have been more sincere about that part.

Rob looked appropriately sheepish, though. "It'll have to do until I can find the real thing, but merry Christmas, Mish."

She smiled up at him. "I can be patient."

"I'm not sure *I* can." He let her pull him to his feet and kissed her again. A kiss that held all the promises she'd ever dreamed of and then some.

Rob slid his hand down her arm and laced his fingers through hers. "Now let's go tell my dad the great news. I can't think of anything that will do his heart more good."

About the Author

DEBORAH RANEY dreamed of writing a book since the summer she read all of Laura Ingalls Wilder's Little House books and discovered that a little Kansas farm girl could, indeed, grow up to be a writer. After a happy twenty-year detour as a stay-at-home wife and mom, Deb began her writing career. Her first novel, *A Vow to Cherish*, was awarded a Silver Angel from Excellence in Media and inspired the acclaimed World Wide Pictures film of the same title. Since then, her books have won the RITA Award, the HOLT Medallion, and the National Readers' Choice Award. She is also a two-time Christy–Award finalist.

Deb enjoys speaking and teaching at writers' conferences across the country. She and her husband, Ken Raney, make their home in their native Kansas and, until a recent move to the city, lived the small-town life that is the setting for so many of Deb's books. The Raneys spend their time gardening, antiquing, watching movies, and traveling to visit four grown children and a growing quiver of small grandchildren, who all live much too far away. Deborah loves hearing from her readers. To e-mail her or to learn more about her books, please visit www.deborahraney.com.